A Suburb of Monogamy

A SUBURB OF MONOGAMY by **Catherine Borders**.

First published by **Omnia Vanitas Review** 2015.

Copyright © Catherine Borders 2015.

ISBN-13: 978-0692502976

ISBN-10: 0692502971

For Lily.
Spluh.

I have always played with God. For me, the signifier Dieu, *as I have always said, is the synonym of what goes beyond us, of our own projection toward the future, toward infinity.*

What I must say also is that clearly, like all writers who invoke Dieu *the word and the word* Dieu *in their texts, I am religiously atheistic, but literarily deistic, that's it. Ultimately I think that no one can write without the aid of God, but what is it, God? without the aid of writing, God-as-Writing.*

– Hélène Cixous.

The Christian is separated from himself; the division of body and soul, of life and spirit, is consumed: original sin turns the body into the soul's enemy; all carnal links appear bad. Man can be saved by being redeemed by Christ and turning toward the Celestial Kingdom; but at the beginning, he is no more than rottenness; his birth dooms him not only to death but to damnation; divine grace can open heaven to him, but all avatars of his natural existence are cursed. Evil is an absolute reality; and flesh is sin. Since woman never stopped being Other, of course, male and female are never reciprocally considered flesh: the flesh for the Christian male is the enemy other and is not distinguished from woman. The temptations of the earth, sex, and the devil are all incarnated in her.

– Simone de Beauvoir. *The Second Sex.*

1.

Acquiescence, then Nora falls into dramatic despair. She sits cross-legged on the abandoned railroad tracks, gravel perforating her skin, whining to Brian about what things were, what they weren't. "I love you. I love you," she says, more pathetic the second time. These words mean nothing. Both hollow and hallowed. Like the chain around her neck made from paperclips and colorful bits of construction paper. A gift he had given her on their four month anniversary.

...

Him, making love to her on the floor. 10:11am, digital time, in red, seared onto her brain. Forever, their vapory outlines shimmering, exchanging virginities at 10:11am.

An almost immaculate inception.

...

Brian is an angry boy, large, unloved by his parents, fists like hams, clumsy. During football practice, he once got a concussion from slipping on a puddle of pee and clocking his head against a urinal.

"Don't complicate things," he says.

A reference to the fragile Maryanne Lindstrom, his girlfriend.

As if they weren't already complicated.

Nora sighs… Brian of long ago, so chubby, so easy to love. Her cherub. Her best friend.

Brian of paperclip necklaces, tinfoil figures, and notes on paper airplanes.

Now, hardened. Inspissated. Eyes up some other girl's skirt.

...

Her father, red, laid her sexuality on the table. Condemning it. Demanding Brian formally apologize for sticking his fingers inside his daughter.

Nora was humiliated. She crumpled the scene into a wadded paper ball, lit it on fire, and still, she cannot shake it. In the name of the Father, and of the Son…

Finger-fucking is a transgression punishable by Hell, and also by parents. It's for her own good, they said. She nodded, having left her body. Still, her father wanted an apology, a confession. Still, after the humiliation. After he had chased Brian, who ran out of the house and down the street without his pants.

She's grounded from the phone forever, for nine months.

Now Nora traces Brian's steps, in pursuit of penance. And of the Holy Ghost.

. . .

A spiral inward. Downward.

"Let's run away together. You and me. We'll get married. I could get a job as a waitress—"

"Goodbye Nora," he says, twisting his lucky drum key into his palm, pushing it through his fingers. A glimmering silver metal cross, hollow like the barrel of a gun. She looks away, toward denial. He sets the drum key down on one of the dull, dirty steel rails. She slackens her vision, imagines being tied to the tracks.

. . .

When Nora was six, there was a mysterious pile of quilts in the living room, nearly as tall as Nora. Disobeying her mother, she peeked through the folds and spied a pile of toys. One of the toys was a doll that drank real water then wet herself. A day and a half later, she tore off the wrapping paper, uncovered Baby Uh-Oh, and lost her belief in Santa Claus.

Two months later KitKat died. The nuns at school told her that cats don't go to heaven because they don't have souls, they don't know the difference between right and wrong. She asked again about kittens. Not even kittens, they said. Perceptibility flooded her as she removed another bumptious weight from the balance of her precarious belief in God.

Nora was quickly given KitKat II.

Her illusion that she was eternal broke into a host of meaningless pieces, as though she had just found out she was terminally ill. She began soldering her own meaning, cutting and pasting a tumultuous bricolage in an attempt to repair. Such was the genesis of Dysthymia.

. . .

Brian asked Nora to call Maryanne's mother and pretend to be his mother and tell her that she, meaning his mother, will be home the entire time chaperoning them, and Nora, with great pain in her sternum, and supposed heroic effort, did this.

. . .

Alone, with a metal tchotchke.

. . .

Large, blinking brown eyes. Dark, regal eyebrows. Pale, diaphanous skin. Nora, a girl, a portrait, the heroine. Afraid of her own age, of her palpitating pulse. Of entrapment, of vulnerability. Loquacious with anyone who will listen, she speaks to hear herself speak, to hear herself being listened to. And she laughs a lot too, with a large mouth painted with hues of clay bricks or brittle rose petals or, sometimes, wet blood. A panther pacing in a teen girl cell, she takes comfort in KitKat II and painting cartoons and phrases on her walls. When she exhales a cigarette, she does so to hide behind a veil of brume. This veil is a protean barrier between obedience and night. She resorts to hysterical realism, perpetually looking between the sheets with an auspicious eye, spinning resentment into purple gold, weaving her independence with her incarceration, thinking she's invincible, then coats her fingers with hand sanitizer to hide the smell of smoke from her parents, who, for her fourteenth birthday had bought her a Mary Engelbreit print of a girl at her desk. A Henry James quote hovers in the upper right corner: It is ART that makes life, makes interest, makes importance, and I know of no substitute for the FORCE and BEAUTY of its process. Her mother even changed the girl's hair from blonde to brunette using a brown felt-tipped marker. This moves her.

. . .

Braiding her thick hair away from her face, she pulls at the plait, the cord, the ligature of youth, of spite, she cuts, the braid, her hair, falls to the floor. An uncanny piece of herself, a lump of bound hair, frayed, splayed open at the bottom, frayed, splayed open at the top. Lying on the floor, away from her. Wrapped in two blue rubberbands, two blue tourniquets. Mea culpa, she says. Mea fucking culpa.

. . .

Gone, she knows, but not really. He's in between presence and absence. A silvery conjunction. Traces of his callused knuckles scratch at her thigh. A voice of vapor speaks silently from inside her ears: the specter of his rejection. A ghost sleeping in her womb. Flying in and out of her vagina as it pleases.

It's just you and me, says the ghost.

The first ghost of boyfriends past.

Nora picks up the phone and stares. Presses the first three digits, then the next two, but she can't continue.

Though abandoned, still proud.

She withdraws, as even pride allows.
She feels the withdrawal in her legs.
The hatchet wound festers down her stomach.
The abyss fosters behind her eyes.

L'appel du vide.

. . .

Her parents aren't home. Nobody's home. She calls six people, to talk about calling Maryanne. No! they all say, but the phone has become a part of her body, an appendage, dressed in psychedelic flowers and fractals with a personalized ringtone.

This is the only way to end all suffering.

She sinks into the grass and dials. Maryanne answers, happily. Pangs of guilt make Nora pull out long blades of grass by the fistful. She talks in circles, circumlocutions. She talks around the point.

Maryanne is an extremely forgiving person.

And easily persuaded.

Click-Dial-Click

Brian answers, he's glad. He wants to be her friend. He listens with a half attentive ear as she nervously blabs on about their mutual friends and some advice she appropriated from Oprah.

She can hear the Nintendo, *RBI Baseball*.

"Okay. Just wanted to make sure we're cool. That everything's okay."

"Yeah, we're cool."

"All right, then I love you, Brian Murphy." Nora has a gravelly voice, deep and raspy, X-rated, as though she were always speaking in the bedroom with a helix of smoke coiling from a wicked smile.

"I love you too," he says from a place of distraction.

Then a sweeter, softer voice. Maryanne, the soprano says: "I love you too!"

"Fuck you, Nora!"

Brian hangs up.

. . .

The unique, supreme pleasure of love lies in the certainty of doing wrong.

– Charles Baudelaire.

It is HE who she pines for, it is HE who fills her daily thoughts, buried in between darker thoughts and lighter thoughts. It is HIM who she prays to, offering up her daily meditations. HE is her reference point for everything. She tells herself, she must forget HIM. HE is dead to her. HE has no name. She pushes HIM deep inside although HE often surfaces, on the street, suddenly in a crowd, in a stranger's face.

– Kate Zambreno. *Green Girl.*

2.

Saint Charles is a suburb very similar to its brethren. Naïve, smug, clean, sprawled, studded with plastic logos. Logos designed to elicit trust, logos colored in classic colors.

It was home to the first Medical College in Illinois. Founded in the nineteenth century, when no one bequeathed their bodies to science. Some medical students, to afford school, resorted to grave robbing then selling the bodies to their own schools. They called these bodies, or rather this process of recycling, "Resurrections." It was in this fashion that John Rood resurrected Marilla Kenyon and brought her body to Franklin Medical College to further his own education. Clobbered with grief, Mr. Kenyon went to Dr. George W. Richards' home and begged for his wife's body. The next time he returned with a gun, and three hundred men, killing a few of the medical students, John Rood included, and wounding Dr. Richards. In the end, the first medical college of Illinois was forced to close after only several years, and although the incident brought Saint Charles fame, ultimately it was detrimental to the town's prosperity.

There are still some bones clocking around the riverbed as boat tours swirl the murky waters.

. . .

Maryanne tells her mom to drop them off at the side door entrance, near the bumper cars. Nora thanks her for the ride in an odd tone, just in case she recognizes her voice as Brian's mother's. The girls go inside, staying just long enough to be assaulted by the noises and smells and rush of the arcade. That, combined with the freedom from adult supervision, excites their nerves. They turn around and go back out into the cold. They each take out a

13

cigarette from their newly matching cigarette cases. Maryanne pulls down her pink sleeves and stamps her feet for warmth. Nora offers her scarf. "I'm not cold," she says. "I'm too amped. At Catholic school we didn't have dances, we had roller skating parties, which were the idea of a dance, just less sinful. And even now I can't help but have butterflies in my stomach when wheels are on my feet."

"Do you know that's the blood pulling away from your stomach?" Maryanne says, shivering, bent, like a flower unable to brace itself against the wind. "We should've worn jackets," she adds.

"Bah," Nora says with Midwestern defiance, "it's only November." But she's cold too; the violence of her chill is just forgotten. Lost, in fantasy, in the ecology of magnetism, in repetition compulsion, in her own reflection illuminated by the neon Bumper Cars sign. She admires herself, her curves, her contours, falls deeply in love with the window pane, the soft, ambient, red glow, but particularly her image, in jeans, a black tank top, and a crushed velour blouse. Crushed to the color of disappointment. The color of twilight. The color of adolescence. An older mauve with younger skin. A full-bodied red wine. A complement to her attempted leopard print hair.

She hands Maryanne a flask. "Do you think I'll like any of these boys?" she asks.

"I have no idea," Maryanne says. "They might be too vanilla for you. Though, your horoscope did say to," and here she changes her voice, "'Prepare your virgin self for the Bacchanalian revels!' Remember? You have to chose between the fire in your loins and the fire in your hearth."

"Loins! Loins!" Nora says.

"Then let the Bacchanalian revels begin!" Maryanne says with the flask held high. Nora opens her mouth and Maryanne pours the warm Jameson down her throat.

· · ·

A gilded lily, Maryanne's sunflower yellow aura is contagious and ethereal. She is both sexy and nonthreatening, a budding Marilyn. She is the day to Nora's night, a canary to her raven. She often stares absently into a warren of narrowly lit streets behind her mind's eye. But when someone speaks to her she stares differently, with quixotic eyes, as if whatever they're saying is pivotal, crucial, amazing. Stretched across the carpet, in matching lavender pajamas, reading an astrology book and a Doors' album lyric book, mashing the two together, giggling about what they should've seen coming, she tells Nora that she's glad to have met her.

· · ·

Saint Charles is the lame son of Chicago's transparent steel-framed tension. White-collar white men, upper-middle money, with robust middles and round shoulders. Their wives glisten, they eat guilt-free chicken and whipped yogurt in pastel cable-knit sweaters. Some of the women look as though they were incapable of orgasm.

· · ·

White leather soles, orange wheels underneath. Her right foot glides forward, her left follows. She whooshes, a whisper, wheels spinning on axels across shellacked wooden boards. She bends her knee, presses onto the tip of her toe, pulls herself over. Off to the side, off of the rink. In the shadows. Transfixed. She is shadow. Reflection and darkness. Looking at the world as if she were three inches taller, remembering what it was like when she was one foot shorter.

This roller rink is much nicer than the one she grew up near, much cleaner. Its graffiti is intentional. Manufactured hipness. The words "fun" and "silly" can hardly be considered tags, or subversive, no matter how much colorful spray paint is used.

Maryanne and the waspish Salo left her alone as they went to the bathroom. Nora's courage, a prophetic sense of anticipation, thinks this an adventure. After spending the afternoon watching television, she feels a promising sense of purpose, of grandeur, as though everything will have been worth writing down. The back of her knees tingle, a parade of gooseflesh breaks out, as it always does when she becomes suddenly aroused.

She pulls at the lace hem of her tank top, an old neurotic gesture of hers, to hide the humiliation of arousal. The shame of suddenly. Of being seen, of being foreign.

She sees the girls stopped by a group of boys. She sees Maryanne motion toward her. She waves, they all wave back. But one doesn't. Instead, he walks toward her.

He looks like a photograph she's seen before. Familiar, nondescript, phantasmagoric.

Nora breathes into her belly, then deeper into her cervix, awakening the somnolent pheromones below the surface of their incautious sisters.

He walks deliberately, in solid steps. Cocksure, but with all the surreptitious grace of a woman.

Nora unapologetically stares.

As does he.

A white T-shirt stretches across his vague chest and army green cargo pants leave too much for the imagination. His tawny hair is gelled to unnatural perfection. A smile breaks from the left side of his mouth and moves across his face.

Nora can feel the mouth between her legs. With the sensation that he knows this.

Because she's on skates, and he's not, they're the same height, at even eye level.

He has the aged eyes of a Titan, a desperado. As if he were always alone, even when he's not.

In one movement he steps toward her, extends his hand, and says "Jake Noyes," in a voice of deceptive warmth, like really cold beer.

He smells like a man, like a carnivore. Like cedar and moss and suede, but more complicated than that.

"Nora Childers," she says, bowing slightly, hands by her side.

But he doesn't accept that. He steps in closer, grabs her hand and pumps.

Ground coffee beans. Cracked black pepper. Cigarette smoke. Orange blossoms. Alcohol. Rum.

"That's better," he says in a rasping, sardonic breath. Still holding her hand.

Then something happens.

A straight curve, an electric line segment, not unlike lightning, binds their gaze, is their gaze. Two electric currents collide in the center. Sucking all matter, all light, all sound, all hormones, all flesh, into its nucleus.

The roller rink disappears. The mephitic smell of child sweat dissipates. Black nothingness surrounds them. Collapses from under its own weight into a speck. A speck of pure light.

It is as if they had given birth to a tiny, hot, dense particle containing all matter and energy. A glowing aleph, vibrating, ticking between them. Reaching a crescendo.

An explosion. A paroxysm. An orgasm. *Jouissance*!

It's beyond words. An unnamable force, a full spectrum. Pure white heat.

They are unable to look away, or step outside its field.

Nora forgets she has a body, until it pulsates.

Anchored, Jake blinks back the *coup de foudre*. Shutting, hiding his equivocal, oceanic eyes.

He takes his other hand and touches her elbow.

"How have I not met you before?" he says.

Just as everyone shows up. Salo holds out a pair of skates for him.

"My dear, dear Salo," he says, dropping Nora's hand, and her elbow. Salo thrusts the skates into his chest hard enough to make a noise.

Nora feels a pain in her chest, as if a pair of roller skates were just slammed into it. She brings her hand to her thorax, covers her heart, thumbs the contours of her padded bra, holds her breast. She can still feel him, just above her elbow, an ache. Until Salo grabs Nora's arm, raises it high. "This is Nora," she says. Nora looks to everyone, and smiles, almost awkwardly, with a hint of anger, as though they all ruined something. Because they fucking did.

"I'm bored," Salo abruptly says then skates away, pulling Nora with her, toward the rink.

There is no moment of separation where Nora and Jake reach out to one another, desperate to feel what they had just felt, psychotic to understand beauty's potential, love's melodramatic music. Instead, she flees the scene. Leaving a trail of breathless gaps in her wake. Buzzing, weak, she is a miniscule celestial body whose electrons are easily grabbed. She is unstable, imbalanced, ready to give. Ready to let him take from her. To possess her completely. To possess her until completion.

. . .

Saint Charles is primarily known for its proximity to the Tevatron, a proton-antiproton collider, a synchrotron that accelerates protons and antiprotons in a 3.9 mile ring to energies of up to one TeV. The town dreams someday of smashing electrons with their antimatter counterparts.

...

The rink is a misshapen ellipses. It looks more like an egg. An egg with two hundred creatures skating in an unbroken ring inside of its shell. The girls follow the current. They skate around and around. Nora watches the mouth of the whirlpool for the rest of their group, for Jake. She can't hold still, can't be still. She overflows, could burst at her seams. Luckily, Salo has fallen into a rant, something Maryanne had already warned her about. Nora likes it though. She sees a parallel spirit in Salo, a fellow termagant.

Her first name is not Salo, it's Caitlin, but she hasn't gone by Caitlin since the second grade. Salo is her last name and is much more fitting for the furious ninety-pound blonde with enough piss, vinegar, and vainglorious pride to flour bomb the old gym teacher, her old soccer coach, in the middle of the Pride of the Fox, while he was waiting in line for the Tilt-a-Whirl. She also destroyed his lawn, forking the grass, toilet-papering the trees, and pouring instant mashed potatoes over everything, which, when mixed with morning dew, makes ones lawn look as though it has a yeast infection. Apparently, the bastard grabbed her ass, many more times than once, which, already, would've been too many. Nora believes her, but no one else does, no adult, that is, and though it could be regarded that her outward rebellion, her lack of make-up or form-fitting clothes, and a penchant for drugs, particularly rolling joints from Bible paper, are merely attention-seeking, the cotton ball cloud of anger festering in her belly suggests a deeper resistance, a private revolt, that goes beyond her mother, beyond her soccer coach, and into a forceful, artistic subversion of suburban culture. Nora, though intimidated by her, liked her instantly, liked her audacity as she round-kicked Nora's locker shut and asked her *who the fuck she was* messing with Maryanne.

"I'm glad Jake's girlfriend didn't come. I can't fucking stand that bitch," Salo says, spitting her gum just beyond the wall.

"What?" Nora asks.

"She totally sucks. Always ragging on him for stupid, paranoid shit. She must have an away game or something."

"What?"

"You're slow," she laughs, "Today, he was totally ogling some chick and Amy came up behind him and did that thing where you cover someone's eyes and go 'Guess who' 'cept he totally guessed wrong. I think he's a player. I haven't had proof yet though, but I'll get it," says Salo, pointing at him with a stiff, enthusiastic finger.

And just like that, there he is again. With Maryanne, with everyone else.

"Salo, how many times do I have to tell you? I'm flattered but I've got a girlfriend," he says, winking at Nora.

What?

"I hate you," Salo says.

And like that, everyone moves on, as if nothing happened.

For a second, Nora thinks an embolism has just popped in her brain. She digs her nails into her wrist, cutting through the first few layers of skin. The cold, greasy, musty air stings, in a good way.

. . .

20

While skating, one cannot directly look at someone else. They must look ahead, beyond their body, to where they will be, to where their foot will fall.

...

Around and around and around
and around and around.

Like cattle. Like sheep.

Jake can skate backwards, but only for a little bit, about enough time to tell a joke.

He asks, "Why do the ladies love Jesus?"

Then answers himself, raising his arms to form a cross, "Because he's hung like this!"

He is the alpha male of the group.

Nick is his best friend. He's objectively better looking than Jake, with his dark hair, brooding complexion, and calculating brow. He's a devout rationalist and a puritan at heart, which is only rivaled by his love of balancing mathematical equations and his irrational affection toward Salo. He and Jake seem to feed off of each other's energy. Nora finds them both captivating.

She steals glances at Jake. Again and again and again and again and again.

Just out of reach.

Unbearable.

She breaks away.

Alone, against the current, she skims across the lacquered wood and skates an invisible radius to the center of the rink, the yolk of the egg. Arms cruciform, laughing in repose, stopping time with a toe, she pirouettes large figure eights directly under the mirrored ball dangling over head. Her skin tingles once more. She feels him looking at her. He is drawn to her. He skates another radius, nearly collides into her, but doesn't, stops short, then encircles her. She lulls her movement to a sway. The blood pulls away from her stomach. The lights go out. The mirrored ball lowers. So round. So fragile. So breathtaking. The music slows. The rink explodes into myriad sparkles. He takes her hand. Her sternum expands. Butterflies aflutter. Cheeks flush. Gooseflesh parade. Arm hair stands on end. Palm to palm, the holy palmers' kiss. She feels his pulse, his rhythm beat into her blood. A total transfusion. She's taken with the poetry, the ouroboros.

"I want you," he tells her.

"Take me then," she answers.

He skates away.

Such is the genesis of Limerence.

. . .

Saint Charles leaves no trace of its past in any wrinkle or blemish or chink in the iron. Everything was built yesterday, created on a concept of this generation's necessities, their luxuries.

It snows palimpsestic plaster year round.

. . .

On the corner of Route 25 and Main there is a religious shoppe. They sell angel sundries and rosaries made from bone. Out front there is a stone statue of Mary. Occasionally she weeps rusted iron particles, particularly in May, after a good rain. People pull over. They get out of their car and begin weeping themselves. They look up to the sun and praise Jesus. They think this is a miracle. That stone is shedding tears of blood for the townspeople of Saint Charles, for their intolerably beautiful world. Flowers, wreaths, letters are all laid at Mary's feet.

For a second, when Nora hears of this, her heart flutters, opens for the warmth of wishful thinking.

. . .

Saint Charles is named after the patron saint of all stomach illnesses, intestinal illnesses, catechism, and apple orchards. But its name is in a endless cycle of re-appropriation.

It's always becoming what it is.

A hamster in a wheel of semiotics.

...

After school, in Taco Bell's parking lot, Amy rests her head on his shoulder, wraps herself around his bicep, and complains how frozen her breath is. *Haaa Haaaa*, she exhales then points to the condensed white cloud.

"Oh, stop. It's not that cold," Jake says.

Amy grabs one of the blankets and pulls it over both of their legs. Maryanne has the other wrapped around her. Salo and Nick are inside buying another round of tacos. Nora sits on the truck's edge, fighting the frost with nicotine.

"Are you guys planning on going to Nathan's party on Friday? I heard his parents are out of town for two weeks." Amy says, more to Maryanne than to Nora, or so Nora assumes. Either way she rolls her eyes.

"I think he's kind of cute," Maryanne says. Then Amy responds and both of their voices fade. Jake looks at Nora. Salo and Nick return. Jake lights a cigarette. Nora doesn't flinch. She stares, unblinkingly, without expression, just looking and smoking and watching. This goes on for nearly a minute. Until Amy's anecdote resolves itself. Everybody laughs. A slight smile crosses Nora's lips. Jake turns his whole body to Amy.

She waves her gloved hand in her face, "Don't blow that this way. *God!*"

Amy is predictable, born in Saint Charles, born of Saint Charles. *Palimpsestic plaster*, or so Nora thinks. In some ways, she and Nora look alike. They have a similar shape. But Amy is less aware, less imaginative, less mystical. She wishes her image was darker, more elusive.

23

She wishes she had a secret. This is why she wears heavy black eyeliner and too much red, but then she'll pair it with khakis or a WWJD bracelet and the whole portrait ends up too clean and boring for further wonderment. She sees Amy as a cheap imitation, as threatening as a polyp. But this is Nora deriving her interior from her exterior. This is Nora decoupaging Amy's plaster, defining Jake's world only as it regards to herself. This is Nora being a teenager.

. . .

They all see a film together. *The Empire Strikes Back*; it was rereleased, but the theater oversold the show. Nora and her eight friends move to the front row, some of them, including Nora, sit on the floor, in front of the others. She sits directly to the left of Jake, cross-legged. At the beginning of the film, when Han corners Leia and says, "You like me because I'm a scoundrel," Jake slides his toe under Nora's thigh, then leaves it there. Between her legs she's all wet. So much it hurts.

. . .

"Confess the name of Christ boldly," she's told. But she doesn't know how.

. . .

Padiddle |pə ˈdidl|
An American game practiced in moving motor vehicles. The teams are generally split according to gender but can be divvied up any way. For every car with one headlight seen the player must strike the roof of the vehicle and yell, "Padiddle." If the player did indeed spot a car with one headlight and cite a Padiddle then all members of the opposing team must removed one article of clothing. If that player was mistaken, then his or her team takes a penalty and each member removes two articles of clothing. Semi-trucks with one headlight are also worth two articles of clothing. When one entire team is naked sexual favors accrue.

. . .

SALO: Shut the fuck up! Where? Where?!

NICK: (*laughter*) I see it! I see it!

SALO: It's dim.

JAKE: That is not dim! I'm turning around. (*Turns truck around, doesn't wait for the next light to pull a legal U-turn.*)

NORA: SALO, that looks legitimate.

JAKE: See, even your teammate agrees.

SALO: (*speaking the same time as* JAKE.) You SLUT! For some of us the point is to actually keep our clothes on.

NORA: No, if we contest, and YOU were wrong WE have to take off double!

MARYANNE: Is that a rule? When did we decide that was a rule?

SALO: (*laughing*) That was always a rule. Maybe if you stopped playing with your vagina back here we'd actually get a PADIDDLE.

NICK: Did she just say PADIDDLE, JAKE?

JAKE: I think she did, NICK. Looks like SALO just cost you guys another article of clothing.

SALO: Oh shut the fuck up. And who says "article of clothing"? You're an idiot.

JAKE: So you believe me? (*Revs the engine, mocking a chase.*)

SALO: Yes, Yes. Fine! But my teammates better shape up! I'm doing all the work over here!

NORA: Oh thank God for her!

MARYANNE: Oh, I know. Thank God for SALO.

SALO: You guys are assholes.

MARYANNE: (*in a high pitched, cartoony voice, almost as if she's talking out of the side of her mouth.*) Hey, POT. Why hey, KETTLE! How are you today? Fine. How are you? I just called to talk about your blackness. Yes, yes. Your blackness.

(*Laughter.*)

NICK: Ladies I believe you should be removing one item of clothing.

(SALO *removes her jacket.*)

NICK: Coats don't count!

SALO: Since when?

JAKE: Coats and jewelry and shoes don't count, and both socks count as one.

SALO: Gay.

NORA: It'll be freezing back here!

JAKE: I'll turn up the heat. (*Reaches over and fiddles with a knob on the dashboard, turning up the heat.* MARYANNE *and* NORA *also remove their jackets.*)

NORA: Thank you.

SALO: Don't thank him!

NORA: Oh yeah! Grrrrr. (*Balls a fist and shakes it at him.*)

NICK, JAKE: Yarrrrr!

NICK: Hey. Hey. A pirate saw a movie today and it was rated RRRRR. (*Turns to the back, hooks his index finger.*)

(MARYANNE *laughs.*)

SALO: Double gay.

JAKE: Strip.

(*All three girls take off their shoes and socks.*)

NICK: Booooooooo!

NORA: What did you expect?

JAKE: Some more imagination!

NORA: On the first rou- (*interrupted by* SALO)

SALO: Be on the lookout!

MARYANNE: You're like a PADIDDLE NAZI.

SALO: That was just a practice round! You all wait!

MARYANNE: Doesn't DAWN live around here?

SALO: Your questions are nonsense! Eyes peeled! Stay focused!

NORA: I should've worn more layers.

NICK: At least you girls get bras!

NORA: Like you two aren't wearing a million layers. Like you didn't plan this all week!

JAKE: We didn't! Scouts honor! We came up with it in the car just now with you guys. It was all of our idea.

MARYANNE: I seem to remember you pushing it quite heavily.

JAKE: And miss a chance to have three lovely ladies naked in my backseat? I would be a fool!

SALO: It is YOU who will be naked! We will be wearing your pants as hats!

NORA: Were you really a boy scout?

JAKE: Cub Scout then Boy Scout. I can tie fifteen different knots.

SALO: She'd like that.

(*Truck erupts in laughter.*)

MARYANNE: I don't get it.

(*The truck continues laughing, but louder.* NORA *whispers in* MARYANNE's *ear what* SALO *meant.* JAKE *looks at* NORA *in the rearview mirror, smiles.*)

MARYANNE: Oooh! OOOOOH! (*Flaps her hands wildly.*) Wait, nevermind.

SALO: Don't warn them! SILENTLY find one! STUPID!

NICK: Turn down Randall.

JAKE: No one has to be home for awhile right?

MARYANNE: Yeah, my curfew is always the earliest but I'm staying at NOR's.

JAKE: What time is your curfew? (*Looks at* NORA *in the rearview mirror again.*)

NORA: Midnight thirty. I might be able to get an extension.

MARYANNE: (*looking at* NORA) Your curfew's-
(NORA *places her hand on* MARYANNE's *leg, squeezes, meaning,* Shut up.)

NICK: No matter, what's it? Ten thirty?

(SALO *rises to her seat, almost stands on the cushions.*)

SALO: (*punching the ceiling as dramatically possible.*) PA-MOTHER-FUCKING-DIDDLE!! Blue car. Coming out of Jewel. Eat it! Off with your sweaters!

MARYANNE: Nice.

NICK: How did we miss that?

SALO: So sad. So true.

JAKE: Truth is only that which is taken to be true.

MARYANNE: You better take this, or we're putting our socks back on.

NORA: What is that from?

JAKE: (*looks at* NORA *in the rearview mirror again, only smiles in response to her question.*) I'll take off my sweater. Save my shoes and socks for later, as it's probably dangerous to drive without shoes in these conditions.

SALO: It's not icy IN the car.

JAKE: Only if you open your legs. (*Adjusts rearview mirror, looks at* SALO.)

(*Truck is laughing.* SALO *is not.*)

MARYANNE, NICK: Burn!! Ooooh! You burned SALO! Oooh, snap!

(JAKE *removes his sweater.* NICK *removes his socks and shoes and then turns up the heat a little bit more.* MARYANNE *puts her arm around* SALO, *who then shoves her off and begins trolling the streets once again for cars with one headlight. There is silence for two minutes.*)

JAKE: (*casually flicks the roof of his truck with his middle finger*) PADIDDLE.

(*The girls see it, they groan.*)

NICK: What'll it be? What'll it be?

NORA: No fair! You guys are all wearing two shirts!

SALO: Should've thought of that before you dressed like a ho in February! Thank God you're not wearing your hooker boots!

MARYANNE: At least you're wearing overalls. Just keep 'em clicked.

NORA: By JOVE, you're right!

(*The girls wait until the light turns green, look right then left for nearby cars, then almost simultaneously they all remove their tops.* JAKE *takes his eyes off the road and stares into his rearview mirror, and* NICK *doesn't even bother to be inconspicuous as he turns around completely and stares at* NORA's *black bra and exposed cleavage. She clicks her overall top back together a little slower than one would expect, almost as if she were disinclined to do so, and then looks into the rearview mirror.*)

SALO: Why didn't AMY come out tonight?

NICK: She's out with her friends.

SALO: I wasn't asking YOU.

JAKE: She's out with her friends.

SALO: Aren't we her friends.

JAKE: You're more my friends.

SALO: I'm everyone's friend.

NORA: Except DAWN, and LIZ, and LEE.

MARYANNE: And GREG.

NICK: And STEPHANIE.

SALO: All those people suck!

MARYANNE: Mean people suck.

NORA: Nice people swallow.

JAKE: Ass, gas, or grass. Nobody rides for free.

SALO: Talk to NORA, she'll pay all our fares.

NORA: Aren't you the burnout of the group?

NICK: Aren't you all quoting bumper stickers?

MARYANNE: You're a bumper sticker.

JAKE: Should we go on the highway?

SALO: We should stay on Randall. We don't want to be too far from 64. I told my mom that we'd be back by midnight so I could beat your ass in GOLDEN EYE. Unless NORA's on the rag.

NORA: *Ugh!* You guys are playing GOLDEN EYE? I'm totally not getting my curfew extended to watch video games.

SALO: Gay.

NICK: (*speaking the same time as* SALO.) You could play.

NORA: All homophobes are gay.

SALO: That's gay.

NICK: PADIDDLE!! (*Punches the roof of the truck and points excitedly at his kill.*)

MARYANNE: You two keep talking!

SALO: You're useless! (*Rips off her baseball t-shirt: SALO, number 9. NICK leers openly at the rise and fall of the beauty mark on her stomach, at her pocket-sized breasts obscured behind a gray sports bra.*)

MARYANNE: I just saw it! I was two seconds behind him. It's hard being in the middle. (*As she pulls off her coral t-shirt, her profuse flesh sighs out its lacy custody.* NICK's *heart rises up into his throat.*)

(NORA *discreetly unhooks the back of her bra and slides it out without removing the flap of her overalls, the cold metal briefly brushes against her nipples causing her to sit up straighter.* JAKE *adjusts and readjusts mirrors, looking back and forth between all the girls. He then steers back in between the white dotted lines.*)

SALO: You failed! Move over! (*Unbuckles* MARYANNE's *seatbelt then crawls over her to sit in the center seat.*) I'm sitting BITCH. YOU can't handle it. (*Leans over the center counsel and looks out the windshield.*) And this way I have a better view! (*Punches* JAKE *then* NICK) Stop ogling us, you bunch of perverts. (*After 15 minutes* SALO *yells that she's bored.*)

...

Obsessive behavior. Checking, rechecking email, signing onto AOL ten times a night. Reading his profile information beyond memorization. He still likes *1984*. He still loves to play lacrosse. He still has a dog named Sprocket. He still fears fear itself.

She thinks she has made a choice. She thinks she's choosing to fall in love like this, under these conditions.

Her father knocks on the door. She can't hear him. She's dancing to the Violent Femmes, and changing, trying on outfit after outfit, and singing to herself, herself as Angela Chase, into the mirror. Her father knocks again.

"What?!"

She turns down the music.

"It's time for church."

"Is mom going?"

"That's irrelevant."

"If mom's not going I'm not going."

"Your mother's going. Get ready."

She sighs an exaggerated teenage sigh.

In church, she crosses her legs tightly, to the point of stimulation, and fantasizes about Jake. Jake pushing her up against the wall, kissing her, biting her, professing his love for her in front of her math class, going down on her in the Confessional, which, she immediately feels guilty about. She makes the sign of the cross, tries to pay attention, resigns to be nicer to her brother, and to go on that CCD retreat. But that tingle, that delightful worm.

. . .

On Tuesday, she sees him in the hallway during her Algebra II hour.

"Pssst," she says.

He turns around.

She motions for him to come to her.

To see if he would. To watch him walk.

"I need a ride home today," she says.

On Tuesdays Amy has Yearbook.

"All right," he says. He knows what she's doing.

. . .

As soon as Nora gets into his truck she takes off her jacket and lights a cigarette. He waits until they pass the threshold, until they're off school property. She makes fun of him for it. He makes fun of her for pretending not to know where the flagpole was simply to highlight that she's not into sports.

"Touché," she says. For a second she turns to look out the window. Her cigarette's reaching its filter. She wants to light another.

"I notice you looking at me," he says. "I know that you watch me."

She thinks for a second. "Do you like it?" she asks, dropping the smoking butt out the window.

"Yes," he says, "Sometimes, I wait a tick before approaching everybody, just so I can look at you. You look really pretty when you're far away."

Nora unbuckles herself and reaches across the center counsel, then slowly, she reaches across his chest, on her knees, she glides against his brown leather bomber jacket, against his nylon seat belt, and plucks the half-smoked cigarette from his left hand. Then returns to her seat and says, "That sounds vaguely insulting."

"Well, you look even sexier when you're that close to my dick."

"My, my, my," she says. "Are you this frank will all your ladies?"

"And I thought I was holding back."

"Turn here," she says. "I live just around the corner."

"That's a shame."

"There's a lot that's a shame with this situation; premature ejaculation doesn't top spoiled nuisance of a girlfriend."

"O ho!" he laughs, his nose pinkens.

"And thank you for the ride, Jacob Noyes. That will be all."

"What? Aren't you going to invite me in?"

"Maybe next Tuesday."

...

An inside joke is often taken too far. It begins when Jake asks Nick if he wants to go Chili's for lunch. "Yar, me be sick of Chili's," he says.

From then on, "Yar" becomes a sentence adverb and occasionally, "Yar" turns into an entire dialogue in piratespeak. It's a game of make-believe, and a game that Jake finds so delightful he can't help turning red to purple and erupting with hilarity. It's not the inside joke itself that bothers Nora, or the way it reminds her exactly how old he is. It's his laugh. High pitched, corrupted, repugnant. Sometimes it's silent, sometimes it's squeaky, sometimes it's a jocky guffaw. It seizes his body. Like he's not fully in control of himself.

At this moment immortality drains from his skin. Once iridescent, now gray. He is no longer a god, not in this moment.

Like when Anaïs's disgust with Henry dethroned him. He, too, became mortal, pathetic. Weak. Nora keeps this image, Jake's laughter, on the tip of her imagination throughout the rest of lunch.

Annoyed, she shuts her eyes and looks away. She tries to locate Jason, her senior crush who carries a knife and would never break character. Jason's laugh is simple, maintained, manly. Then she looks outside for the hot tattooed janitor that mows the lawn shirtless. Jake catches her ogling and as he calms his tittering to a couple of belly shakes and sighs, Nora, still looking out the window, says "Everyday of the week and twice on Sunday." To which every girl emphatically agrees or sighs with her head in her hand.

Then, Brian walks by.
"Lesbian," he coughs, decidedly at Nora.
"Fuck you," Salo says, throwing a
French fry at him.

Mortality escorts a sense of urgency, a kind of dumb impatience; one that sharply contrasts with the uniqueness, the pomposity of divinity. It was in that farcical moment, when the ichor mixed with blood, that Nora was given another choice. That choice was a gift, an opportunity for disregard. That she disregarded. But it was because of his otherwise engagement, his unavailability, that Nora chose to like him all the more, to elevate him, seduce him, ensnare him, steal him, convert him into a prize. A spoil of war. Nora chose cognitive dissonance, competition, safety, danger.

...

Late for class, and since late is late, Nora slows her pace to a lento, to the pace of the rain shower outside. She likes being alone in hallways, inside the silence, like a pause in between breaths, especially when there's a soft, gentle tapping at the windows.

The echo of her chunky black boots in such a grand, empty space stirs her into whimsical expectation.

Heel, toe.

Even through concrete, she can smell the rain, the wet earth, the thick clouds misting daylight into dusk.

Heel, toe.

The heel is hard like a consonant. The toe is a soft tap, an aspirated h, like in thought. She thinks, she remembers hiding from the world here with Brian against these lockers during the Winter Ball, make-believing they had been locked inside the school, the feeling of her nipples erect against silk.

Just when she opens a set of double doors leading to a staircase, she hears someone else open the doors at the opposite end of the hallway. As she turns, she sees the white T-shirt, the faded cargo pants, his rusted hair. As the door clicks shut behind her she pinches her cheeks then spits her gum out against the wall, toward the corner, where hopefully no one would step in it. She smooths out her pleated plaid skirt, rolled once at the waist, just like in Catholic school, and unbuttons another button on her white blouse, making sure he'll notice her lacey black bra, as if it wasn't already a stark contrast in between her pale skin and the semi see-through blouse.

When he opens the plexiglas door, she turns and begins ascending the first set of stairs. He lets her round the corner. The backs of her knees tingle. She feels his eyes transfixed onto that paradisal space covered by a thin strip of black cotton. He puts his hand on the back of her bare thigh, fingers reaching toward paradise. Reaching, touching, he grazes her sex with the tip of his middle finger; the very thought of its proximity contracts her entire body. Her wet mouths dilate, work through a restricted compulsion. An aggressive emergency. She turns around and leaps down to the platform between the first and second floors. Down to him, where they collide, where their lips converge and her cunt aches with the pleasures of impropriety. With his face in her hands, he grabs her ass and kisses her insatiably; the kind of kiss that would rather be fucking on this stairwell toward neither ascent nor decline until the movement that shakes their futures descends into madness and poetry. She discovers, colonizes the texture of his tongue, caressing, learning the interior of his mouth, as he learns hers, she thrusts her knee in between his legs. His clothed cock is conscious against her naked thigh as he moves his hands up, over her shoulder blades, up her neck, weaves them into her bristling roots and takes a fistful of hot pink hair, yanks at it from her scalp, pulling her away, keeping her close, holding her in purgatorial passion, astral *jouissance*.

Until they hear footsteps.

They fly apart. Someone opens the door. A boy neither of them recognize.

She takes her middle finger and wipes the spit from the corner of her mouth.

"Today... tonight," he says.

"Can't," she says.

"Why not?"

"Friday," she says.

"How am I going to do that?"

She shrugs. Walks away, ascends.

"Okay, okay. Friday."

When she reaches the top of the stairs, as he gallops back down, he calls, "I love your new hair!"

...

His truck smells like old car upholstery, mentholated cigarettes, and him. Clover, oranges, leather, cedar, and salt. She inhales deeply, already aroused.

Padiddle! First him: her socks. Then her: his socks. Then him: her cardigan. Then her: his hoodie. On and on and on.

Pretense. Throat clearing. Foreplay. Teasing. Stalling. Playing. Chivalry.

Milky teenage skin, luminous in the moon light.

Every time they drive through traffic lights, headlights, neon lights, suburban lights, a stripe of clarity skims across their bodies. Like flickering candlelight. It won't stay still, stay put, which is both a curse and a blessing.

Each flash is ephemeral, formless, musical.

She can read the side mirror, her mirror, reflected on his face.

WARNING: ASSHOLES IN MIRROR ARE CLOSER THAN THEY APPEAR.

Wearing nothing but black underwear, she unbuckles her seatbelt and moves in, **CLOSER**, as marked across his cheek.

She takes a cigarette from the dashboard, lights it then places it in his mouth, rubbing her gumdrop nipples against his thigh along the way.

He reaches his sinewy, freckle-dusted arm over to turn up the heat.

"I'm not cold," she says, on all fours, leaning closer. "But I'm incredibly wet."

With his palm up, he moves his hand from her diaphragm down. She moans into his ear as he slides his finger along her labia.

Her skins feels electrified, like her very bones were lucent.

At the sight of one headlight approaching, she turns and lifts herself, punching the ceiling and yells, "Pull over, Mother Fucker!"

He does, in an area where the houses are spaced apart by acres.

The terrifying intensity of magnetic force!

She takes his cock in her hand, like stiffened silk, and rubs it against her face, around her mouth like a cat. She begins to go down on him, coating his sex in all of the words that she's ever thought of him, thought for him, a thick verbose film, murkier than saliva. A gesture ahead of itself, they ascend time. He looks for her again. Her lower lips are swollen.

Cruel, serious, immoral, vicious. She cums then sucks his cock to end all movement.

He is her musical instrument. Delicately fingering the fleshy nodes, pulsating, sponges of sanguine arousal, singing a love song unto his mushroomed ego, the winking eye of prima facie. She cannot help herself.

40

She loves him.

She loves his cock.

He comes with an irascible fury, and tastes like strawberries and dried tobacco. Buttery ichor of the gods.

She swallows. Keeps him inside of her, like a fetus, rising and eddying, suppressing the secret, she puts her hands on her stomach. He lights two cigarettes, then gives one to her. The thin, hoary smoke curls from the tip of his cigarette toward the ceiling of his truck. It creates enough of a screen that she doesn't feel uncomfortable at all getting dressed. For the moment, he stays in his boxer shorts and blows smoke rings toward the moon, then one at her. She breaks it with her finger. It feels cold.

"I like you," he says. "I like you because you are just like me."

She turns, hides her face, the embarrassed notes in her cheeks. When she drops her shoulder back down he traces his knuckle from her jaw to her clavicle then back up her neck.

"What are we going to do?" he asks.

"That's kind of your problem," she says.

...

She says it, out loud, "I love him."

But *love*, that word…

Its anemic language… It's always too much and too little.

Untranslatable.

An avalanche of sincerity trying to be authentic.

Love for the sake of love, an idea caught in Queen Mab's eye, like a shard of glass scratching at her cornea. *L'amour pour l'amour.*

To love love is to love an action, a verb, an elusive, incorporeal mist of vapor.

Love for the sake of love negates the loved object.

In this case, Jake Noyes.

He, like everyone else, is the sum of his parts, and Nora, like everyone else, can only know some of his parts, his qualities, tangible pieces that she can attach her love to: the smell of citrus and wood; tawny hair; feral, unbridled eyes; deliberate gait; mentholated cigarettes; yellow backpack; Amy, but here, it clouds ominously.

Nora has to resist the gravitational pull of his body in public. She has to deny their obvious attraction. Sidestep him. Escape into bathrooms to rub away her tumescence.

He stands before her, dripping in unspeakable discourse, waiting to be recorded in a journal.

Small acts of kindness burgeon into venerated professions.

Once, he gave her an Ibuprofen. Instead of swallowing the requested drug, alleviating her pain, she suffered the headache, and now keeps the white pill inside of her jewelry box, next to a miniature diamond ring she received on her first communion.

L'art pour l'amour.

. . .

She sets down her things in the hallway, in the way of anyone who wishes to walk through. She goes into the kitchen, opens the refrigerator, pulls out the bowl of last night's Jell-O. The doorbell rings. Still able to see the front door, spoon of red Jell-O in mouth, she looks through the flanking glass doors. Jake lets himself in. He's carrying a single red rose. She swallows, looks confused.

"Is your brother home?"

She shakes her head. He walks over to her, lays the rose on the island, and kisses her, licking the outline of her lips, kissing her softly, softly with compassion, like the lapping tongues of the tides. Usually he's so rough, desperate. This kiss is unlike the others, out of place, cloying, maudlin.

The phone rings.

She answers.

"Is Jake there?"

It's Amy. Nora doesn't know what to say. She's speechless.

"I know he's there. I followed him to your house. Will you just put him on?" She says. Jake waves his hands "No."

Nora improvises. "He just brought over my mittens I had left in his car from *Great Expectations*."

Amy begins to cry. "Today? It's Valentine's Day, Nora. Why did you need those *mittens* today? Why couldn't you get them at school? What's going on?"

Nora feels terrible. She doesn't know what to do. "Nothing, honey. He already left. He's probably on his way to your house right now. Don't worry so much."

"Don't fucking tell me what to do, slut. I see the way you look at him. Just watch your back!"

"Holy shit," Nora says. The line's dead.

"IloveyouIloveyouIloveyou!" Jake says.

"This isn't funny! She just threatened to kick my ass. I think she suspects something."

"I'll talk to her. Don't worry," he says, wrapping his arms around her waist.

"You should go."

"In a minute."

...

"Do you want to watch something?" Maryanne asks.

"Television makes me too anxious," Nora says. "It's like, you're watching someone else's best and worst moments—the climaxes of their lives—condensed into two hours, and then afterwards you shut the TV off or a commercial comes on and you think about how you just spent two hours watching them, and how boring your own life usually is. I think it's called The Madame Bovary Effect, or something."

"For me, it's more that moment, right when the light sucks itself back into the box, and you watch it disappear. But after it's gone, you're left looking at yourself in that black reflection. It's like an evil copy of you. The negative sides to who we really are."

Nora thinks about it then looks into the black television screen. She sees herself and Maryanne sitting on the couch, studying their evil reflections.

"What would your evil self be doing right now?"

"Well, right now, I'm sitting here. This is where our worlds intersect. But, when I get up, I don't know. I would probably steal some money out of my dad's wallet then buy that dress we saw yesterday."

"I blew Jake," Nora says.

"I could see that."

"No, no, I did it. Two weeks ago. And we've been fooling around every Tuesday," at this Nora clamps her eyes shut, as though she doesn't want to see Maryanne's disappointment in her, or worse, to dredge up what Nora had done to her.

"That's fucking awesome!" Maryanne says.

Nora opens one eye.

"High school relationships don't last; you taught me that," says Maryanne, nudging Nora in the boob.

"Oh my God, I thought you were going to be so mad!"

The girls embrace one another, Nora even sheds a tear. "No," you're my friend. "I mean, I like Amy, but I like you more, and whatever makes you happy. Wait," she pulls back, "Oh my God, is he leaving her?"

"I don't know…" Nora says, with a kind of coquettish giddiness that she doesn't usually display.

"They have been fighting a lot more recently. Did you notice?"

"Of course I did. But you did too? Omigodomigodomigod! You have to promise not to tell anyone!"

"Pinky swear," Maryanne says, holding out her littlest finger, its nail painted a pretty pearlescent pink. Nora does the same, except her fingernail has chipped black polish. They hook them together then shake. A solemn oath.

"What's his sign?" Maryanne then asks, leaping into her purse to pull out a tattered copy of *Sun Signs* barely held together with masking tape.

"We have the same birthday," Nora says.

"Jesus, Mary, and Joseph!"

. . .

The next Saturday evening, Jake suddenly springs on Nora, via AOL Instant Messenger, that Amy is playing a tournament in Milwaukee, and, if Nora were available, he would love to take her to a movie. In Elgin, he suggests. The town to the left of Amy's friends.

Nora, of course, makes herself available.

They never make it to the movie, stopping for two hours within the labyrinth of frozen fields near his house. Jake tosses his bomber jacket into the back seat, Nora throws her fitted black leather coat on top of his. Both of their car seats recline onto them.

Afterwards, Nora reaches in his jacket's pocket and pulls out two cigarettes.

"Your curfew isn't until midnight?" he asks.

"Maryanne works around here," she says. "We could go visit her and steal some candy."

After twenty minutes of wrong turns down dirt roads, they finally reach a main road, populated only with rickety barns about to crumble from dry-rot. She perches, almost uncomfortably in a tight pink top, not her best color. It brings out her acne, her rosy cheeks. She presses her pubic bone down, letting the gentle bumps in the road stimulate her mind. They come upon a sign: **DO NOT PICK UP HITCHHIKERS.** Then a massive, unmarked structure surrounded by football fields of dead grass.

Hauntingly blank, this place looks like a depository for nightmares. Completely fenced in, with barbed wire and metal spikes; there were even barbed wire walkways connecting rooftops. Narrow slits for windows. Dilapidated plaster, twisted and rusted metal.

"I didn't know Saint Charles had a prison."

"Technically, this is Elgin, and it's a juvenile delinquency facility."

They stop at a red light. His tires spin black muck onto the pristinely blanketed sidewalk. It is almost colorless, gray and ugly, but then, immediately pulling Nora's gaze to the right, she notices a withering, gelid, unbound bouquet of roses, lilies, and spiders.

"Pull over," she says.

"Why?"

"Because I want to take a picture."

"It'll never turn out."

"At least let me try."

She pulls out her camera, a cardboard box that's to be gutted and thrown out once the film is used up. With a finger on the flash, the camera makes a high pitched noise, she presses the shutter then winds the roll of film. She imagines why the flowers are here. A woman must have thrown them out of the window after, or during, a lovers' quarrel. Or a man was about to return home, apologize with flowers when he gets the phone call not to bother, that it's over. Or the prisoners aren't allowed flowers.

The petals are curling, browning at their edges. Some of their pistils are coated with ice. Both frozen and dying, like cold, frigid, sad vaginas. Looking through the glass window, she tries to guess how close she can get without blurring the photograph. She clicks. Winds. The flash burns her retinas.

Within ten minutes, they pull into a massive parking lot, one big enough to house three hundred cars, but it's eerily vacant. Nora hops out of the car, playing a kazoo and dancing.

Surrounded by glass vases and vibrant flowers, Maryanne methodically prunes and arranges baby's breath into corsages.

After the initial merriment, Maryanne grabs both of Nora's wrists, "Next to the pharmacy there's a set of double doors. Go through them. Upstairs is our break room. No one should be up there now. The manager's checking customers because he just fired Kelly."

"Who's Kelly?" Jake asks.

Nora grabs his hand and starts running again. Past the makeup aisle. Past the freezers. Through the dairy. Into the pharmacy. Through the double doors. The secret cove for Jewel's employees.

They jump onto the rickety table. Arms out, she steadies her balance, he draws her close. His arms clasp around her waist. She leans into his chest, scratching her face with his sweater's woolen fibers. Everything metamorphoses. The lights dim. The Coke machine disappears. They move in a circle. They dance. The ballroom floor shakes, the table quakes. Nora falls, lands on her left side and grabs her ankle. Jake is over her, breathing down her neck. She smiles up at him and stretches her body out to lay down; shoulders square against the table, legs squeezed tightly together. He reaches into his lower left cargo pocket and pulls out a small, glinting knife. Nora does not move, doesn't even flinch. He lightly presses the knife into her navel, drags it along her silhouette, drawing little circles with the sharp tip, until, reaching her ever-expanding sternum. He twists the blade to tear a small hole in her T-shirt. And in one swift motion he splits her pink shirt to the collar. The fabric flaps open, exposes her heaving chest, her blushing cleavage, her tie-dyed bra.

Without hesitation he rips the rest of the shirt in half.

He traces the knife along the curves of her stomach and along the edges of her bra, stopping at the middle clasp, letting the honed tip linger over her heart. He slips the knife under her bra, slightly puncturing, dimpling her flesh. He runs the cold steel over her nipples. She squirms underneath. In another prompt motion he pops open her bra, exposing both of her breasts. He looks down at her with teeming, almost paternal love, shuts his eyes, and thrusts the knife into her abdomen, slicing her up to the diaphragm. The wound gushing forth, blossoming like Gallica Roses from the monastic herbaries of the Middle Ages. Red, Maroon, and deep-purple crimson.

Nora barely lets out a moan.

She turns her head to the left then right while Jake reaches inside her body and tears out her still beating heart. Blood dripping down his arm, he holds the heart up to the sky. The terrible beauty, the sublimity of it all, makes her pass out. Her dangling arteries, her spurting aorta, all begin to flop lifelessly. Blood pours out of Nora onto the black and white floor, spurts forth like a fountain from her gaping cavity. The table creaks and sways from the sudden flood. Jake is on one knee, bloody arm still raised high. He takes her heart to his mouth and bites the left ventricle, tearing at the organ, smearing gore all over his face.

...

The heart. The symbol. The emotional lynchpin.
The Valentine. Red and pink
construction paper. Paper doilies.
The cliché.
The gift.
The cynosure of discourse.
Weighing eight ounces. In the center of the chest, in between the lungs, slightly tipped to the left, pumping five quarts of blood each minute. Two thousand gallons a day.
One hundred thousand times a day.
Dub-blub. Dub-blub.
The heart, as a beating, anatomically correct, human heart.
The sacred heart of Jesus. The immaculate heart of Mary.
The black heart of Mephistopheles.

♥

...

If the punishment is worth the crime, Nora will gladly take the punishment.

She doesn't get many nights with Jake, only afternoon's scraps.

This is why she's twenty-four minutes past curfew.

Both her parents are still awake.

"Where were you?" her father asks. Her father is the head of the family.

"We paged you like six times," her mother says. She is the heart.

"I was at Jewel. Maryanne had to push the carts in that parking lot all by herself, and I didn't want her to be alone at that hour in Elgin. *Jesus.*"

"I thought you were on a date," her mother says.

"Don't take the Lord's name in vain," her father says.

"No, it wasn't really a date. I was just the first he picked up."

"Still, next time I want him to come to the door," her father says.

Nora nods, apologizes for being late, but this isn't Nora. This is her double, an android, some semblance of an obedient daughter.

"I don't like this boy," her father says.

Nora is off in the air, twirling, singing.

Padam. Padam. Padam.

. . .

Jake smiles a private smile in public to Amy that Nora thought was hers alone. This dreaded sight, its perennial indefiniteness visits her in the night, and much like King Hamlet, this questionable shape can be deciphered as either a demon, a ghost, or the tortured soul of a false memory.

Remember me...

. . .

At Jake's New Year's Eve party, Amy is still on his arm. (In with the old and out with the new.) Wearing a tiara, Nora sits in the corner, alone, unhappy. A tristesse princess. She takes out her notebook and scribbles in the plagiarized language of teenage love. A language of chance and desperation and the lack of language. *Look at me*, she writes.

Look at me. Look at me. Look at me. Look at me. Look at me. Look at me. Look at me. Look at me. Look at me. Look at me. Look at me. Look

50

at me. Look at me. Look

at me. Look at me. Look at me. Look at me. Look at me. Look at me.
Look at me...

> *Look at me and lower yourself.*
> *Look at me so I can't look at you.*

. . .

Earlier, when Nora met Jake's parents she did not really look at them. She did not want to count them as real people who passed down their traits and neuroses into their offspring. Real parents with rules and discipline. She wanted to think of Jake as ready-made, always himself. The original, hatched from a celestial egg of his own making.

The holy Oedipal trinity: Daddy, Mommy, and Me. They say this promotes a conventional and repressive family structure; it also channels polymorphous desires into narrowly restrictive ones.

. . .

Now, here, sitting at a table in the mall cafeteria with Chinese food, Jake periodically darts his eyes over to the jewelry store boutique, where Amy works, though she has the day off.

"Look, I'm sorry! A thousand times: I'm sorry!"

Crestfallen, Nora slouches into her brown vegetables, the carrots cut with pinking sheers.

"I made you a picture."

He rips a sheet of paper out from a spiral notebook then slides it over to her.

It's a doodle of rose done with red and black pens.

"You still suck. This," she gestures with her chopsticks to their table behind the carousel, obscured by a green, plastic potted plant, "all sucks!"

"It won't always be like this. Amy and I have just been fighting all the time."

Everything seems false, unnatural, out of place. The carousel is turning, only four kids are on it, and their parents are taking pictures.

52

"Don't make this anything other than it is. I am only your mistress. Being stood up comes with the territory." She stabs at a piece of broccoli with a chopstick. He stares at her. At her outlines, as if he wanted to sketch her face.

"Don't look at me like that," she says.

He puts on his sunglasses.

"Now you're incognito," she smirks. "Amy'll never figure it out!"

"Chill out, Chopsticks," he says, taking her hand, kissing it. "You have so much hostility. Let me make it up to you. I can't stand you being mad at me. Tomorrow?" He offers.

She protends, portends, pretends.

. . .

Like Europa, Jupiter's moon, Nora has a liquid ocean under a thick crust of ice.

. . .

The snow has all melted, and still, Nora waits. She's at the park where Brian carved their names on a picnic table. She scratches it out with her house key. Jake is five minutes late. Ten minutes. Fifteen minutes. She counts from one hundred backwards. Still, he doesn't show. Maybe she had the wrong time? Maybe something's happened to him?

Everything seems ugly, dismal, and empty. There are no children jumping on the bridge, spinning the wheel to nowhere, jumping off the swing-set with its chains covered in plastic. The sun is masked by low-hanging, wispy, gray clouds. She wishes it would rain, so she could write about it. So it could seem more tragic.

Fifty-five minutes. Two women speed-walk by. In nylon track suits. They pump their arms, sway their hips obnoxiously, exaggeratedly. They are not waiting for anyone. This is what they do. Someone is probably waiting for them.

Seventy minutes. Nora sees Jake's face, his body, just over the hill, but it's a different boy, one that looks like Jake. One with equally nondescript features. The same casual clothes, navy and army greens, the same Irish complexion, Cubs hat. **BOYS LIE**, she carves. Killing time. Feeling stupid.

...

```
    Cancel, just cancel! Don't keep me waiting
like  a  fucking  fool.  Just  page  me  71-000  or
something. I'll get it.
    Asshole.
```

She messages him then signs off.

...

All the kids run out of Salo's house. Someone had attacked Jake's truck. Taco Bell sauce, mustard, catsup, and whipped cream. Circles of bologna rotting on the hood, to stain the paint. One of the headlights had been smashed, and his left window was rolled down to a crack.

"No! Fuck! No..." He opens the door. "God-mother-fucking-damn it!"

"It smells like pee," Maryanne says, nose scrunched.

An icicle disk of urine was slipped into the cracked window to melt, to fester—already fetid—in the backseat.

Jake turns on the windshield wipers, smearing the condiments into a diarrheal mess.

The next day at school someone leaks that Brian did it.

Jake and Brian have never met before, had never spoken.

Nora becomes so giddy, so happy, so high. But this space, where Brian still loves her, is only an abstract metaphor, untethered to anything tangible, conscious, and therefore, real. This act is a juvenile declaration. His last love letter. Her closure.

When everyone busies themselves with sleuthing Jake hisses to Nora.

"My headlight is out!"

"Don't be paranoid."

"Did you tell anyone?" Jake asks her.

"No," she says.

A cancer has now infiltrated their alliance, their clique, and it has metastasized. Sides are drawn.

. . .

In distress, enflamed, engorged. She wants to belong to him. She wants it more than she lets herself when he isn't around, when he isn't fingering her, and kissing her neck.

"Call me your whore," she says. "Call me your whore."

"You're my whore," he says, "my little whore."

At this she relents.

. . .

As a child, the world was a flat painting. Heaven above, Hell below. Unable to discern fairy tale from fairy tale, to call a spade a spade, at six, Nora became a vegetarian because she really believed in Bambi. She really believed that animals had thoughts and feelings as complicated, as symbolic as her own. She also believed Satan had feelings and wasn't all bad. She didn't think it was all so black and white. She didn't understand that God created Satan. He always just was. Was just always there, like God, omnipresent and magical. So when a snake approached her once in the park, she believed she was special, she thought it was going to start talking to her. She told the snake that she didn't want to talk to it, that she couldn't, but secretly, she was happy the snake choose her.

. . .

"Wait, you—of all people—didn't know?" says Salo.

"What's that supposed to mean?" Nora says.

"Riiight…"

Everyone laughs, becomes grotesque.

Nora digs her nails into her naked thigh, pops out a chunk of skin.

. . .

Then, alone, her heart thumps, leaps, dances, careens. She must find him. She runs to his classroom. Jumps, kicks her legs out, waves her arms. *Jake! Look at me!* He doesn't look up. She writes, *Later*, on a piece of notebook paper. Sticks it to the glass panel on the door with her gum.

. . .

The bell rings. He's walking with one of Amy's friends, they're talking intensely. She looks angry. They pass Nora in the hallway. Amy's friend glares. Jake doesn't look at her.

He must not want to make it obvious. He still doesn't want Amy to know, Nora thinks.

When they pass, she feels him slip something into her back pocket.

She runs to the bathroom, takes out the note.

Meet me at four, at our park, sub rosa.

The permanence of ink, a bandage to the painful interludes!

Later, she feels just as ecstatic.

Finally, Her and Him.

"I didn't want you to find out from anybody else…" he says. Solemnly. "It all happened so fast…"

Heather.

Who the fuck is Heather?

"She's Catholic you see."

"Don't give *me* that Catholic bullshit!"

"I still want to be with you, Nora."

They start talking over each other.

"But why fuck with a good thing, right?—"

"This is how we roll isn't it?—"

"How could I be so fucking stupid? It's cliché!—"

"I didn't think you cared. I was just going to be with Heather for a little while, it's really no big deal."

"This is how we *rolled*, Jake. I actually wanted to be with you. And I thought you wanted to be with me too. I mean, I should've known. This works for you. But I can't do it. Not anymore. I can't be your whore. I can't be your whore without hope that I will ever be your girlfriend."

"Nora—"

She turns and runs to her bike.

"Nora!"

She's gone.

...

Takotsubo Cardiomyopathy,
ignoring the symptoms can be fatal.
And they *say* nobody's ever died from a broken heart.
Nor a cracked, bandaged, or sutured heart.
They also say everyone dies alone.

...

The abyss, all over again, a tenebrous ink stain, blotting out the fantasy that once was.

The necessity of darkness, of bed.

Complete dyscrasia.

Two weeks, four days.

Nora is beside herself.

The painful, inhuman process of intercision.

(When a soul is caught in a pill cutter.)

Her body, split in two, cleft in twain. Separated from itself. Othered itself. Complete meiosis.

Nothing can collapse the crevasse, can bridge the gap between virgin and whore.

Her head is hot, sweating, swollen, pulsating buckets of vascular tears.

Her stomach is cold. Her internal organs are cold. Her vagina is cold. A place once alive, pink, blooming with bubbling brooks and amber waterfalls; now desolate and cold. The Sahara at night. Not a cloud in the sky, just endless blackness, manifold nothingness, cold bile.

Black nail polish. Black sweaters. Black coffee. Black circles under eyes. Black ascension. Sipping black milk at the dinner table.

She compulsively signs on to the internet. Scrolls up and down. Rereads old emails, old conversations. Dissects old emails, old conversations. Words stripped bare. Words multiplied, multifarious, multifaceted. The more she translates, the more he slips away. Only a few grains of sand left in the palm of the hand, queued up in the lifeline.

She wonders if he has her letters saved as well, wonders if he reads them.

Wondering if there's any use wondering.

Complete ataxia of the mind. Lying upside-down off of the bed's cliff. An attempt to homogenize. To meditate. To define. Mistress.

. . .

mistress |ˈmistris|
1. a woman who has authority, control, or power, esp. the female head of the household, institution, or other establishment. 2. a woman employing, or in authority over, servants or attendants. 3. a female owner of an animal, or formerly, a slave. 4. a woman who has the power of

controlling or disposing of something at her own pleasure: mistress of a great fortune. 5. (sometimes cap.) something regarded as feminine that has control or supremacy: Great Britain, the mistress of the seas. 6. a woman who is skilled in something, as an occupation or an art. 7. a woman who has a continuing, extramarital sexual relationship with one man, esp. a man who, in return for an exclusive and continuing liaison, provides her with financial support. 8. Brit: a female school teacher; schoolmistress. 9. (cap.) a term of address in former use and corresponding to Mrs., Miss, or Ms. 10. Archaic. sweetheart.

Maystresse. Maistiress. Mastres. Maistricce. Mestresse. Mastresse. Masteres. Maestriss. Mystres.

. . .

Bound to a definition, hands tied to the wheel.
Hypnotic spiral. Glutinous sleep.
Hynogogic images. Dizzy with vertigo.
Jake is just out of reach,
fully erect in the eye of the storm.
"Pain is the annihilation of the world,"
she whispers.

. . .

It was a rainy day, when Ella Corbino fought Nora three blocks from the school yard. Nora wasn't ready. Rage strained her fresh chest, her eyes. She couldn't see. Ella pushed her to the ground, someone was kneeling behind her. Michael. Nora's skirt flew up over her head. Three drops of period blood had stained her underwear. The boys laughed. The girls said "Gross!" Nora lunged her lithe body, with the force of suppressed tears, and punched Ella in the face, feeling the girl's bone, her skull, resisting Nora's knuckles. Ella screamed, she cried. Nora pulled at Ella's hair and spat on her uniform. She raised her hand, about to slap her again, but Ella blocked it with her forearm. Nora's ring, her Claddagh ring, the ring that currently is turned outward, upside-down, telling the world that her heart is available, flew off her middle finger into the battlefield.

The next day, her legs swinging through mass, Nora looked over to the window. Catherine was crying. And in that moment, she believed Catherine's stained glass image was weeping for her.

Nora wasn't listening to the homily. She was turning her ring, pulling it off, putting it back on. She believed it was lucky because that morning, walking, now by herself (as she was a pariah), on her way to school, she had found it, her amulet, resting in the dead grass. She felt lucky, like her guardian angel was wrapped around her finger.

. . .

Salo draws Nora a cartoon. She gives everyone a character. Nora's character wears a fishing hat and knee-high hooker boots. She has square boobs and pines after Jake, a large walking, talking penis. He is devoid of facial features and has long sticks for arms and travels on his balls. Merely a horizontal line separates his head from his shaft.

"Lynch them! Lynch them all!" Says the diabolical Salo. She draws herself in red as a stick-figured Lucifer atop a red bannered cliff.

Prominently in black ink, Jake and Nora swing side by side, X's for eyes, lynched with black chains. Hat still on her head, boots still on her feet, Nora's mouth is agape either in agony, or in reference to the blow job, the betrayal. Pointing to Jake, whose stiff with rigor mortis, Salo bellows: "You are bringing down the heavens and raising a whore!"

Posters are strewn throughout the cave. Red circle, Jake qua penis struck through with a red line: the international symbol for No: not wanted, not welcome.

NO. No penises, no Jake. Little devils dance below, shouting that they love Salo, that they are restored. They call her a god.

This circulates through out the school. It doesn't bother Nora as much as it should. She's really amused more than anything, which only encourages Salo, driving Nora to a space even farther from reality. Now her transformation into a fictional character is complete.

...

Three months later.

And then, one day, suddenly, the computer beeps a low bell-sounding beep and a box appears on the screen.

Noise71: I'll leave Heather for you.
    Noirchat: Go fuck yourself.
    Noirchat: You should've left Amy for me.
Noise71: I lost a lot of friends because of you.
    Noirchat: Soooo not my fault. You lied. I told the truth.
Noise71: You're SO full of it.
    Noirchat: Whatever.
Noise71: I would give anything to fuck you.
Noise71: Hold you, and kiss every inch of your body. I want to make you feel special.
    Noirchat: Come over.
Noise71: You'll fuck me?
    Noirchat: No.
Noise71: Then why would I come over?
    Noirchat: Goodbye.
Noise71: Wait!!!! That sounded bad. I just thought you wanted me.
    Noirchat: I do.
Noise71: Really?
    Noirchat: Come over.
Noise71: I can't.
    Noirchat: Can't or won't?
Noise71: Can't.
    Noirchat: You're pathetic.
Noise71: Are you calling me a pussy?
    Noirchat: Totally resent that terminology.
Noise71: Chill out Chopsticks, I was just saying.
    Noirchat: Saying that it's degrading to be a woman.

Noise71: It's just an expression.

    Noirchat: Well don't use it like that around me.

Noise71: How about: Can I come over and lick your pussy?

    Noirchat: We'll see.

Noise71: Are your parents up?

    Noirchat: Obviously not. Park three houses down. I'll be in the backyard with the dog.

...

When Nora looks into the mirror she looks at herself from Jake's eyes. She objectifies herself to herself. Through his eyes, like this, she sees herself as sexy, important, desirable. The person in the mirror is Nora, but *Nora qua Jake*. Nora is both looking and being looked at. She is both Jake and Nora. Both subject and object. And this dialectical loop ribbons off of the mirror, onto her body, and into her eyes where she absorbs the tableau and whisks herself into a fantasy of tonight.

...

As if it were day, wearing a sundress, Nora lays out a blanket. The moon is so close tonight, so candid and illuminating. On her stomach, she scissors her calves back and forth as she reads *Calvin and Hobbes* by the insect-infested light on the side of the house. Cicadas, katydids, and crickets serenade. She's already been bitten twice by mosquitoes. She sprays another layer of pungent bug spray onto her skin, no doubt covering the smell of the lotion she lathered all over her legs right after she had shaved them. She then hears a car coming down the cul-de-sac. When the engine cuts her heart swells. She becomes nervous her parents will wake up, that their window is open.

When he sees her he smiles as if there were no other place he'd rather be, as if he were home.

"I've missed you," he says.

"I've missed you too," she replies, automatically, wishing already that she hadn't.

He pushes her back. She has never felt his weight on top of her before. He notices that she's not wearing any underwear and unbuttons his fly. Nora puts her hand over his distention, blocking entrance. So he thrusts his fingers inside of her instead, but continues to motion, gives the illusion, as if he were fucking her. But she's anxious. She listens for her parents.

A moth flutters past his face, its shadow mimics a beauty mark, in the same location as Sister Margaret's, on her chin, the way the skin sagged down her neck, Father Barnes' hairy neck, his collar, a white rectangle on a strip of black, the cloth draped over wooden Christ's uncarved genitals, over the colossal wooden cross, metal cross, gothic cross equipped with fleurs-de-lis, held out in the face of a vampire, sizzling flesh, branding, burning, Madonna dancing in front of crosses, Brian dancing to Madonna, *Like a Prayer*, her father's intrusion, *Pappa Don't Preach*, his anger, her fear, now, she dips her head back, looks at her backyard, double-checks, but exposes her neck, Jake preys, kisses, "My love, come for me my love." She tries to block everything out; she looks at his face, concentrates on his eyes, his muscles, she contracts, moans, Koko, the dog beside them pants, a mosquito bites her thigh. Nora fakes her way through the next few seconds.

She feels empty, dirty, sinful. Alone.

. . .

When Nora was a child she could not accept Hell. There was work and there was Heaven. To wipe away venereal, or even mortal sins one merely had to shine stars for their allotted sentence. She also thought that the nighttime sky was a large blanket God threw over the earth, and that the stars were the slivers of light peeking through the wool. Oscillating between these two myths, she felt no contradiction.

She also liked thinking of God as having a mother.

. . .

"Oh shit! Salo will be here in five minutes!"

Jake puts his feet on the table.

"Fine, that's cool. I'll just call Heather. And you know I will."

"Okay—I'll leave. Don't want to upset *Salo*." He says her name in a tone of mockery, but Nora knows he's not mocking her, he's scoffing at the feud, at the sanctity of monogamy.

Nora's pager buzzes: 99-666-99-99-666

"That means she just left, and she's pissed. Go!"

"Dude, she's like ninety pounds, you can totally take her."

"Are you kidding? I once saw her run all sideways on the lockers. She'd totally fuck my shit up," she says.

"Dude, I *love* when her irises turn silver. She could be so fucking hot if she wasn't such a bitch."

Nora crosses her arms, knits her brow, looks at him as if this were a romantic comedy.

He leans in to kiss her, she turns her head. Continuing the cliché.

"I like your shirt, by the way. The irony is astounding," he says as he turns to leave.

And it's almost as if Salo jumps onto his chair the second the double glass doors finally click shut.

"What's up, slut?"

As the girls walk past Shoes Your Own Adventure she scowls, her eyes become slits (not silver). When a man in a yellow hoodie looks up from his magazine, she points at him. Nora hopes he doesn't recognize her.

"Hey! Hey wait!" he yells

"There's evil inside your store!," Salo bellows, "Purge thyself and we may consider speaking with thee!"

The mall's gulch echoes her scream. People are staring. An old couple walks by.

"Evil? What evil does thou speak of, fair maiden?" He's tan, rugged, has a goatee. And clearly not in high school. Both his ears and his eyebrows are pierced, pieces of dyed hair stick out of the mouth of a backwards red baseball cap.

"Is Jake working? I can smell his vile specter rotting about your flesh!"

"Jake went home about an hour ago. What's your deal? Did he dump you or something?"

"Or something," Nora says, is ignored.

"Dump me? Me?! How dare you insult! He has scorned this woman!" Salo says, pointing to Nora, "but he has never poisoned my veins! My little lady! I am clean, free of his viruses!"

Nora rolls her eyes.

"I thought you and Jake had a thing," he says. "I couldn't get him to tell me."

"What?! Has she been here? Have they been *canoodling*?" Salo demands, venom in her voice.

"I've seen her once or twice," he says, smirking.

"Great, thanks," Nora says, crossing her arms.

"Shameful! Repulsive! Long ago, days afore, she bowed down and worshippedith his *disgusting* cock! She will never be clean! NEVER!"

"And yet, you hang out with her," he says to Salo. "You, my lady, are a walking contradiction."

She looks as if she's been slapped. "How dare you!"

By now, another employee rushes out, a heavier one, his two hundred-and-thirty-five pound frame is barely contained within a thin, worn blue T-shirt that reads, *I'm With Stupid,* with an arrow pointing down to his dick. His chest puffs out like a pigeon's. He has the size and stature of a Coke machine.

"Hi," he says to Nora.

"She can't talk to you," ninety pound Salo tells him, pulling on Nora's arm to leave.

"And why is that?" he asks.

"Because there's *evil* in our store," the manager says, jazzing his hands.

"Dude! We've got to get rid of it!" the Coke machine says.

But the manager grabs Salo's hand, "Go out with me," he says.

"No fucking way!"

"You have to! Do you want me to fire him?"

There's a flicker in Salo's eyes. Her pupils widen. She smiles.

"And hire me!" Nora blurts out.

"Done," says the manager, extending his hand. "I'm Justin."

Salo shakes.

Like a complete Neanderthal, the Coke machine picks Nora up by her waist and throws her over his shoulder. Her legs kick in futility. He spanks her. "Hush woman! I must show you around."

He takes her away from Salo, to the back room of the store, and introduces himself as Tony, assistant manager. He then introduces Nora to her new job.

"Okay, the most important thing you have to remember is where everything is."

"Don't you have a labeling system?"

"No. No. Where everything *is*," he maintains, but then stops, looks at her and says, "Do you know how cute you are?"

She blushes. She likes this giant of a man. "Where *is* everything then?"

He grabs an Airwalk shoebox off one of the many metal shelves lining the backroom's walls. "This is our most popular shoe," he says and opens the box. Nestled in the shoe, underneath the tongue, is a bag of marijuana larger than Nora's ever seen. "Holy shit!"

He laughs. "Each brand has a different drug. Well, just adidas, Doc Martens, Airwalks, and the Birkenstocks."

"I would think the pot would be with the Birkenstocks."

"Hell no! Fucking hippies."

"So, what's in each? Wait—did Jake know about all this?"

"Not all of it, but yeah, for the most part. He didn't really partake. He's kind of a tool. Did you really go out with him?"

"No," says Nora, "I just blew him."

Tony laughs, "Lucky guy. Okay. There's ecstasy in the adidas because, duh, all day I dream about sex. Then there's mushrooms in the Birkenstocks, and Special K in the Doc's because Special K is special and Docs are special because we get *hella* commission on them."

"What's Special K?"

"Nora. Nora, we have much to discuss!"

"I feel like such a square."

"Well, maybe I'm lying."

"Are you?"

"No, I'm just commenting on your shirt. Not all boys lie you know."

By the end of the week they're fucking.

Noise71: I take this as an act of war.
 Noirchat: Le travail, c'est comme la guerre
 : et si personne n'y allait?

She assumes he's translating, but then a half hour passes and she signs off.

...

Anthony Hunt is not of this world, this epoch. He's a crusader, a heroic heretic, severing heads and limbs with hearty whacks from a nicked axe. Grunting at the moon. Beating his barrel chest into the night. Or an executioner, face masked in a black bag, ripping Madame du Barry's chemise, showing her only his lupine teeth and hairy arms, spitting on a basket of bloody heads. The anachronism, the threat of violence, feeds Nora's fantasy as much as the reciprocity of it all: he'll protect her gates and she'll feed him with fork and cunt.

...

Tony handles Nora's body as if it were a kitten, his fragile new pet, bones as brittle as a tortilla chip. He tells her he loves her. She fucks him in his Jeep Wrangler. She sits on the Xerox machine for him, prints out pictures of her vulva. The next day, she slips Jake one of the copies, with a note written in red marker: *Our warehouse, 4 o'clock. I'm sorry I stole your job.* He's there early.

...

"I'm not going to fuck you; not here, anyway," she says, her voice echoing, bouncing off their eight by ten cell. They are inside a huge, aluminum box, uncomfortably sitting on its corrugated metal, dangling their legs over the edge. She takes another drag from her cigarette, "It's not perfect yet."

"There is no such thing as the perfect moment."

"This place is so forgettable. I need to be able to feel the importance, the significance, of the moment when you're first inside of me," she smiles, hiding her anguish with irony.

"What's wrong with the hollowed out end of a semi-truck? Clean though it is."

"You don't get it."

"Sure I do: an epiphany of romantic communion." Because he gets it she says, "Well, not now anyway. I love Tony."

"*Ugh*, you're annoying."

. . .

It's Jake and Nora's birthday today. Neither called, nor sent the other an email, nor a page, nor an instant message. But Nora wanted to. As she opens Tony's present she wonders what Heather bought for Jake, or if she was one of those pruriently prudish girlfriends that give a blowjob instead of buying anything, as if her body is so fucking special, as if this blowjob is going to be any more special than all the others.

. . .

At a red light, Jake looks down at Nora and tells her to come up.

"Not until we're off 64, and especially not when we're stopped!"

As if she heard her, Salo hops on the hood of the truck.

"Holy fuck!" They yell.

Salo points at Nora, "You fucking slut!" then she narrows her eyes at Jake and points at him too. She jumps off the hood and runs around to the passenger door. She pulls Nora out from underneath the dashboard.

"I'll talk to you later," Nora yells as she runs away.

"No she won't!" Salo yells back.

"My lipgloss!" Nora says when Salo slams the door.

"It's dead to us! Keep running!" Salo says.

Both girls are laughing hysterically. The light turns green. Jake fumbles with the gear shifter then drives away. As they're running away Jake yells, "I miss you, Salo!"

...

Her taunting agency, how she holds her supple body against him, becomes too much. Thrown onto her back, literally, thrown, he knocks the wind out of her. Kneeling on her thighs, he holds her arms down, bends in to kiss her, bruises her biceps.

She squirms, laughs, cannot escape, pinned. Dew soaks through her dress. Tossing her head side to side, she tires, gives a look, signifies discomfort. But he's not there. His eyes are fogged over, his pupils are large.

She bucks her hips. He uses his knees to open her legs. Still, she's confined, her aegis removed. Merely a panting object, a writhing thing.

"What the fuck is wrong with you?"

"If only I had duct tape," he says then kisses her on the mouth, forcing his tongue to the back of her throat. Her skin itches wherever it's exposed to the cold grass.

"Don't worry," he says, pushing her dress up. "I won't fuck you."

"But I could," he adds. "And I will, someday. Not yet though. No, not yet. *It's not perfect.*"

She tries to spit on him, but it comes out in more of a spatter.

"You wet?" he asks, as if the phrase fell from his hand into her lap. "Ooh," he says, "You are wet."

Furious with herself, at the treacherous creamy display. As if she and her vagina were not on the same page. She's confused, miffed. Where is this desire coming from? A longing to mitigate the pressure, the throbbing mystery between them, between her legs.

"Get the fuck off of me!"

He takes out his cock and begins masturbating, the tip of it already beading, dripping. She's tormented into silence, unable to separate from her aching clitoris, she eyes his dick with an animal watchfulness. He cums in seconds, on her face, in her hair. He cums so hard he lets go of her and holds one hand to the earth to steady himself. She wiggles out from underneath him, and there, with his dick still erect and poking out of his fly, she wipes his semen off with her hands and kicks him in the testicles as hard as she can. He falls over and she runs. When she gets home she grabs a handful of dirt and smears it all over her face and into her hair.

She could not be more relieved that no one in her family is home.

. . .

He calls. He writes. He stands at her locker, waits on the hood of her car in the mall parking lot. If he sees Tony he flees, or hides. She sees him run, so she pulls Tony close and kisses him, popping her leg, walking her hands up his massive pectorals. She giggles, he picks her up by the straps of her overalls, and drapes her over his shoulder.

> "Take me to bed or lose me forever!" she says in her best Southern accent, just loud enough. Polyvalent utterances—utterances sent off in different directions, intended for more than one interlocutor.

. . .

Noise71: Stop punishing me.
      Noirchat: Leave me alone.
Noise71: For how much longer?
      Noirchat: FOREVER! I hate you.

. . .

"Who are you looking at?" Tony asks.

"No one," Nora shifts her gaze quickly, trying to hide the terror, the excitement at being caught.

Tony looks where Nora was looking. "Is that fucking Jake? That faggot?"

"Don't say faggot."

"Is he still bothering you? Salo said he was bothering you."

"No, it's fine. He came by my work once. I told him to go. Salo's such an exaggerator," Nora pushes a small laugh out her throat.

"I'll kill him. I will fucking kill that little twerp. You tell me if he ever so much as looks at you."

. . .

At night Jake parks his truck outside her house, across the street from her bedroom window.

The first night she pulls her curtains shut with an emphatic snap of the wrist. Cirrus rectangles of see-through white, impossibly still, a silken veil between them, a barrier.

The second night she leaves the curtain open but pretends she doesn't notice him. She turns on the radio and enacts her Sunday ritual where she puts together a couple of different outfits to wear during the week. She starts with a pencil skirt and pairs it with something that matches, but then decides it matches too much. She tears off shirt after shirt, skirt after skirt, dress after pants. Keeping her bra and panties on, she bounces into one look after another. One masquerade after another.

She feels like an actress, acting for her director. She moves for him, dances for him. She strips for him, changes for him. She paints herself blank, makes a canvas out of her soul. She's a thousand different women, every woman he could ever need. His gaze on her feels like an embrace, as if beauty were reaching out to her, coating her in its sweet love, touching her beyond what he could see, an unlimited space, a continuous eternal place of abundance that gives and gives, and loves.

To be engulfed by Jake's gaze fills Nora with a sense of occasion, an overwhelming feeling of purpose, of pride. She can now be because she is being watched, being seen. Her being has meaning through translation. As she strips, as she becomes, she begs: *Interpret me!*

Me!

Love me!

The third night she pauses, stares at her own reflection in the window, then out into the night sky, the dark, looming trees, the never ending blanket of stars, but really she's trying to stare into his truck, trying to see through his windows. But she can't. She cannot meet his eyes; she can't find them. So much glass between them. Standing before him in a black chemise with white eyelet trim, she pulls the nightgown over her head, then backs up and removes her underwear. Completely naked, she turns around and faces a standing mirror. She loses herself deliberately, focuses on him, through (in) the mirror. She takes her time twisting her short, black strands of hair and pinning them atop her head, with the bleached ends sticking up like an array of peacock feathers. Once her hair is in place she lines her eyes with dark kohl eyeliner and glosses her lips blood red. She also adds a little bit of the lipstick to her cheeks, to really rouge them up, give them that afterglow look. After about twenty minutes she looks like a harlot, a whore. She walks over to the window and kisses it. Then shuts the curtains. Her voyeur honks the horn as he drives away.

The fourth night he doesn't show but pages her late in the evening with 71-000.

Distance, after all, is the condition of seduction.

. . .

"How many times do I have to tell you? Don't change in front of the window with the curtains open! Anyone could be out there and you're just giving them a free show of your hoochie-coochie!" her mother yells, walking over to the window. "Oh hell, Nora, what is this? Paint?" She goes to wipe the kiss from the pane, smudging it, when Nora jumps up.

"DON'T!"

Her mother backs away but still draws the curtains. "Shut these curtains," she points.

. . .

Maryanne lays the cards across the floor in an arc.

King of Cups. Queen of Cups. VI of Swords.

Hermit. VII of Cups.

"This is who you love," she points to the grim VI of Swords: a soldier standing, strokes the water, steers the boat forward with a woman, slumped, depressed, imprisoned, haggard, sitting at the bow, looking down to her knees, barred from seeing ahead by a make-shift cell: the six swords, standing fully erect, stab into the wood of the boat, blocking a clear sight into her future.

"You're a part of him. He's a part of you," she's muttering, thinking, consulting the book. "You do share a birthday, Nor."

"Wait, Jake's the dude pushing the boat?"

"No, they're both you. Listen. You're sad, but not outwardly. Inside. You get by. You think you're getting better. You think you want to heal but you don't. Why?"

"We're impossible," Nora sighs, flops. "I don't even like him half the time."

"Do you want to know your immediate future?" Maryanne says, finger on the Hermit.

"No, it looks bleak. Skip to the grand future."

74

"See this?" Maryanne points to each of the seven overflowing goblets, "Too many choices."

"That sounds like a cop-out."

"Castle. Castle in the sky? Fantasy. The serpent means lust, or is it temptation?..." Maryanne's speaking to herself again, thumbing the pages. Then, "This electric-ghost-looking thing is your true self, everything else is a false idol. You cannot follow him. You cannot follow Jake. He's an illusion. If you go after him, you will suffer more than you have. That path is cursed."

. . .

In an over-sized threadbare T-shirt, with her ears piqued and her brow knit in maternal concern, Maryanne exudes femininity. She crosses her legs and places a hand on Nora's thigh. If Maryanne wanted to she could ensnare the hearts of both the sexes, but she isn't interested in leading, she finds it too manipulating. Sometimes Nora wonders if her naïveté is just an act, that she's really as Machiavellian as everybody else, feigning ignorance while lording her blushing tits over anyone that so much as offers her an aperçu.

Maryanne has the type of body that exists beyond itself, onto the covers of vapid magazines and into insecure women's heads before they fall asleep. Her skin, her breasts are enticingly ripe and soft, begging to be stolen. Such cunning exploitations would be entirely believable if she didn't bleat at the first sign of dismissal, fainting on the train tracks into the hands of a sinister thug before he even ties the first knot. This is what men love about her: the possibility of breaking her. Though she has been caressed, ravaged even, by many lovers since Brian, her body retains its innocence, its maiden glow. She still seems untouchably pure while also easily conquered. A virgin/whore mirage. These men, these vanquishers, map out their journey all over her flawless skin. They think they have settled an undiscovered country, colonized Eden, that's just when she leaves them for another.

This all makes Nora want to confide in her, tell her everything. She wants to help her. To slaughter every boy that touches her inappropriately without her consent. Sacrifice them to the altar of countless Maryannes sacrificed in the name of some forgotten god. She wants to guard her and hold her, rock away the reasons she refuses to eat more than eight hundred calories in a day.

She wants to share Jake with her. Let her in on this pleasure beyond love that shoots straight for the nerves. A pleasure unto death. But nothing about Maryanne radiates death. Her cheeks are too rosy, her hair is too golden, her façade is too happy.

. . .

Jake does not appear at her window that night. Nor the next one. Nor the one after that. She checks her inbox. He has not written her either. She begins an email. Erases it. She begins to dial but hangs up. Her path is forked. She turns on the radio, their song comes on. (Meaning, one of the many songs that reminds her of him.) For her, this is a sign. She drives to school without hitting a single red light. Another sign. She makes a game out of these auguries: *if this song comes on in the next three songs he'll love me. If he pages in the next hour we'll get married.* All this, to avoid making the decision herself. She drives past the park. It is unchanged. Yet corroded, an amalgamation of itself. Memories chipped. Memories fused. Brian grafted onto Jake. Tony grafted onto Brian. Nihilism nipping at her heels. *11:11, make a wish.*

. . .

Nora quits her job. Breaks up with Tony. Avoids Salo and the mall and drugs. Some girl at school calls her a whore as she walks past. She looks like one of Heather's friends, but Nora can't be sure. All she can muster in return is, "Bitch, please."

So underwhelming.

. . .

"Yeah, I just don't see why a guy can fuck fifty girls and be a hero, but *mon Dieu!* if a girl fucks two guys, or—heaven forbid—blows a guy outside of dating, she's a whore! This kind of mutated sexuality is the essence of fascism!" Nora says just before biting off one of the candy beads on her necklace.

"My boob itches," Maryanne says.

"I wanna die," says Nora.

Instinctively, Maryanne extends her arm, "Hon, you're both Virgos, probably the same rising sun. A tragicomedy was bound to happen."

. . .

Down the hall. Classes are in session. Moving as slowly as possible. Lost in thought. Stuck in a trance. Nora hears everything as if it were magnified. A scuff of a shoe. A rattling cough. Pencil pressing, the tip breaking, scratching the paper. She goes to the bathroom, changes her tampon. Checks her make-up. Her hair. Reapplies concealer to the dark circles under her eyes. A toilet flushes. Amy steps out of the stall.

They make eye contact, Amy quickly breaks it. Nora rewashes her hands. She's sure they both want to speak, ask each other questions only they would know the answers to.

But Nora also wants to hold her, tell her that she's sorry.

Amy presses the plastic bar and dispenses a lot of bright, liquid pink soap. Her hands are covered in a thick film. Lathering and lathering.

"I..." Nora begins, the word hanging in the air, pathetic, sheepishly in between them. Amy flicks the water off her hands.

"You know what, Nora? Don't. Just because things between Jake and me didn't work out doesn't mean I have to like you."

Nora thought they could bond over their mutual hatred for Heather, but Amy's right. She's at the receiving end of this blunt quadrangle. Nora's sorry she even uttered a word. Amy dries her hands with the loud automatic blow dryer. Nora wipes hers on her jeans and leaves first.

. . .

At lunch, Jake is seated at her table. He normally has Gym, but somehow he had gotten out of it. He's chatting away with their mutual friends. None of this should seem extraordinary, but Nora has not really seen him, nor really communicated with him in any real way since that night outside her window. Three months ago.

He says her name ecstatically, she responds in kind.

He gets up to hug her. It's awkward. Everybody's looking.

He then continues talking, not looking any further at Nora.

He gesticulates when he talks, possibly for compensation.

Nora likes watching his hands. She wishes she could do it for a week, before Maryanne asks her, "Which would you rather?"

Missing the first part, Nora asks her to repeat the question.

"Would you rather be forced to scream at the top of your lungs for an hour or have your eyes glued shut for a day?"

Suddenly, and probably not accidentally, Jake's foot grazes her shin. Because it was intentional, the quick touch felt all the more intimate. She wants to reply. Needs to. She feels it in her shin. She slips off her shoe and finds his foot again, runs her toe up his sock until she feels hair, skin. They wait, for a certain second, when they know everyone else is occupied, and then they look up, smiling briefly, without any teeth. This small gesture, right now, means everything.

"Scream for an hour."

. . .

The person you are trying to reach has a voicemail box that has not been set up yet.

. . .

Nora finds an inspiring costume dress in a thrift store, her prom dress. A powder blue polyester gown with a sweetheart neckline that's stained with blood on the abdomen and the upper right thigh. Five dollars. She then has a dream about a brown dress. The next day she dyes the dress a chocolate brown. The blood is masked and the shimmering silver threads now sparkle gold.

Hand in hand with Sean, her latest beau, she passes Jake and Heather, who are in line for pictures.

Suit as dark as night, the silver tie brings out his eyes and the crispness of the worsted wool. Stretching his neck, feigning comfort, he removes his sport coat, not because, Nora assumes, he's hot, but because he can't look at her right now. So she looks at him. The white linen shirt hangs on his chest in a way that accentuates what growth he's accomplished. Vaguely, she can see the outline of a T-shirt underneath. She exhales loudly and introduces Sean to Heather, but Jake cuts in, cuts across Heather, with his hand out, and introduces himself to Sean, to his spiky blue hair, his thin black tie, his chain wallet and metal collar, his hammer and sickle tattoo bleeding through his collared shirt rolled loosely up his elbows. Sean extends his arm, two vertical stripes cutting across his blue veins. Compared to Jake, Sean looks like he's never seen the sun. They shake hands, and Nora notices how cold and business-like Jake seems. In this moment, she's unsure which guy she finds more attractive. She never imagined they'd meet. She falls quiet and wants to disappear, but Sean smiles broadly, happily, with ignorance. Although he has a rebellious casing, he's as bright as a stone, an unfortunate byproduct of bad genes plus the lingering effects of repeatedly mixing ecstasy with acid, or "candy-flipping."

Nora can see Jake sizing him up as such so she interrupts the tension with a laugh.

A small, sarcastic exhalation of air.

"You look great tonight," she says to Heather, who is wearing a pink Jessica McClintock nightmare with a matronly jewel collar and French tipped nails. Her headache hair looks like it was lifted from a bridal magazine. With one match, her entire head would combust in flames.

"So do you! Where did you get your dress?" She looks like a Disney princess next to Nora in her DIY mahogany dress, hugging her hips, breasts heaving, thrust forward, silver padlock around her neck. She fingers her necklace and notices Jake tossing a nod toward the double helix staircase.

"It was my mother's," Nora says, before she rambles. "God, I'm so happy they're not being assholes about smoking tonight. Otherwise I'd only be able to survive here for an hour. Sometimes it's like every hour on the hour I need one, you know?" she looks at Jake, then to Sean, "I wish you smoked."

"That's not a nice thing to wish on someone," Sean says, but only Heather's paying attention to him. She's deferential, petite, potato-fed.

Nora assumes that Heather is stupid as well. She's at least naïve, smiling tightly with her perfect teeth and dry cornflower blue eyes.

Nora pulls a rhinestone studded flask of Goldschläger out of her purse, tilts it to Jake, in salute, and drinks. "Have a goodnight, guys!"

"It was good to see you, Nor," Jake says. Pulling her in for a hug, he whispers "Third floor," into her ear.

Nora laughs and waggles her sparkly, gold-flecked tongue. Jake takes the flask from her hand and drinks. Both Sean and Heather seem uncomfortable, like they're politely waiting for this moment to pass.

At 9pm, Nora excuses herself to smoke and go to the bathroom. Sean is sitting on the air conditioner. Maryanne's on his lap. She kisses Maryanne's forehead. Finds Jake and Heather. Walking past them, she walks to the double helix stair case. She shoots him a glance then grabs the hem of her gown and ascends three flights.

Three minutes later, he appears. As he walks toward her, he loosens his tie, but instead of meeting her, he turns and opens a wooden door with a golden knob. Inside the room is dark and smells like lemons. When she opens the door he seizes her, kisses her, clutches her ass, lifts her leg, slams her up against the wall, fondles her succulent flesh. Her eyes adjust, they're inside a woman's bathroom.

He guides her to a deep-buttoned, plush fainting couch, lies her down, lifts her dress and kneels before her. In a gesture of prayer, he removes her black lace panties, delicately, tells her to open up for him. She is here, nowhere else, here. At last! Turbulent, defiant, unruly, disorderly, he grabs her, with unquenchable violence, by the back of the knees, by the throat, pulls her body toward him, into him, spreading her legs, making an offering.

Inside of her he mobilizes, explores the resistance of her flesh, finds her sex with his tongue, licking, lapping, loving, slapping, he draws deeper, locates her unconscious. She locates one of the buttons and pulls, rips it out, feels the threads snap. She clasps her fist around it so tightly, her nails dig into her palms. With his nose pressed at the crown of her crease, she pulls him inside, closer, wetter, hunger, lover! She swoons, collapses to the arm of the couch, hits her head on the hard peaks of Victorian molding.

"I'll go first," he says, drinking from her flask.

Disoriented, "So soon?"

"It's been seventeen minutes," he says, and swings his suit jacket over his shoulder. Without expression, he says, "You look stunning, by the way," then leaves.

She wonders if she could get away with smoking a cigarette up here, but decides it's not worth it. She gathers her wits, her things, pocketing the little green plush button, she takes a long drink of Goldschläger then reapplies her lipstick. Feeling intensely private, she makes a beeline for the parking lot to smoke, avoiding Sean and as many insincere smiles as she can.

. . .

The town, obviously, is not the same when he's gone off to college. It's much, much grayer. Sitting at the park, picking at grass, she has a sudden image of her body as a bloodless corpse. She feels painfully embarrassed, dirty, slovenly. She throws up into a garbage can. After she wipes her mouth she looks up to the sky and thinks of God, not outer space. She feels constricted. Trapped in a body that's trapped in a dome. She spits one last time into the garbage can then lights a cigarette. If Nora knew what *litost* meant, she would describe this feeling as *litost*.

. . .

Nora wants to sleep with more than half the men she encounters, and she wants all of them to want to fuck her, even if she isn't attracted to them, even if they're middle aged. The ones she likes, she wants to worship their cocks. She wants them to bend her over their knees and punish her for looking at other men. The rest she wants to worship her, to deify her body, lick her cunt clean, and beg for her touch. When she has a boyfriend she feels like a cat in heat: face down, ass up, caterwauling in pain for pleasure. She loves walking through the grocery store, hand in hand with her lover, making eyes at the boys behind the butcher's counter, walking in such a way when an older man is behind her. It's a problem, she knows. She's not nymphomaniacal, she just has tasted the fruit of the forbidden and lost her appetite for normal sexual passions.

. . .

She is bored walking through the pharmaceutically lit hallways without the prospects of Jake suddenly appearing from around a corner, in his bomber jacket, nodding toward the staircase, in the direction of the parking lot, even though it isn't yet 11am.

Nora reaches into her bag, to open her book, *The Sun Also Rises*, to her bookmark. She slides her finger along the stiff card stock—a postcard from Iowa: on one side a picture of Manet's *Olympia*, on the other, scrawled in blue ballpoint pen, Tu me manques—feeling better, just knowing it's there, this close to her body, that he misses her. For a couple of weeks this slaked her, but soon enough a fraying postcard wasn't enough, and Nora found herself bent over one of the bathroom sinks, sniffing lines of Ketamine with Salo during Gym class, which, of course, makes her miss Tony.

...

"Santa won't come unless you go to mass!"

Often Nora's defiance is treated with humor.

She looks around and wonders how many of these adults *really* believe in Christ. She pictures all the couples having sex, usually doggy-style, tits flopping, flapping. How many are cheating on one another? Which ones chronically masturbate? Which ones are addicted to pain killers?

As Rob kneels in prayer, he begins to bang out a Marilyn Manson song on the pew in front of him. Nora laughs, her father shuffles to sit in between them. The crease in his brow, that crinkle of disappointment, frowning down on her. This frown still affects her deeply. She slumps in her seat, takes out the Book of Hymns, and reads, concentrates on the lyrics, the music.

> *Word of the Father,*
> *Now in the flesh appearing,*
> *O come, let us adore him,*
> *O come, let us adore him,*
> *O come, let us adore him,*
> *Christ the Lord.*

A low hum of white noise, lots of coughing and cough drop unwrapping. The acoustics, the ambiance, are more unsettling in the middle of the night, without the daylight shining through the streaks of stained glass. Instead, all the candles are lit and the incense is heavily smoking, so much so, that it burns Nora's eyes and nostrils, she too coughs, so does her mother, and her father. Her brother seems immune.

Staring ahead to an empty altar, the golden tabernacle shimmers to the left, protecting the delicious circular wafers, "The Body," which bear the stamp of the crucifix, a stamp, that some factory, somewhere, implemented.

Mozart's *Requiem* XOR György Ligeti's *Requiem*?

Carved from wood, stained in parts, Mary, Joseph, and toddler Jesus stand off to the right. Joseph's hand on the tyke's shoulder, as if he knew. As if he could turn around, turn behind him and behold, his step-son's future, larger than life, sculpted, cloth draped over his cock, defying gravity, suffering, eyes rolled back, captured in mid-moan, in horrible pain, his son, Jesus.

Nora thinks she is sitting in the most boring place in the whole world.

Then, her father puts his hand on her farther shoulder, wrapping an arm around her. "I love you, kid," he says.

Dies irae...

She puts her head on his shoulder, pressing into his suit, its shoulder pad, and suddenly she feels sick, guts twisting into knots, like something she ate isn't agreeing with her. She thinks back to what she ate: Cranberries, spinach, turkey, mashed potatoes, and cookies. Last night she was on ecstasy, but she was certain she threw that up before they went bowling, and it's been over twenty-four hours. She had felt fine by this afternoon, but this shit lingers, she remembers Sean saying.

If Daddy could hear me, he wouldn't recognize me. Thank you, Lord, for protecting my thoughts, though, I guess, they're not sacred, as I'm thinking them right now, to speak to you, but I mean, not that you're not sacred, you're sacred amongst sacred, but I guess I mean, I'm sorry. I guess. I'm sorry for lying to my parents, lying to the boys that I sleep with—even though I shouldn't—the men that I think about sleeping with, even though I shouldn't, and the women that I think about undressing, and fucking, as if I were a man, I

85

shouldn't think on, but it's like my prayers and my thoughts have merged, and I can't stop, unless I stop thinking that I'm thinking to you, for you, because I'm in your house. This is why I don't pray anymore, and because I assume you're busy, too busy to listen endlessly about the people I'd liked to sleep with, all the boys I asked you to make like me, as though you were some genie that could manipulate feelings of love, or my mother's head pain, which hasn't budged, at all, even though I asked every night as a child, which cannot even take this ridiculous incense you like so much, but I'm not mad. I hear you work in mysterious ways. But I'm on to all this. Fuck! I bet you're angry with me, because of a lot of things, because of Jake...

Jake...

Jake...your face, your smile, your skin, your hair, your cock, your bones, your teeth, your handwriting, the way you touch, the way you eat, the secrets you hold, that shirt you wore, the one with the pockets, once, when you bent low, your sweater grazed my chin, you asked me if my stomach was rumbling, I wanted you then, I needed you then. I needed you last night! I wish I could've called you, just called you, like it was normal, like you could take me away from now! I hate him so much! He thinks he loves me. I couldn't be more disgusted. I wish it were you. I wish he were you. O God!

As it was in the beginning, is now, and ever shall be.
World without end.

Her father coughs.

de Die Judicii Sequentia...

Come, Desire of nations come,
Fix in us Thy humble home;
Rise, the Woman's conquering Seed,
Bruise in us the Serpent's head.
Adam's likeness, Lord efface:
Stamp Thy image in its place;

Second Adam, from above,
Reinstate us in thy love.

Wide-eyed, fearful, watching the serious faced couples genuflect to the dead hand of an anachronistic authority, to the dead man floating above, his son's likeness hanging morbidly in cruciform.

Her pulse gallops, her heart flutters, pounds off tune, as if it were skipping a beat every now and again. She presses two fingers to her neck, surreptitiously, and *listens* in a panic.

I love one but fuck another. Both acts will lead me to Hell.
Both acts are worth it.
I'm sorry.
I'm so sorry.

Look not on our sins, but on the Faith of our Church, and grant us the peace and the unity of our Kingdom where we'll live Forever and ever and ever and ever and ever and ever and ever and ever and ever and ever and ever and ever and ever...

Lacrimosa...

She leans back, "Mom," she whispers, "Mom, I don't feel so good."

"What's wrong?"

Ecstasy. "I feel faint, and nauseous."

A dream is a wish your heart makes.

Mea Culpa. Mea Culpa. Mea Culpa. Mea Culpa. Mea Culpa. Mea Culpa. Mea Culpa. Mea Culpa.

"It's just the incense. Put your head between your knees."

She does, and breathes, *Hail Mary, full of grace,* looks at shoes, clamps her eyes shut. She can smell her own menstrual blood. And baby powder. Her father *who art in heaven* rubs her back *Hallow be thy name. He thinks I'm faking it.* She feels hot. Too hot. Sweaty. Clammy. Off. This must be a latent side effect. Something's wrong. An embolism is bursting. Her left arm tingles, aches. This sweater must come off. Vomit climbs her esophagus, sloshes against the back of her tongue, falls back down, falls like dead weight into her stomach. This is punishment. For not getting caught. The urge to confess rises with the second tide *as we forgive those who trespass against us.*

"I've got to go," she says, and leaves, fleeing, flying past a great deal of people she doesn't recognize.

Outside or the bathroom? If only there weren't any people.

So much green velour and patent leather.

She kicks the door, thinking only after that a small child could be on the other side. The fear stirs her bowels. The door swings open, onto air. There's no line. No one. She's all alone. She falls. Palms on the linoleum. Head against the thick clay tiles. She lifts up her sweater, exposes her stomach, presses it to the cold floor, sits up, inhales the bleach porcelain, blows the air out of her mouth, rippling the water, thinking about the thickness of food and thinness of alcohol, trying not to think about the inevitable. She focuses on a scarlet stain in the grout. Wine? Blood? Juice? Lip gloss?

First the mashed potatoes and cranberry juice.

The door opens. Her mother's heels. She calls, "Nor?"

Then the scratchy, chunky, pink cookies. They cut her throat. Petals of blood fall into the toilet.

This is my blood, the blood of the new and everlasting covenant, it shall be shed for you and for all so that sins may be forgiven. Do this in memory of me.

Her mother knocks on the stall, then pushes it open, as Nora had failed to secure the metal latch.

She squats down and rubs Nora's back, tells her everything will be all right. And Nora believes her because part of her still wants to think that her parents are infallible. Because, just this one time, she wants her mother to take care of it all again.

With her forehead pressed to the black, plastic seat, Nora flushes the toilet and allows herself one wail as the water reaches its highest pitch. Her mother was unraveling some toilet paper and didn't hear her, or didn't say anything except, "Here."

Nora wipes her mouth, then looks at her mother, bile still fresh on her tongue, "I love him," she says. "I love him," more lachrymal the second time.

"I know, Baby," her mother says, rubbing her hand in circles across Nora's back.

She throws up again.

AMEN...

. . .

She sends Jake a postcard. Frida Kahlo's, *Las Dos Fridas*.

Je m'en viens. Two Fridays from next.

. . .

There is everywhere in the long run a certain sexual impulse felt as unclean. From then on it is no longer a matter of beneficent sexuality "intended by God" but rather of malediction and death. Beneficent sexuality is close to animal sexuality, unlike eroticism which is man's own and only genital in its origins. Eroticism is a sterile principle representing Evil and the diabolic.

– Georges Bataille. *Erotism: Death and Sensuality.*

3.
Set to Philip Glass's *Glassworks*, in six movements.

1. Opening.

A piano intermission. The notes strike the pavement like rain.

At 11pm the hydraulic doors sigh open. He's already there, leaning in brown Doc Marten boots underneath the orange light from the heat lamp. Protected from the moon's icy stare, his cheeks, his ears redden, he rubs his gloveless hands, the blood returns. Nora feels as if steam is visibly wafting off of her. For the last eight hours, five without sunlight, the overheated bus bounced along its complicated route, comingling the smells of outmoded machinery with sweaty flesh. Nora had clung to her puffy jacket, wrapping herself in a dizzying happiness of an imminent future, replaying the same CDs, smiling at the memories, lost in her own frenetic obsession.

Once he sees her a familiar smile breaks from the left side of his mouth and moves across his face. This is the same smile he always gives at the beginning of their illicit encounters: indefinable, chimerical, ephemeral. A smile of pain and nostalgia. Of invention and loss. Of appreciation and love. A sort of sigh of release, then of awe and mischief. Nora adores this smile. She has contemplated it to the point of annihilation, to a moment beyond *jouissance*, beyond thought.

Between them is a gulf, a vertiginous, hypnotic, insoluble space.

She laughs in response, then runs toward him.

They kiss hello, like a normal couple, then he takes her bag and they walk seven blocks in subzero temperatures to his dormitory. Covered with only a thin layer of purple nylon, her thighs ache inside the arid heat. She has trouble walking up the stairs, but wouldn't complain even if she were frostbitten, so much has she anticipated this night, or rather, the next fifteen hours before she has to return to the bus station at 2:30pm.

The doors open onto a hall of shirtless boys constructing a trapdoor involving a great deal of clear moving tape and a cup of ranch dressing. They're laughing like fools at hypotheticals but one of them takes the time to compliment Nora's legs, the others whistle. These are his friends, one of them is his roommate, who, apparently isn't coming home tonight.

The door opens onto a space between adulthood and adolescence, a ten by twelve foot recycled room with a hollow door and a striped tie tied around the knob. And bunk beds, just like summer camp, except the counselor is a drunken RA with an undeclared major and mottled acne.

Opens onto black lights, Christmas lights, blue icicles with rubber cords, and emptied bottles of liquor lit up with electric water. Crisp posters for bands long since retired and John Belushi drinking a bottle of Jack Daniels. Plaid, flannel bed sheets, freshly washed. A marked calendar of naked women on cars, their asses shaped like hearts.

She puts her hand to her eyes and hisses. He plugs in the blue lights and flips off the oppressive fluorescent light. He flips another switch and the black lights come on as well. The highlighters float like science experiments in their rum and whiskey bottles. They glitter like trophies.

The door opens onto a lie, a compromise, an inauthentic prescription for teenage sex. Drunken fingers trembling in the dark, parting lips, forgotten names, his roommate pretends to be asleep, jacking off all the while.

The door opens onto a threadbare carpet and a room without a view. An air conditioner blocks the window, and a Bob Marley blanket blocks the air conditioner. The whites of Marley's eyes glow blue and the smoke hangs in a fug. Every fiber of fabric smells like must and cigarettes. She finds this masculine.

He apologizes for his roommate's mess. She takes off her wet boots and cracks her toes. This is the farthest she's ever been from home without a chaperone. She lights a cigarette in triumph then unscrews a bulb, but the strand remains intact.

"They don't make them that way anymore," he says.

She looks at his teeth. "What?"

"When you unscrew one bulb the whole string doesn't go out anymore."

"Oh."

She doesn't want to look at him, at his blue teeth.

A second passes. She taps her cigarette again then hits the top button on the ashtray to make all the ash go away, into the hidden chamber below.

"How was your ride?"

"Long."

She sucks her cigarette, pays a great deal of attention to its neon tip, the way the paper crackles and disappears.

The door opens onto inquietude, vulnerability masquerading as ineptitude. She crosses her legs then takes an orange out of her bag.

"You look," he stammers, playing with the zipper on his hoodie, "gorgeous."

"Thanks," she says, sitting seiza-style, dropping the orange from one hand into the other. Like she's playing Catch with herself.

Feigned nonchalance, indifference, all desire is moved to the orange she undresses, inserting her nail into its navel, deep enough to get just under its skin, where the juice seeps, stings her cuticles. She pushes forth, raking, peeling, shrinking, stripping, ripping, tearing, licking, suckling the sweet, sticky orange water dripping off her hands, running down her forearms.

The orange opens, the pulp radiates unnaturally, as if the fruit was covered with a spider's web. Through this silly lighting, Nora hunts for the authentic, some symbol of Jake as she knows him, as she lusts for him. She locates a tattered quilt folded in the corner with a stuffed elephant, Frumpy, or Frumps, depending on his mood, sitting, slumped on top. Her shoulders slacken. She relaxes.

He relaxes too then puts on some music. And shuts off the black lights.

"Thanks," she says.

He looks at her, stops fidgeting, holds still like a silvery note piercing her body, entrancing, beguiling, seducing, digesting, moving from her head down her throat, quickening her heart, the note repeats, flushes her face, flashes behind her eyes, looking back at him, with love, in love, with him, with this moment, this space, where everything melts into a pile of fresh orange skin curled into a spiral, spiraling out, ensnaring their bodies, and still, the note repeats, holds. *Undress me. Open me.*

2. Floe.

Nothingness.

The origin of all creation.

A sheet of paper. A blank computer screen.

The reflection of all visible light.

White salt. White T-shirts. White tea. Fresh white lilies, fresh white snow. A glass of white milk. A mountain of glass. Cocaine cut across a mirror. An Ibuprofen, crushed into powder.

White so pure, a child outlines it in blue. So cold, it's hot to the touch.

This too, too sullied flesh.

Somethingness.

A chunk of white floating in the ocean.

Alone, isolated, melting, merging.

A cold marriage bed, until now.

An arrhythmia of hormones, cardiac confessions on the tip of the iceberg, melting with the floe, into one another, in the moment, impatient for osmosis, to become one, to exchange fluids, to gush, to flow.

The orchestra isn't visible.

Piano, electric organ, bass, synthesizer, piccolo, soprano sax, clarinet, bass clarinet, tenor sax, French horn, viola, cello.

They climb the rungs on the ladder one by one, their feet slapping, tapping, like notes striking the pavement.

Like an ice floe, the top bunk floats on the ocean of space, a pool of unmitigated abyss, the void of a thousand beloveds drowning, dying, digested, the paranoid sea of reasons that prevented this moment, the thalassic expectations leading up to it. The same sea that can give birth to another Nora at anytime. A sea that they don't have to deal with as long as they're in this bed, on this mattress, floating toward each other and away from all else. The same sea that sloshes as a mirror.

> Pelagic: *This is exactly what I want, no strings attached, a prophylactic, a numbing palliative, an addictive narcotic, to be your mistress, your secret other, inoculating my heart, precluding love, with you, with anyone else. Unfiltered jouissance, pure fun, all the time.*
>
> Demersal: *I love you.*

She feels his absence in his touch. This excites her.

A cold marriage bed, until now.

A bed of down and cotton. A bed of past lovers and both of their parents.

A bed of ice floating on, above, away from a sea of words and pretext. The sea of past lovers and parents.

She exhales a curl of smoke off a rolled tongue, filling the room with hot, tangible breath. Spiraling out of control, an arrhythmia of hormones, cardiac confessions on the tip of his dick, going with the floe, impatient for meiosis, to become one with the ocean of space, to exchange fluids.

"Is this really happening?"

"Yes."

Nothing is as important as the immediacy of this arousal. But the moment of collision cannot be seen. It's too fast. Too urgent. Too ethereal. Irreal. The material of dreams, an admixture of liquid and gas, condensing into a drop dripping off the tip of an icicle. Nora reaches out, into the impossible ether, to touch beyond the tease of a drizzle. Her hands fall through the hazy outlines of unearthly desire, wet with amnestic disappointment, playing in a loop, dizzying, intoxicating, trembling. Nora the nymph. Maybe he takes her in his arms, or when her lips press against his she trembles, or maybe she jumps him and pushes him back down to the floor, or he scoops her up, carries her, weaves her legs through the ladder. Their whole bodies sighing, sweating, turning into fog turning into mist. Pounding. Faster. Harder. Closer. "Fuck me."

3. Island.

Preferring illusion to all else. Even to him. (*The more you think of something the more it disappears.*) Nora abandons herself so fully, so wholly, that something happens, something begins. Jake brushes the hair out of her bourbon eyes and becomes sentimental, and, as if being sentimental weren't crime enough, he says to her, "You are the most beautiful girl I have ever seen." But this love is an intrusion. It's an unwelcome betrayal and has no place in this pelagic fantasy, this fantasy of fantasy, this immortal moment isolated from the ocean. An island of moment. Not of this world. Outside of time. Amoral. Immoral. An island of immortality. An Olympus of down and cotton. Blue stalactites dripping off the wall. Islands of blue glowing, blue tears leaking blue out of the corners of her bourbon eyes, his blue eyes. Disillusion. Dissolution. Discontinuity. Between them is a gulf, a vertiginous, hypnotic, insoluble space. One island to another. Fusion would be fatal. But nonetheless. Impatient for meiosis. Mitosis, masquerading as meiosis. Bodies open out to an illusion of continuity, suppressed repression, an uneasiness, the nausea associated with the disassociation of identity. The illusion of individuality. The ebb and flow of waves surging into one another. Flesh made up of eyes. Eyes made up of fingertips. Exposed nerves, quivering at the thought. Her very bones are lucent. He attaches himself, gnaws at the marrow. The blood, the ichor coalesce in a flow of renewal. Her skin covers him, grows over him, absorbs him. The sacrifice. He ties her to the tracks. She rides his cock, her body ripping itself apart, another self rises from within—a glowing amalgamated self—exposing the truth to a disfigurement, a decay, a love. She must separate passion from banality, now from before, metaphor from desire, lust from love, beauty from bromide. She glows.

4. Rubric.

Yelling, floating, hallucinating. Her body, buxom and defiant, hoisted and proud, burst into a million multi-colored, metamorphosing images of wavy lines and brilliant visions. *This is my body, it shall be given up for you.* She cries, claws at the ceiling. Jake takes, she gives her will, her reason, her imagination, her memories, then her voice. Disembodied, she convulses, levitates, explodes in the white heat of harmonious honeyed agony, a pain of pure happiness. An hysterical paroxysm. Oscillating back and forth between the terrible fiery glow of submission, complete impuissance, black unconsciousness, and a spell of strangulation, of fire, needles, lacerations intermitted by an ecstatic flight into space. Shaking her soul from her throat, he drives his long golden spear into her chest, her *geist*, a beastly fire glows from its tip. As he thrusts the passion into her heart, he pierces her entrails, her essence, her very will to live, disintegrating her ego, her sense of anything. Except pain. And love. As he pulls out, Nora's body, her viscera, her honey, her soul comes out with it. She moans. She wails. She tells him that she couldn't be any happier.

5. Façades.

Until they repeat themselves, twice, to the point of beautiful exhaustion.

He sleeps with his penis tucked in between his legs. Everything else is oblivion.

6. Closing.

A fiction of presence. Holding hands in this gray, foreign land. Obscured by fog and dirty snow. Waiting curbside for the bus. She moves to the bridge, the river. Frozen into sharp angles. Thick, blurry, turbid angles. Green, gray, blue angles. The river reminds her of his eyes. He kicks a flattened can of soda toward her. She kicks it back. The banality is painful. The bus arrives, the doors sigh open. They hug. *Tell me you love me.* They kiss. They peel apart. They wave. A different kind of happiness washes over her. Contentment. Quondam, quixotic minutes. It hurts to sit down. She writes. Refuses to become anxious, to worry about destiny. Quixotic moments. Relived. Rewritten. In taxing detail. Her sternum tingles, expands. She strokes her inner thighs, twirls her hair. Records. Repeats. Melts into languor.

. . .

A consistent proof that religion is man-made and anthropomorphic can also be found in the fact that it is usually "man" made, in the sense of masculine, as well. The holy book in the longest continuous use—the Talmud—commands the observant one to thank his maker every day that he was not born a woman. (This raises again the insistent question: who but a slave thanks his master for what his master has decided to do without bothering to consult him?) The Old Testament, as Christians condescendingly call it, has woman cloned from man for his use and comfort. The New Testament has Saint Paul expressing both fear and contempt for the female. Throughout all religious texts, there is a primitive fear that half the human race is simultaneously defiled and unclean, and yet is also a temptation to sin that is impossible to resist. Perhaps this explains the hysterical cult of virginity and of a Virgin, and the dread of the female form and of female reproductive functions?

– Christopher Hitchens. *God Is Not Great: How Religions Poisons Everything.*

4.

Crowded out by the Ave Maria, Nora writes *Tu me manques*, in small letters on the back of a postcard of the Virgin Mary looking up to the clouds. Some charity was giving the cards away at mass to promote their cause, to encourage a more generous donation. When the baskets of cards came to Nora she took three of them. She decoupaged one onto her dresser, another on a journal for Maryanne, who collects images of the Madonna, and the last she saved for Jake. But she never sends it.

. . .

To even say the word is to have the mouth open in the shape of an O, a hole, a vagina, in penance, in holy patience, for the cock. Whoooorrre.

Lord, I'm not worthy to receive you, but only say the word and I shall be healed.

. . .

Nora wakes up feeling as if she has just bled all over herself. As if her period had engulfed her. So thick, so viscous was the sweat between her legs. Jake had just beaten her with a wooden baseball bat. Beaten her against the curb outside of her parents' window. Beaten her to death, to revival.

. . .

Drunk, Nora tries using God to speak to Jake, or rather, using God as a telephone wire unto Jake. She often uses God in such a way when she's intoxicated and upset. At this moment in time, Nora's upset that she has a crush on Garrett, who, at this moment in time, is making out with Maryanne, who, at this moment in time, has no idea that Nora has said crush.

Lying outside in the grass, arms cruciform, bored, cold, pining, praying. She wants him to think of her the way she thinks of him: unattainably high. Jake, her drug. Both medicine and poison. Her *pharmakon*. "Call me," she repeats. In an endless cycle of obsession. Call me. Call me. Call me…

And he does, just because he was thinking of her.

For awhile, for now, Nora holds onto this coincidence as proof of God's existence, and also as a sign that her and Jake are cosmically connected, or "meant to be together," as her mother would say. "Star-crossed lovers," as Maryanne would say.

. . .

Jake texts, So you think you can tell heaven from hell.

She sends nothing back, binds her enthusiasm. She'll see him in three weeks.

. . .

Then she can't help herself. She sends him a present, a woolen baby-blue blanket with silk trim, a replica of childhood, of home, along with a Joan Miró postcard: *Dancer*: pierced heart, waxing moon, dangling spider, lunar spirals, on a rectangle of blue.

Happy birthday.

He responds, almost immediately (four days via post), with humility, perhaps hostility, with Picasso's *Les Desmoiselles D'Avignon*. Women made out of sharp lines and ninety degree angles, but he had pierced each of them with a pin, with over a hundred tiny holes poked into them, through them, through their eyes and breasts, through their wide mouths and sharp corners. Written on the other side (despite the perforation), in smudged blue ink, couched inside quotation marks: "The assassination of painting." Then, in black pen, without quotation marks (but still transpierced), I am undeserving of such a gift.

In quiet delusion, Nora sees this as a threat, as proof that he is sleeping with other women. But that none of them are as good as she.

She knows she has no right to be jealous of his other conquests, but still, she regrets exposing herself as ever being a little girl.

...

Iowa City is a quaint, cozy town, like a freshly steamed cup of Chai. It's also a beacon of white light, unwaveringly pure. Devoid of parental supervision. Walking down Iowa Avenue she looks at her feet, into the copper, "AND THE COLOR YELLOW REGRETS IT WAS NEVER GREEN, AND THE EAST AND THE WEST LONG TO TRADE PLACES, AND THE SHADOW WOULD LIKE JUST ONCE TO COME OUT ON TOP." Marvin Bell, stamped into the sidewalk, part of Iowa City's literary walk of fame, where so many have done the walk of shame. From Brown to Burlington and the Iowa River to Governor Street: a tiny box made out of ivy and cobblestone. Couches on porches, Beer Pong in driveways, bean bags tossed on streets. The sweet smells of corn, night, and summer's autumn wafting in through windows, sometimes alongside the drone of an over-worked air-conditioning unit, always alongside the cicadas and crickets.

Hippies, jocks, and Chicago's suburban royalty are all zippered in together. The latter is shiny, makes up a majority of the sorority system, and wears a lot of frosted pink. The hippies and anarchists play guitar or Hacky-Sack in the Ped Mall. Sometimes they panhandle, often with a dog in tow wearing a sign that reads, "Why lie? I just want beer." They say one man owns six of the eight popular bars downtown, it used to be nine but one had to shut down because an under-aged girl's face caught fire. The drink required flames. They say it was the hairspray and cosmetics. They say her face melted onto the bar.

Back when the spirit of Vonnegut walked and Kerouac spat his unkempt spittle, this town, the Gaslight Village, used to mean more than getting fucked up or a rant to end consumerism. Before the Writer's Workshop crowned itself and rested on its traditionalist laurels, it was something brazen and intrepid. That was the time Nora wished she was writing in the Ped Mall. Even if for a moment she could eat an apple on that sidewalk and confirm her meddlesome suspicion that nothing, auras especially, ever really changes. When she looks over to the swarm of liberals camped beneath the golden dome of the Capital Building protesting, smearing themselves in black paint, she wonders if that's where she's supposed to be. If political activism really is her calling, but, as always, she settles on scribbling in the shadows. Really, she thinks these neo-hippies fools, and finds them annoying with the way they disturb one of the best places to sit and think, with their insistent chant: *No blood for oil! No blood for oil!* She walks past them and tilts her head up, hoping that they don't catch a whiff of her patchouli skirts and ask for her sympathy and a signature, or worse, to join their drum circle.

. . .

The bathroom is white and silver. Immaculate. Pristine. Antiseptic. All white tiles, tubs, tissues, toilets, sinks, curtains, and toes. There is always water running, dripping, slipping. Nora lets it overflow and splash onto the floor, where it thins, spreads, falls down the drain just before the white plastic curtain that separates her from all the other bathing girls.

She thinks of Joan Bevelaqua's *Ophelia*, and drowning in a wedding dress, popping out of existence as if she had been shot by a phaser. She consults her oracle, pushes thoughts of marriage, and the ghosts of Tony, Sean, and *O God!* Brian, to the side of her mind. She rubs herself to the sounds of water dripping off of all these faceless women. Their turning feet and shapely calves. She wonders what it would be like to fuck them, to push into them, making them moan for her, for Jake. She thinks of his clandestine smiles. How easy it is for him. A pulsating montage of his mouth breaking across his face. His eyes alight. His balls swinging as he walks. The possibilities of tonight, of explaining herself to no one. Of not having to come home to an angry and suspicious eye.

Tonight!!

She dunks her head under water until tiny bubbles cram into each of her ears, tickling the drums, sending shivers up her arms.

Only an hour before did she place a text: For it is morrow! Come, put on your dancing shoes, your fair maiden awaits!

Now, on a heavy red bathrobe, on a white plastic chair, next to the clawed white bathtub, Nora's phone lies in silence.

It silently lies.

And so his fair maiden waits.

. . .

After three days of unpacking, decorating, exploring her dorm, the town, the campus, Macbride Hall, meeting Rusty, the giant, three-toed ground sloth at the Natural History Museum, basically avoiding her vacant, uptight, depressed, and intensely Lutheran roommate, he finally returns her text.

Have you unpacked yet? Settled in? Can you play?

This text isn't a response, it's a new topic. It's as if her text never happened. It's as if she never waited or that night never was. As if he never got the text.

Meet me in the Stud Room. In the tunnel underground connecting our two dorms, she replies. The Stud Room is an abandoned study room adjacent to the abandoned cafeteria, which, to Nora, stands as a relic, an homage to The Max or The Peach Pit, dusted over with the ghosts of the recently graduated and their dotcom successes. Nora's been down there twice and so far she hasn't seen a soul, though she couldn't ever imagine why. This place is special, as sacred as it gets. She feels like for once she stumbled upon a bona fide secret space worth having. It was around 1am her first night when she pushed open the metal door, descended the stairway, and traversed the windowless corridor by herself. She could smell the caked-on grease from the old kitchen trapped within that musty basement stench. The smell of bats, old children's books, decaying cloth, and things forgotten. Nora became excited, like her dream of being locked in a mall with a boy is finally coming true.

I moved. I live in the fraternity house now, he responds.

Gross, she types, but then changes her mind, backspaces and sends, The Stud Room is the study room with the Y scratched out. It's more underneath Quad than Hillcrest. 10 o'clock.

And so the fair maiden waits, again.

...

She arrives early but he's already there.

...that indefinable, chimerical, ephemeral smile...

"I can't believe I never knew about this place!"

"Could you imagine actually studying down here? It's like a dungeon. Or a brig!"

"Do you remember the Dungeon?" He asks, already nostalgic for high school. Nora doesn't understand. She understands the question, the reference to the freshmen's locker room, but she doesn't understand why he cares, and why he would ask her if she remembers something so obvious, so banal, so not that long ago.

She steps on one of the desks that reminds her of Catholic school, the kind whose table is the top to a hollow box. She ducks to avoid hitting her head on the ceiling. Jake grabs at her ankle, runs his hand up her leg.

"I'm on my period, you know."

She doesn't know why she said that, and in such a manner.

"That hardly matters," he says. "You're here. That's what matters."

He twists his finger into one of the holes in her stockings, rips it open.

"Hey! Those are like ten dollars!"

"I'll buy you more." Kissing her leg, he pulls her down off the desk, or attempts to. She wobbles, scowls, then jumps. He is unfazed. Tearing at her fishnets, shredding them right to the elastic waistband. He unbuckles himself, falls back down, kisses her, sticks his dick inside of her.

She leaps away. "Are you fucking crazy?"

"C'mon. You're saddling old rusty."

"What? The Sloth?"

"Waving the Japanese flag. Taking Carrie to the prom."

"Condom!" she points.

"It was worth a shot," he says and he walks over to his pants. She surreptitiously pulls her tampon out from her drain pipe. Her anger dissipates quickly as he folds her skirt up and fucks her over the school desk, slapping her ass, and telling her how much he's missed her.

Afterwards, each of them standing on a different desk, they smoke with their heads out of the cracked window near the ceiling until they hear something. Resolute footsteps. They throw their cigarettes out the window then lay flat on the floor, trying not to breath. The security guard walks past, completely absorbed in something other than his job, but this is enough to spike their adrenaline into arousal again.

Caught up in the excitement, without even zipping up his pants, he lowers himself on one knee.

"Nora Childers, will you be my girlfriend?"

He takes her Claddagh ring, turns it around—closing her heart—and then puts it back on her finger.

"Why Jacob Noyes, I do declare!"

. . .

Nora acquires boyfriends to maintain her "relationship" with Jake. When she's single she clings to Jake, leaks a bit of her girlfriend personality, her dependent side. It starts with a follow up text, a phone call for no reason. She can see his phone vibrating endlessly in his pocket. She'll call again, asking him where he is, where he was, until he places one foot out the door and makes himself a wraith, disappearing into the whispering winds. This is why Nora needs a boyfriend, so she can get what she wants from Jake, so he stays. She tries to choose a guy with a wandering eye, one who won't fall in love with her. One she can lie to and cheat on with the least amount of guilt possible, but this latest stunt has thrown everything for a loop. She feels very uncomfortable.

. . .

Jiji Sandmore marched onto the scene in jack boots and a pink skirt made out of cellophane. She was carrying a sign that read: **Art is DEAD!** when someone threw a tomato at her and yelled "Support our troops, Hippie!" Nora stopped and offered her her hoodie and a small bit of marijuana. Jiji saved Nora's name in her phone as "Weed."

Jiji is the type of girl you notice before you notice you're noticing her. She's magnetic, fascinated, and always caffeinated. She attracts artists, brooding men, and seems to repel the kind of person that would call her humor pretentious. Without missing a beat, Jiji could tell someone exactly how their anecdote reminds her of Proust, or when something smacks of Foucault, and when she says this, she'll probably be wearing an old wedding dress, whirling about and fidgeting with her tulle skirts. Jiji speaks with authority, as if everything she says were obvious, even when saying things like: "You know, everything in its own way is an homage to *Teen Wolf*," or, "The very nature of an antithesis is that it's couched inside the thesis."

Nora is simply captivated by her. Every book that Jiji had mentioned on their brief walk home Nora went out and bought the next day. *Middlemarch*, *My Life* (Hejinian not Trotsky), *Invitation to a Beheading*, *Watt*, and intro books on Derrida, Freud, and Existentialism.

. . .

"How long did you wait before calling Jake?" Nick asks Nora.

"Shut it," Nora says, shielding the sunlight from her eyes.

"Ope! She's already fucked him!" Nick says.

"That doesn't count for the crown does it? New rule! No Jakes! Jakes never counts!" Salo yells. The crown is an uncomfortable plastic novelty awarded to the friend who most recently had sex.

"I second the motion!" Nick says.

"I didn't even reach for the it!" Nora says.

"That's right," Salo points then adjusts the golden crown atop her head. Its brilliant studded jewels cast red, green, blue, and magenta shadows on the wall.

"You both are assholes," Nora says.

"Don't insult your queen! Now pledge thy fealty, indentured whore!"

"A pox on both your houses!" Nora says, then slams the door to have a cigarette, but out on the front steps she decides to leave.

...

Jake introduces Nora to everyone as his high school
sweetheart, and this means something to her.
Because it doesn't mean anything to anyone else.
It's like a secret turned inside-out.
Perverse and peeling.

...

When Nora shuts the heavy metal door to her dorm room the dry-erase board falls to the floor, again. She picks it up and presses it to its usual spot, pushing hardest on the areas where the ticky-tacky tape holds. Futile. The board falls again, this time cracking the corner of its cheap, plastic frame. She throws her backpack onto the floor and rummages through Anna's desk drawer for the duct tape. She tapes the board back on the door, covering the entire frame in dull silver, ensuring that this fucker will never fall again.

Tuesday is the only day she gets home before her vacuous roommate, so it's the only day that Radiohead won't be on the speakers. She goes to her computer, opens AIM, Napster, and her Media Player. Her downloads resume. She highlights and clicks on The Cranberries before opening her drawer and pulling out a wooden box made to look like a book, *Wuthering Heights* painted on the spine in gold lettering. Unlatching the brass hook, she opens the box and takes out a glass pipe swirled turquoise and navy, a cardboard toilet paper tube, and a baby food jar half full of marijuana. She breaks off a small nug and crumbles it into a fine dust on the book box. Using the pad of her middle finger, she packs the bowl, filling it only partway, then smells her fingers. She then rolls a Minnie Mouse beach towel and lines the crack at the bottom of the door and switches the fan in the window on and sets it to reverse, so it will suck the air out of the room. She grabs a couple of Anna's dryer sheets and stuffs them into the toilet paper tube. She takes one more and covers one end of the tube, using one of her hair ties to keep it in place. Anna would freak if she knew Nora smoked in the room, so Nora climbs onto the back of their floral loveseat, getting as close to the fan as she can, and sparks the pot, inhales, holds, then exhales into the tube, toward the window. What lingers is like an earthy distortion of the dryer sheet's chemically fresh scent. After each hit she looks into the tube and examines the expanding rusty-brown stain. To ward off feelings of hypochondria, she hums the music and thinks of the way her mother folds laundry, how it's so different from the way she does it.

Nora has recently discovered the delights of being comfortably stoned, when the drug's effects are dulled and manageable. She loves it. She loves the effortless hilarity, the gentle compression of anxiety relief, the profound levels of concentration, but especially the way everything seems more important, more profound. Worthy of complete devotion. While high, Nora can get lost in any narrative, she can see their skeletal structures outlined before her, their characters opened, autopsied, organs, souls, flesh unlaced, unpacked. Nora can let go of her body or become nothing but her body. Through this oscillating detachment, she sees the pale and beautiful world with acute clarity: full, terrifying, existing as it really does: infinitely, without remorse. Absurdly.

When she goes outside to smoke a cigarette she holds on to the railing at the side of the stairway. Outside is vertiginous, not home, unsafe, nothing seems to stick. This dizziness isn't like the drunken spins, it's more philosophical, emptier. It's as if the veneer cracked and everything reveals itself to have always been two-dimensional, easily understood. Hidden in plain sight. In the cobblestones streets, Nora can see the ancient roads sandblasted, beaten, trodden on by horses and bare feet. The past and present seem to converge, without Nora, who is still curled around the railing, smoking a second cigarette, out of laziness more than anything.

The anxiety, the dread, sits in her stomach like an undigested lump of her mother's rock-hard meatloaf.

...

With her legs straddled across his bare back, and her knuckles kneading into its knots, Jake, without turning his head around to face her, says, "Hey, you know, next month is my formal. We should go. I mean, you're probably going to hate it, I know it's not really your thing, but since, before, we could never—"

"Sure, I'll go. Why not? It could be hella fun. I'll wear a dress made out of Saran Wrap or something."

...

Jake and Nora are both asleep atop her extra long twin mattress, with gray, jersey sheets and an egg carton foam pad underneath. A piece of masking tape on the ceiling reads, NO JAKE, in Salo's script, in black permanent marker.

In their sleep, one of them kicks their leg from a dream and knocks a vibrator off of the bed and onto

Anna's nightstand where it buzzes on, waking up, first Anna, who screams, then both Jake and Nora, who stifle their laughs, until Anna's begins swatting at it with her pillow, in a futile attempt to make it stop but only manages to knock it onto the floor, in a crack between their beds and the wall. Nora climbs down, laughing hysterically as she does, and grabs one of those plastic swords with compartments that collapse in on contact giving the illusion of penetration. She unclicks the sword to full, stiff capacity and uses it to reel in her vibrator. "Sorry, Anna," she mutters with equal parts of embarrassment and mirth.

"That's effing disgusting," Anna says.

In the form of a question, Nora makes a cigarette analogon, bringing two fingers to her lips and exhaling. Jake climbs down from the bed and Anna releases an exasperated sigh of disgust.

. . .

PORTRAIT OF A FRATERNITY HOUSE: A dead Christmas tree. Decorated, littered with empty beer cans and empty liquor bottles acting as ornaments, slid over the tree's branches like a condom. A trash heap in one of the corners on the second floor that rivals the character on Fraggle Rock, sans the wisdom. There is a bathroom with eight toilets and no stalls or walls but up to three inches of slimy, dirty water that barely trickles down the drain. A pair of rubber "community" galoshes sit outside its doorless doorway. It has been said that this is a place of circle jerks, where three or more boys stand around masturbating over a centerfold or a Hustler magazine. It's a race really, one of those covertly disguised rituals of bi-curiosity. Just as the other incidents of men dancing around each other in diapers while one sits in the middle cutting an onion, or the simple task of melting blocks of ice with ones naked body.

116

As she tip-toes out of Jake's room, she passes two of his brothers returning from a cigarette on the patio. They tell her that they just masturbated to her carnal sonatas. One of them even thanks her.

As she walks, she swishes, feeling a twinge of pride and a tingling behind her knees.

...

I won't be able to meet you tonight. I have to study. :(

Nora has Jiji over instead. In the underpass they smoke weed and burn the names of people that once scorned them. "Hell hath no fury!" they yell, dancing around an enflamed coffee tin.

"Hey!" Jiji calls out to a boy rushing past without a jacket. "I'll give you twenty bucks for your hat."

"Dude. Sold, I've got three of these," the guy says, handing over his fedora.

"Here," she says to Nora. "Put this on, and give me your hat."

"Why?"

"Because you look like a ill-conceived clown."

Nora's wearing Kermit the Frog pajama pants, a tie-dyed shirt, an open yellow cardigan with a cherry pattern, two mismatched gloves, and a woolen pink hat fully equipped with ear flaps and a white fluff ball up top.

"I look awesome. I like color."

"Ya think?"

Nora takes the fedora, buttons up her cardigan and performs an anecdote. She only stops when she notices Jiji's attention has been averted to a drunk couple stumbling up the stone steps toward the underpass. The guy's arm is around the girl's waist and the girl has one arm around his neck and another holding her strappy heels. She can barely hold her head up, but she looks like the type that isn't supposed to keep her wits about her, the type that laughs before she finishes her sentences.

"It's not what you think!" Jake says. "I'm just walking my buddy, Paco's, girlfriend home."

The girl laughs a frothy laugh into his chest, like she's laughing with the back of her tongue, hiding from Nora's gaze; she knows Jake's in trouble.

"Is this your girlfriend?" she asks.

Nora's myopic veil is pulled away.

Neurasthenia.

"See," Jiji says, "life *is* a novel."

"He's walking me home," the pretty girl hiccups with affected sincerity.

"How special," Jiji says, as if she were talking to a three-year-old.

"Five minutes," he asks. She doesn't know if he's pleading or offering.

Nora lights another cigarette, watches them disappear down the corridor. She feels like a tiny cup of espresso, steam swirling to the moon, snowflakes falling in her crema.

. . .

Her nose, ears, and cheeks blush with anger and sudden warmth. She passes two sorority pledges in the hallway outside her room. She asks, "Have either of you seen a tool-looking frat boy knock on my door?"

She can feel the anger pulsate behind her left eye.

"Jake? JoJo's Jake?" one of the girls says. Her friend looks confused, so she elaborates, "Yeah, you-know-who, the one that JoJo hooked up with in the closet at that last party."·

· This particular phenomenon will happen several more times throughout Nora's life, most notably with a woman in the process of waxing Nora's stomach. Life is a novel.

Two girls, ten minutes. *Amazing.*
After all, she is the girlfriend now.
The girlfriend.

Existential vertigo.

She starts to cry, softly. She doesn't want anyone to hear, especially JoJo's friends.

A different kind of hysterical paroxysm, a rupture. Rapture.

She turns left instead of right and uses her key to unlock the bathroom. Alone, she walks slowly, contemplating every soft angle and jagged curve of porcelain. In front of the mirror she stops and rolls her shoulders back, popping each knot along the blades. First she looks in her red eyes, then to her torso, her bloated stomach and obscured breasts, she marks the curves in her ass, but again travels back up to her distended face, her mascara streaked, acne smattered cheeks. Her sallow complexion and shiny pink nose repulse her. She lets out a pathetic whimper and her face collapses, sinks into a noxious maelstrom of failure, pity, and unrequited love.

A cerebral cul-de-sac of circumlocutions. An aspiration that respired only to be aborted.

A relationship that survives on force and will alone sits where it spins.

Around and around and around and around and around.

The hubris!

She's a mistress, not a girlfriend! The perpetual lover who outlasts and has already outgrown her role as girlfriend!

Trembling, the scorpion sting of rejection burns in her belly, moves down below, her mouths growl the wails of war, of endless difference. She is better than him, eternal to him. He needs her as she is, in that precise, precious way.

The failure to date, to name, cannot change Nora's irreplaceable uniqueness to Jake, because then it would alter the allusion to, the illusion of the irreplaceable uniqueness of herself as an individual, which would then question the presupposed cells of infinity whorling along within the self, herself, everyone's self.

War, the illogical logic of *him* versus *her*, or *she* opposite *he*, as man intended, or God, whichever came first. Still, in conflict, even with backs turned they will still be fact to face. Their identities comingling, fucking. Forever side by side. Never alone.

Codependent to the point of self-effacement, which is why she divides herself again, and from this bifurcation, she peels layers, creates paths, lives.

Nora with Him.

Nora without Him.

Nor with him, nor without him, peeling, deferring to the other, different from herself. In war with the other.

There's a knock at the door. She pulls the fedora down to hide her eyes.

Everybody on this floor would have a key. Wouldn't rely on someone being in the bathroom, especially at 2am.

She hears his voice, distant, muffled. "My girlfriend's in there."

Girlfriend.

She hears a chuckle, then a key inserted into the door.

"No, no," she says and grabs his arm, "Come on, we're going to my room."

"Are you crying?" he asks, stealing her hat and putting it on his head. He looks fantastic in the blinding white light. The shadows fall over his left eye and the bridge of his nose.

She unlocks her door as he's trying to look at her face. "You! Nora Childers! Crying? I can't believe it. I won't believe it!"

"Get in the fucking room!"

"You look like a cute little punk rock chick," he says, pointing to the black tears beneath her eyes. She grabs him by the shirt and pulls him close. He smells like gin and juniper. She kisses him just to see if she can taste pussy on his lips.

She can't. She pulls back. "Did she blow you?"

He guffaws, vacantly. "Since when were you the jealous type?"

Sobriety is such a harsh critic of intoxication. Every stagger, every blunder, each excessive blink cancels out his effrontery, his ferociousness. She can tell he's furtively desperate to keep his wits about him, to keep this insipidity a secret.

"Did. She. Suck. Your. Cock?"

"You're serious?" He tightens his forehead and stretches his eyes. He looks visibly shocked, then straightens his face, with great deliberation. "No," he says.

With her arms folded, she watches him nervously laugh and explain, kind of, in an affected and borrowed way, how and why he didn't fuck that girl tonight. She imagines herself Amy, or Heather, hearing him explain where he was when he was with her.

She cuts him off, "Two girls in ten minutes! Ten. Fucking. Minutes!"

"Chill out, Chopsticks. What are you even talking about?"

He lights a cigarette in her room. She panics. "Are you fucking thick? I'm two doors down from the RA!"

121

She lunges to take the cigarette, he maneuvers, takes another drag then smashes the butt against the wall, leaving a seared black smudge of soot and ash next to her cork board, close to a picture of her parents on their wedding day.

"You can't get away with your normal shit with me! I wrote your antics. This is our game, our story." She throws her hands up. "Un-fucking-believable! I trusted you. I'm the fool. And what kind of stupid circus name is JoJo anyway?"

"Nora, I care so much for—"

"You're not as amazing as you think you are, you know. You are thoroughly ordinary, and often intolerably so."

...

Jake disappears with a trace, always with a trace.

Because lovers can never disappear completely.

They are human, for the most part, embodied time, and though time is infinite, the cradled flesh is finite, unless, time is cyclical and this has all happened before: Nora with her arms crossed, lying to Jake, telling him that he's intolerably ordinary. He leaves. She cries. Lather, rinse, repeat.

Tourbillon de la vie.

After the tears, the insight. The girl who hesitates between men, will decide to love all.

...

According to Milan Kundera there are two types of womanizer. The lyrical womanizer seeks his own personal ideal in each woman, whereas the epical womanizer seeks the knowledge, the experience of the infinite variety immanent in the feminine mystique, the gentle solar system.

Jake belongs to the former category. Drunk then on his own lyricism, drunk on the litany of interchangeable bodies stretched before him. Drunk with power, with false romance, on boxed wine and classic rock medleys.

Whether or not time flows in a loop, whether or not it repeats everything again and again and again is irrelevant. It's all intolerable and loathsome.

The unbearable lightness of being, the unbearable weight of eternal return.

Application. Continuity. Connectedness.

Eternal return. Eternal sunshine. Eternally begotten of the Father.

God from God. Light from Light. True God from True God.

. . .

Nora's father climbed down from the attic with a box cradled in his arms. "This is the last one," he told Nora's mother, "and if it's not in here, we're going to the store."

He unwound the string around one of the plastic knobs keeping the box shut, and when he opened it a rush of stale Christmas charged into Nora's nostrils. It was the smell of ornaments, of plastic pine needles, of dust. Her father removed a set of bubble lights, the ones her brother picked out last year. He smiled as he laid them on the ground. Then he removed fifteen feet of plastic popcorn string. Then he dug and he dug, until he pulled out twenty feet of sparkling garland. Gold and silver tinsel. Perfect for a halo. Nora's mom grabbed the garland triumphantly with a "HA!" and attached it onto a loop of wire with a hot glue gun. She then looped some more wire around a head band.

As Nora watched her mother her eyes widened, she lit up and ran around in circles with her hands over her head, because she knew she was going to have the best halo in the class.

And later, as she walked down the same aisle brides and coffins alike traverse, Nora felt like the prettiest angel that ever was. She was making her father happy. She was making God happy.

> As she walked down that red tongue of Christ, fidgeting with her white dress, she waved emphatically to her parents, security, accomplishment, swelling in her chest.

...

God is Dad. God is Dead. God is Deed. God is Dad. God is Dead. God is

Deed. God is Dad. God is Dead. God is Deed. God is
Dad. God is Dead. God is Deed. God is Dad. God is
Dead. God is Deed. God is Dad. God is Dead. God is
Deed. God is Dad. God is Dead. God is Deed. God is
Dad. God is Dead. God is Deed. God is Dad. God is
Dead. God is Deed. God is Dad. God is Dead. God is
Deed. God is Dad. God is Dead. God is Deed. God is…

. . .

Nora meets Ben through one of her failed lovers.
They are friends, in a way, Ben and this soon-to-be-ex, but
only in a way. Ben has the somber eyes of an Alaskan Crab
fisherman. She thinks he is the only man she's ever met
that could survive alone, without the love of a woman for
the rest of his life if he had to. Each time she sees him it's
under the same conditions: beer in hand, quiet
accomplishment encased in an understanding smile. He
listens. Greg has had too much to drink, which for him is
only five beers. Ben is on his eighth, and there isn't a sliver
in those warm fisherman eyes that told her so. She only
knows from the empty cans she counts in the recycle bag
next to the cooler.

"There are few things sexier than a man that can
hold his liquor," she says.

"You mean, there are fewer turn-offs than a man
that can't."

"Fair enough," she says, which is how she always
feels around Ben, like she can let the world just be.
Because it will still be there in the morning.

Tonight, they sneak away from the party. Ben tells
her that he's crazy about her, and she tells him the same.

"How should we tell everyone? Should we just start
making out at the next party?"

"Greg's still in love with you."

"*Ugh.*"

"He's my friend—I can't—it's got to be gentle, sincere," Then he pauses to think. "All right. I'll tell him. It'll be better that way, coming from the friend," he says. "I'll tell him that I really like you, that it wasn't a dick measuring contest or some shit like that. I mean, he knows you're not really that into him. You guys barely hang out, and when was the last time you slept together?"

"You just want to know that for your sake. But fine, two/three months ago or something."

He smiles sardonically. "It's not like the poor kid doesn't know you've moved on."

Nora looks up at him, somewhat indignantly at what he's implying.

"Nor, you haven't slept with the guy in two months." His voice is like Xanax to her. "It'll all be fine. He'll understand." He takes her hands. "I'll take care of it."

Nora trusts him. Completely. So much so that at this moment Jake doesn't even cross her mind. Everything seems so simple.

But the tequila goes from her head to her thumb, she types, hello.

. . .

"You're what?"

"Seeing somebody," she says.

"So."

"So?"

"So what," he puts his arms around her waist.

She wiggles out of it. "So that means that you can't do that."

"You're un-fucking-believable!"

"He's great. You would like him. A sports nut," she smiles and looks out the window like people in love do.

"Why did you even text me?"

"To tell you this! To talk, like people do sometimes. Because sometimes coffee is just coffee!"

"Coffee is never just coffee."

"It's just coffee, God damn it!"

"Then fuck off, you ignorant slut." He says then sips his coffee. Nora's still staring at him. She can't tell if he's kidding. He opens his *Quarks and Quasars* textbook, winds his finger as if to say, "Wrap it up," all while keeping his eyes on the page. She leaves with a huff.

. . .

Late one Friday night, with a bright red nose and a goofy smile, Ben stumbles into the dorms, laughing, shivering, without a coat. He had gambled it away in a game of cards. He *was* winning, on a roll even. "It was that pair of bitches," he kept saying. "It's always the bitches."

His hoodie is soaked through the back, muddied stiff at the elbows and down his left leg. He must have fallen.

Nora takes off her sweater and covers his frostbitten ears. Later, those ears will fill with fluid and turn grayish black. Ben will also find this funny. He laughs but his laughter is controlled, because, as Nora will learn, Ben is always in control. And when Ben gambles, win or lose, he couldn't be happier. Once, he even gambled away his microwave. "Best night ever," as he'll recall.

Simply put, Ben merely wants a beer, a game, and to see something naked.

Nora likes that she doesn't find this annoying, that she doesn't find him annoying. She likes that she's not worried, that she doesn't have to tend to his wounds, though that makes her want to all the more, and he doesn't stop her. He never stops her. She likes that too. It almost makes up for his libertarianism, or the way he and his roommate spit sunflower seed shells onto their carpet, waiting for the salty dregs to attract ants before raking them up and starting the process all over again. They also smoke and dip, spitting greasy tobacco into any ash-laden, empty beer can lying around.

...

    Okay. I forgive you. Let's have some "coffee."
        I'm still in love. Go away.
        Or rather, Fuck off, you ignorant SLUT.

...

After finals, after all the parties and tickertape, the children of the dorms, and the princes and princesses from the Greek community, all return to their respective Chicago suburb or small Iowan town. Of course, there are others from elsewhere, Jiji, for instance, but most, as with all colleges, maintain a short driving distance from their parents. By June, Nora declares Saint Charles maddening and rents an apartment in the Gaslight Village. Jiji hadn't returned to San Francisco, and neither had most of her friends. Nora spends most of her time on a rickety porch, sweating in a sundress, fanning herself with an old Chinese paper fan from childhood, smoking joints and discussing Mark Rothko or Theodore Adorno or Virginia Woolf over blackberries and freshly picked, butter-fried morel mushrooms. Ben is in Hartley, Iowa for the rest of the summer working at a factory, moving giant planks of wood from one place to another. He'll make enough money there to last him through most of next year, and he'll come back stronger, leaner, smarter. He'll perfect his brood.

...

Today is the day.
A day like all the rest.
Except today, Nora is going to quit smoking. She is just going to stop. She will twist her last butt into this ashtray that her brother made, a clay pot made to look like

a bird. As its beak holds her smoking sin Nora thinks not if she should do it, but if she could do it. The anxiety brings the cigarette back to her lips, she inhales. It hurts. This must be her twenty-third cigarette of the day. She always over smokes when she's reading.

She twists and twists the butt and plays with the black ash, the few Indian red tobacco shavings that had gotten away, gone unsmoked, then, forever, drawing a circle, then another, and now, she's decided she's going to try. No cigarettes tomorrow. If she can manage it for a week, she'll call Ben and convince him to quit too, which shouldn't be too hard for him considering a pack can last him a week, unless he's gambling, but maybe he could only smoke when he gambles, when Nora isn't there. Feeling empowered she grabs the almost empty box of Lucky Strike Lights, rattling with four fragile, unsmoked paper cigarettes, and wraps it in silver duct tape then throws it into the community freezer, stuffing the little package in back behind some frozen Ziplock bag of semi-liquid berries, which Nora and Jiji had always called "ex-girlfriend," because it was George's and George creeps them out.

She falls asleep reading *Madame Bovary* every night for the next three nights. On the third night she finishes, crying herself to sleep, and the next morning she wakes up thinking about how the book continues for thirty pages after Emma dies. She's swept away by the continuity of life, the double-standard, the trick, the gaffe; that life is, really, discontinuous, for Emma, for everyone, for herself. She goes downstairs, pours herself a cup of coffee and grabs the Luckies out of the freezer. Then sits on the front porch, by herself, for which she is very grateful, and stares at the little silver package glinting in the sunlight.

She tries to unwrap the box but ends up using the Swiss Army knife on her keys to cut through the ribbed and gooey silver tape. Then she takes one cigarette out and places it on the table next to her. It's cold, the cellophane fogs. She stares at that for a while. *They won't think I've failed. I did quit for three days, those are the hardest days, and if I can do it then, then I can do it whenever, but now, in college, especially my sophomore year,* now *is not a good time.*

To forget, to immerse in everydayness, she checks her inbox.

Golden Sin.

A shockwave blows through her body. Everything's awake now, everything's activated, including her bowels. Unconsciously, the cigarette is between her fingers.

Golden Sin

Sing my Sin, my heart, that you do not know what I

    cannot know.

    Like metal poured into a glass, opaque, unattainable.

My secret stuffed in a locket, your locket, close to your heart

    Locked behind a gate, the golden gate, of things we do not deserve.

    This life of pain, no one is to blame, but me.

I am the serpent. I am the apple. I am the lie between your legs.

Less of a man, more than

    a secret, one sweet caress. I will never regret.

With the cigarette dangling from her mouth, she holds the flame far from her face, waves it around, makes it dance. The *danse macabre*. Brings it slowly towards her face. She shakes with anticipation, fighting off the guilt, smelling the dried apricot aroma of the toasted tobacco. She lights the cigarette. Pyrolysis. Her mouth tingles. Paresthesia. Like her mouth lost circulation, fell asleep, like she's just bitten into a banana. It tastes differently from what she remembers. Staler. She inhales, slowly, a thin stream, a small puff of silver grey smoke, of tobacco, of acetanisole, acetic acid, acetoin, acetophenone, acetylpyrazine, amyl butyrate, amyl butyrate, benzoin, resinoid, benzyl alcohol, bergamot oil, bornyl acetate, butyl isovalerate, butyric acid, caraway oil, cardamom seed oil, carob bean and/or extract, celery seed oil, chamomile flower Hungarian oil, chamomile flower Roman extract & oil, cinnamaldehyde, cinnamyl isovalerate, citral, citric acid, d l-citronellol, cocoa and cocoa products, coffee extract, green cognac oil, coriander oil, beta-damascone, davana oil, delta-decalactone, gamma-decalactone, decanoic acid, diacetyl, para-dimethoxybenzene, dill oil, 2.5-dimethylpyrazine, ethyl acetate, ethyl butyrate, ethyl hexanoate, ethyl isovalerate, ethyl lactate, ethyl maltol, ethyl octanoate, ethyl phenylacetate, ethyl propionate, ethyl vanillin, fenugreek extract, geraniol, geranium rose oil, glycerol, guar gum, gamma-heptalactone, 2-heptanone, hexanal, hexanoic acid, gamma-hexalactone, hexyl acetate, 4-(para-hydroxyphenyl)-2-butanone, immortelle extract, alpha-ionone, beta-ionone, isoamyl acetate, isoamyl butyrate, isoamyl formate, isoamyl hexanoate, isoamyl isovalerate, isoamyl phenylacetate, isobutyl acetate, isobutyric acid, isovaleric acid, lactic acid, lemon oil, lemongrass oil, licorice extract, lime oil, linalool, lovage extract, maltol, l-menthol, 2-methoxy-4-methylphenol, para-methoxybenzaldehyde, methoxy-3-methylpyrazine (mixture of isomer), methyl-cyclopentenolone, methyl isovalerate, 4-methylacetophenone, 3-methyl-butyraldehyde, 2-methylbutyric acid, mimosa absolute, mountain maple extract solid, gamma-nonalactone, oakmoss absolute, gamma-octalactone, delta-octalactone, opoponax oil, orange oil distilled, sweet orange oil, orris root extract, palmarosa oil, phenethyl alcohol, peppermint oil, phenylacetaldehyde, phenylacetic acid, piperonal, propenylguaethol, propylene glycol, rhodinol, rose oil, bulgarian, true otto, non-alcoholic rum flavour, sclareolide, d-sorbitol, spearmint oil, storax, styrax extract, invert sugar, sucrose, tangerine oil, 2,3,5,6-tetramethylpyrazine, 2,3,5-trimethylpyrazine, gamma-undecalactone, valerian root extract, valerian root oil, vanilla extract, vanillin, veratraldehyde, water, carbon dioxide, and ethyl alcohol.

It all immediately hits her lungs, travels through her blood stream, tingles the patterns of her fingerprints. She grunts from the delight of failure.

Later, she'll print the email, and reread it, guts churning, thinking, knowing, that reading his poetry is a Eucharistic act. Through his words she imbibes part of him, feels impossibly close to him, especially because it's about her. Sinking into ink and sin, her total attraction brings her to roll with waves of ecstasy from within.

. . .

Legs folded underneath her, she sits on her ankles, Seiza style, then bounces up. She leans closer, thrusting her chest toward him, nearly leaning her rack on the table. He cups his cigarette, inhales, then lets his arm fall to his side, outside of the booth. She asks him for one. He gives her a look of distrust, flashes his gaze to her purse but says nothing. Slowly, he sits up and grabs the pack of Marlboro Menthol Lights off the table, flips open the box, and pulls one out. One of his cigarettes is upside down. He still considers this act, this inverted cigarette, lucky. He hands it to her with the filter pointing toward her, she takes, smiles, places it in her ruby mouth then leans forward. He straightens his back, tucks his chin in, then straightens his legs, grabbing the lighter out of his pocket. He flicks it, cups his hand around the flame and leans into her. She grabs his hand and looks into his eyes as he lights her. She looks from under her lashes, widening the whites of her eyes, and her pupils. She doesn't blink. She doesn't smile. He holds her gaze. Places the lighter on top of the pack. She inhales, lifts the corners of her mouth, as if she were about to smile but then blows the smoke toward the ceiling of the bar. The curls of silver and gray scatter immediately under the wind from the ceiling fan. She smiles, lowers the cigarette and exposes her wrist, turning her palm toward him, sending him a wave of pheromones and patchouli scented oil. He eyes the carmine crescents staining her cigarette, then reaches out his fingers, requesting a drag.

. . .

Outside smells like burning leaves and firewood, like shoe leather and blank leaves of notebook paper. With another bottle of wine—this time a spicy Shiraz—swinging from his leaky grip, the two of them walk in the middle of the street, summer heat thick in their throats, arms clasped, leaning on one another, breaking out into song every now and again, comparing memories, falling into the grass, lighting cigarettes every fifteen minutes. Nora's hay fever scratches at her eyes, they can't stop watering. She continually drinks herself into denial, mayhaps relief, and with every sip, she lets a little of Ben leak out of those tears, and thinks that this is the happiest she's been in months, though the liquor claims forever.

They arrive at the cemetery just after 3am. Even in the near complete darkness, the Black Angel's easy to spot. Once as golden and promising as the sun, now she stands, eight and a half feet tall, oxidized, cursed into cosmic blackness. Shaded in charcoal, personified chiaroscuro and tawdry, hopeful superstition. Her eyes are black as coal, black as soot. Black as cinder. Her wings hug her body. She looks to the ground with her palms down: she bars the ascent into heaven. Shrouded in enigma, as enticing as a Ouija board, Iowa City's Black Angel, the Feldevert family's gravestone. They say once Teresa Dolezal Feldevert, a Bohemian immigrant, buried her husband's ashes beneath the angel's feet, she vowed that she would remain faithful until the day she died, swearing that this death angel would turn black if she cuckolded his memory. They say that any girl kissed at her feet in the moonlight will die within six months of the contract.

From the moment two pairs of lips touch, a silent contract of love is sealed with a kiss.

Towering over the other gravestones, the angel's arms forbid them to walk any further. She commands respect, and Jake immediately drops to his knee and genuflects. Nora grabs him by his shirt's collar and pulls him in, smashes him into her lips. Aggressively, she slides her tongue into his mouth, works her hands up his body, into his hair. She's become wild, rabid. He pulls away, flips open his phone and orders a cab back to his place.

. . .

The first door on the left. A cracked and crooked sliver of gray light leaks into the hallway. Not the shimmery moonlight, but the dull, matte gray of Charlie Chaplin; the reels are spinning, slapping. Someone tip-toes towards the hot flashes, knocks on the door. Opens it. The screaming stops. Sheets are pulled up and over.

"Jake?"

"Jesus Christ! Tuba."

Apologies. Tuba shuts the door all the way. Sviridov begins again, in the middle. *Time, Forward!* Just in time, to remain still. After a moment Nora's eyes adjust. A room bereft of all color. Black, blurred edges and the white, simple facts. Until Nora puts the back of her hand to her forehead. Puckers her dark lips. A damsel in distress, a porcelain doll, a femme fatale. Carrying the heart of the world in her chest. His pale face blends into the pillows. "I want to rape you in your wedding dress," he says.

Stiff and flawlessly she moves before him. Graceful and fragmented. She's here. She's there. His face. His cock. The scene is rigid like a flip book, accelerated, like a gland upon the brain.

Shifting her bedroom eyes, she's concentrating on giving herself to him, creating the illusion of bodily perfection, emptying her own desires, becoming a cum bucket. He is injecting her with his fantasies. Tonight, a French harlot during the Depression. With an open mouth, Nora climaxes at Sviridov's first crescendo.

The page turns.

He flips her body. Pulling her to his mouth, pushing her back down. She climbs to the top, props him up on his elbows digging into the mattress, grabs his stomach, brandishes her breasts. She is a cat killing a mouse. A Venus Flytrap. She wants to draw out this moment, play with it, tease herself. The world disappears for her, for him, her audience. She puckers for the camera, fucking her chimera. There is no thrusting, only wiggling, belly dancing. She feels the bumpy, fleshy folds hugging her urethra. She feels full with emotion, with child, with penis, with expiry, complete. She screams, aloud, over Sviridov, through time.

She had forgotten *this*, this feeling, rising, into her chest, her throat, her liver. To say an explosion would be a cliché, would make it ordinary. To say an orgasm would negate the feeling.

An hysterical paroxysm.
A passion unto death.

An erotic fait accompli. Life ascending to destruction, a resplendent feeling of accomplishment. Impurity, unfiltered. She deflates. But he isn't finished. He flips her over again, she lies there, he pushes in, out, in, out. Her well is drying up, she'd absorbed into her own orgasm. The rubber squeaks. *Don't break,* she chants in her head. Then: *What have I done?* His weight presses into her, slick flesh on sticky flesh. He isn't paying attention to her anymore. He's lost in his own pleasure. She could be anyone now. She concentrates on breathing through his body, through the pain. He grunts, again, an octave higher. *Finish!* She hurries him along. Moans, teases the cum out of him. *Oh my God! Oh my God! Uuuah!* "I'm coming, baby," he says, disembodied, his voice whimpers, sputters. His sex pumps, pulsates, swells against her. Latex creates a distance, a barrier. She peels herself away, lights a cigarette, and sits up. Glowing, exhilarated. He grabs a plastic bottle of water. It crinkles in his grip. "Oooh, give me some."

Love cannot be without possession, the will to possess.

. . .

The summer when Nora was ten, she didn't understand why her mother didn't want her talking to him. If he was so bad then why would she let him into their house? Why would she hire him to paint the garage? He was standing on the paint splattered silver ladder, and Nora looked at him with a disconcerting feeling in her stomach. That was her father's ladder. Not this guy's. He smiled at her as she passed. He smelled like smoke and nail polish remover. She gave him a half-smile, the kind that lets people know you're acknowledging their existence, but little more. Then his phone rang. Nora could hear a shrill voice, so she went and hid behind the garage to spy. He forcefully said, "No. No." Continued protesting, said he was working. Then he called her a "fucking harpy." That night he ate dinner with the family. Said he was just about finished with the branches. Nora couldn't help but feel uncomfortable sharing a meal with a man she wasn't supposed to talk to. She sat with her hands under her thighs, barely eating any of her meat. He asked her to pass the salt. She did. And he salted and salted and salted. He salted the steak, the corn, the potatoes, the green beans. He salted before every bite. Three months later he committed suicide. She spent countless nights awake wondering if somewhere, maybe below her feet, he was being tortured, if he had been turned into a tree.

...

Three new text messages.
`Come over.`
`I miss you. I want to see you.`
`All of you.`
Nora smiles then looks around the room, looks to see if Jiji saw her smile. `I'm at a friend's,` she types.
`Come over.`
And then, immediately afterwards, he sends another, `I'll see you in 10 minutes.`
`No.`
`Every centimeter of you.`
`God damn it.`
She puts the phone down and picks up a pen, puts it back down, runs her fingers through her hair. She looks around the room then picks up *The Iliad*, flips through to the end of the chapter. Twenty -six pages. At least forty-five minutes. She picks the pen back up and taps its tip onto her notebook. She looks at the clock, then her phone

again, pressing a side button so it lights up. She looks back down to the book. *God damn it.*

She calls over to Jiji who doesn't hear her. Jiji's sitting in a grand velour armchair across the room, twirling her hair and reading *Midnight's Children.* The chair is burgundy, ashy, and has clawed feet. It was once somebody's trash. When Jiji found it she carried it six blocks to her apartment then fixed it up outside (to make sure it was without mice or piss). Now it looks both ancient and beautiful, as if it had always belonged to her. She sets down her book in her lap and sighs, "The scene where the doctor inspects a naked woman through a hole in a sheet laid over her body! The perforated sheet! The holy lens laid on profane nudity, accentuating her nakedness, raising her then to the level of divinity not because of piety but because of the taboo. And at the same time the sheet functions as a veil, a taste, a tease, religious and tantalizing, obscuring her body, her nakedness, making the act—for both Aziz and his future wife—more elicit, more taboo, reminding us how one must be ashamed of the body, ashamed of our desire, how unholy our bodies actually are according to the laws Rushdie's direct text subverts! Pure genius."

"Awesome... But I'm... I'm gonna go," Nora says.

"You sound unsure."

"Yeah..."

"Who did you get a text from?"

"Maryanne. She's freaking out about some guy."

"Doesn't she have a boyfriend?"

"Yeah but this guy is way better. I've got to convince her that leaving Matt for him is a great idea."

"Okay, I have to get up early tomorrow anyway. I have to be at the Clinic at 8am" Jiji says.

"Rough!"

"Yeah, but at least I like the job. You want to smoke a bowl before you go?"

"Sure."

...

Back in her room, she sets down the shower basket and disrobes. Caressing her own skin, seducing her own face, she falls in love with the sight of her naked body as she stares at its surfaces, forgetting for a moment the psyche eternally trapped behind its confines, and simply marvels at her own loveliness. She smiles, giggles, turns to the left, the right. She cannot believe she's looking at the same girl who cries over any of this. Even her stretch marks seem charming.

She looks at her closet, at her clothes, at the perfect dress.

The dress she was supposed to wear to his formal.

A starry night, without the vibrancy of Van Gogh's palette, more like the terrifying vastness of a country night sky. It once had dreams of dancing under those stars, now it will only hang from a hanger, with its thin straps, taut and freakishly long, clinging to tiny plastic hooks. Its back is entirely made up of straps, strings, but without the width of a person those straps stretch taller, leaving the skirt huddled in a glittery puddle of itself. It is an evening gown slumped without a figure, weeping like a wallflower.

She had even bought the perfect pair of matching heels, complete with seven rhinestones on each strap, so she could exhume her old clip from the depths of an even older Caboodle box.

Feeling melancholy, she looks at the time and throws on an old baseball shirt.

She goes outside, lights a cigarette, and walks the two blocks to his fraternity house.

Once at the door she can hear voices occasionally rising over Sublime. She hates Sublime. She sighs then punches the pathetic, predictable code: 42069.

"Nora! Nora! You came!" Jake stretches his arms out with affection, but she doesn't look at his face, she looks at the two enormous forty ounce beer bottles duct taped to his hands. The stench is thick with yeast and ranch dressing.

"It's called Edward Forty-Hands!"

Everyone in the room is laughing. Even Nora cracks a smile, though a little of her patience slips out that crack in the process.

"Nora! Nora! I'm so happy!" He runs over to her and hugs her, sloshing cheap beer onto her jeans, the floor, his pants, and the back of her shirt. "Nora, you've got to do me a favor. Nora. You've got to help me smoke a cigarette. Would you do that? Could you? I've been dying for one!" He's overly animated.

A cigarette sounds like an excellent idea.

She needs a moment to think.

"You wanna play?" this bro asks her from across the room. Though she suspects he's only asking her to get Jake's attention because right after he asks this he slams the remaining drops of his beer and everyone yells. Some cheering, some groaning. The guy shakes his hand, violently, trying to get the tape off by sheer force of gravity, which doesn't work. So then he smashes his own hand into the wall, then into the couch. Then steps on it, hoping he can separate glass from tape. He grunts as the tape rips his arm hair. He sounds like a body builder at the gym, like a character from one of her brother's combat videogames. The rest of the boys are hopping around him, both cheering him on and telling him he's never going to do it. So far, he's the first to finish a bottle and they're all incredibly interested in the quickest way to remove it.

"I've got to piss so fucking bad," yells one of the brothers.

"Like a horse race!"

"Oh my God, you have no idea!"

"Maybe Nora'll help you with that," another brother says, at which each boy calls, "Nora? Nora! Help me! Help us!"

"Why do the ladies love Jesus?" Jake asks, doesn't wait for an answer, "Because he's hung like this!" Arms cruciform, beer escaping.

"Cheating!" one of the guys yells.

Jake then falls over laughing at himself. Tears are streaming down his cheeks. Beer spills out onto everything.

She couldn't be happier that Ben returns next week.

But at that thought the guilt settles in. She grabs a bottle of Captain Morgan's and drinks until she throws up.

...

The universe is expanding, cooling.

...

```
        I can't.
Why?
        It wasn't a good idea. I told you.
        Stop texting me, especially at this
        hour!
But this is when Angela's asleep.
```
Who the fuck is Angela?

...

It's true, the pleasures of domesticity have staled. She is too comfortable. Restless. Ben is like a pair of pajama pants worn for so long they feel like a second layer of skin. Some days the depression is so fierce she clutches her chest, eyes wrung out, twisting her shirt, trying not to check her pulse that she knows is beating way too rapidly.

141

She tells herself it's the marijuana. That if she wouldn't smoke every day she'd feel better, less restrained. She starts running a lot, but only at night. To counterbalance the pot. She runs home from class. Home from work. Home from Salo's. She runs as if she's running away from someone, from an alleged attacker, some disheveled, feckless wastrel, desperate to assert some dominance, to feel like a man with a cock. Nora's always on the lookout for this man. She carries a bottle of pepper spray with her, sometimes with her finger on the trigger, especially when she runs through the parking lots behind the apartment buildings. She could take the main road but she doesn't feel safe there either. Probably, because she's mainly running from herself, some villain inside of her that she can't disembody. That she can't justify and analyze away because everything points to her own fears and failures. When she gets home she often flops onto her concrete steps and cries.

. . .

She's running late. Class is in three hours and she's behind on her reading. Ben's horny, which at the moment, probably because she's otherwise engaged, she finds endearing.

"Okay," she agrees. "But you have to read out loud."

He'll agree to anything for an imminent blowjob.

He begins John Locke's *Essay Concerning Human Understanding*, "Book II: Of ideas. Chapter i: Of ideas in general, and their original. Section 4."

"These two, I say," he's animate, he continues "*viz.*," he says, "external, material things, as the objects of SENSATION and the operations of our own minds within, as the objects of REFLECTION, are, to me, the only originals, from whence all our *ideas* take their beginnings. The term *operations* here, I use in a large," he pauses briefly to sigh, "sense, as comprehending not barely the action of the mind about its ideas, but some sort of passions arising sometimes from them, such as is the satisfaction or uneasiness arising from any thought." He finishes with a flourish.

She laughs, and for a moment, she forgets herself. Until she sees Jake crossing Dubuque Street, his manufactured blond hair glinting in the sun. She smiles, thinks, *I can't see you*, then ducks into The Deadwood, a bar with her kind of people, a bar where she can become a silhouette against the light.

After a pause, she sends Jake a text.

You are made out of paper.

She orders a Bloody Mary, skips class, smokes way too many cigarettes, and writes:

Imaginary Lover.

Of all that is seen and unseen.

Eternally begotten from the past.

Imperceptible by day.

Haunting at night.

Jake by Jake.

Light from Light.

Like a ghost, or a memory.

. . .

Choking from the sour air under the bell jar, Nora can only sleep about four, maybe five hours a night. She takes a second job. They put her on twenty milligrams of

Fluoxetine a day to "keep her head above water." They don't know about her self medication. She takes the pills with oatmeal and a glass of milk everyday at 6am. She spends the rest of her mornings in hospital garb, counting glass phials, readying them for the autoclave. Hours upon hours, counting crystal clear glass phials and rubber stoppers in rubber trays, a hairnet atop her head. The smell of rubber is almost painful and the silence frightens her. Brings about tinnitus.

Maybe Silvia was right. Maybe marriage really is a lobotomized death.

She used to joke with Jake that they'd be ninety, locked in the same nursing home. They would develop a special knock, a secret rendezvous, even then. Sometimes Nora fears this is who she is, that she will never be able to settle down, no matter how badly, how much she wants to at times. Other times, this is her default boast. She's as hard as a man, they'll think. Durable, coveted, beddable. Totally independent.

She hasn't had sex with Ben in over two weeks. He's very patient with her. She doesn't deserve it.

...

She dreams of being tied up. To headboards and trees. The bark scratching her back, raking over her skin. She persistently dreams of being beaten, raped, and shot in the head. Jake's not always the culprit. Sometimes it's a stranger, some man she's never seen before. The man she's been running from. Sometimes it's Brian. It has never been Ben or Tony, nor has it ever been her father.

She also dreams of nuclear holocaust, of being thrown into a mass grave, à la Mozart, but still alive. The intolerable stench, the vacant and clammy flesh bronzing, rotting in the sun. She dreams of her mother being curbed, brains splattering the pavement, and Maryanne being hanged, purple pierced tongue protruding from her slacked mouth. She dreams of awaiting execution, trial by fire, drowning in the sea, kneeling before a towering chamber of elders, neck in chains, little girls in bonnets screaming "Witch! Witch!" She wakes next to Ben and scrambles to the other side as if a rat were in the sheets. "It's okay," he says, over and over again. He holds her, strokes her hair, calms her down. "It's okay."

. . .

In the Natural History Museum, two hours before her Psychology lecture, tucked away on another floor in between halls, Nora falls asleep next to Rusty. Her favorite spot. Stretched out along the bench, with a backpack as a pillow, she sleeps, clutching a sweater as if it were her teddy bear. Her face half covered by a mess of tangled hair, she's dreaming, but in such a way as one dreams when one is napping after not sleeping nearly enough the night before. Fitfully. Aware yet fixed. Sleep Paralysis, painted by Fuseli. A sudden disturbance in her calves, but not from within, someone has sat down, moved her feet back. His arm is on her back then pushes the hair out of her eyes. She flitters, the leaning tower of dorms, an insane asylum, the fiftieth floor of an old Chicago building, the kind with hand-cranking elevators, where her father used to work, pops out of existence, or rather recedes, fades, back into her subconscious, as does Jake, whom she didn't actually see but was chasing, searching for, arguing with people to see, slicing through them like an infantry of melons. Did he die? Wasn't she trying to get to his funeral? She cranes her neck, he speaks, "You know, if you needed a place to sleep…"

"You're not dead," she says, stupidly.

She didn't know how good it would be to see him, how serene and turbulent, how she needed this, how he needed this too. But really, part of her did know, she could tell, by the way her face lit up, by the way her temperature rose, by his mirrored responses. By just knowing, really.

. . .

Nora never thinks her life akin to a novel as much as when she's drunk.

Coincidences abound.

Her histrionic heart flutters a little every time the doors open, especially when Ben is procuring her a drink or using the bathroom.

He returns with a tequila sunrise. From the rest of the night on all her cigarettes will taste like tequila and immediacy.

"Where are you?" Ben asks.

She can't lie to Ben.

"I wanted to tell you. Because. It's not a big deal. But. Normally I wouldn't tell. I ran into an ex from high school the other day. We were just going to meet for coffee this Wednesday. I could cancel but I didn't think it was a big deal. Is that okay with you?"

He smiles. "Nor, you can drink coffee with whomever you like."

. . .

"I've become a Buddhist," he says. He believes in reincarnation, he says.

He tells her that they were once lovers in another life, in many other lives, and that it isn't fair to them—or to their potential lovers in this life—that they keep seeing each other.

"We already had our time," he says.

Nora laughs, it's the only response that makes any sense to her.

His head is bent. His shoulders are slumped, rounded. He's fidgeting with a Rubik's Cube, without hope

146

of getting anywhere. He never does. She moves from the chair to the floor, beside his leg, placing a hand on his thigh, near his groin, too close for him to misread the gesture. She looks up at him with the sad eyes of a mourner, a supplicant.

Maybe he's thinking about all the women he should be fucking instead of her.

Maybe he's thinking that in other times Nora would've never lasted. She would've been burnt at the stake ten times over.

Stoned at least thrice.

Flogged, raped, beaten, beheaded. All for crimes against male supremacy.

She walks her fingers up his thigh, pressing her nails into the hard, cold denim, arousing his cock. The cock that she's apparently fondled too many times in too many past lives.

"Fuck you," she says. "Fuck your God. Fuck your Buddhism. And fuck me, right now."

And he does, again, then again, then goes flaccid on the fourth try.

· · ·

a. Around ninety thousand years ago, a hairier, more simian Jake spots Nora sipping water at the creek. Bent over, using both hands to drink, her round ass yawning before him, the water glistening down her hairy arms, her tanned flanks, her tired legs. He couldn't help it, grabbing her by her long, dirty hair, and fucking her right then and there before she even had a chance to see his face.

· · ·

"What a good-looking couple," an old man in a gray hat says as he passes the liberty bell, under which Nora and Ben are breaking up. A smooth break-up, she'll later say. She wishes they could all be like this, like Ben.

147

She told him she was sorry, that she wasn't happy, that maybe it was him. He said "Fair enough," and asked her if she was hungry, upon which, they went to Sam's and ordered a half pepperoni half mushroom pizza.

...

6. Nora never sleeps with Jake without a bun already in the oven, otherwise her husband is bound to figure things out. As it were, Nora has seven children, though two of them perished from Typhus, which makes for five children, excluding the one currently tucked in her belly. Though there's a lot of talk about town that her second eldest looks a lot like Jacob, the fishmonger. The poor child, he's covered in freckles. He looks as if he's been splattered with blood. There isn't a single spot on any of his kin. The work of evil spirits, the town cries, sacrificing a bleating goat before the olive tree. Nora weeps for the evil she's created with her infidelity. She weeps for the pain she sees in Jacob's eyes when he looks upon his son.

...

She hasn't called Jake in two weeks. Two weeks intended as never. But never disintegrates in drink, like sugar, like salt.

Her: Words to memorize. Words hypnotize. Words make my mouth exercise.

Him: Words all fail the magic prize. Nothing I can say when I'm in your thighs.

Her: I miss you.

Him: Come over.

...

c. Nora kisses her trembling thumb then proceeds to bless herself, her rosary dangling and slapping against her fist. She takes a deep breath, then says, "Forgive me Father for I have sinned it has been seventy-six days since my last confession. I accuse myself of the following sins..."

"Yes?"

Nora looks up, looks to the wooden screen, tries to see through it. She doesn't recognize the voice, she got the new vicar. She swallows. "I accuse myself of adultery."

"You have lain with another man?"

"Not lain, no! I had refused him! But he came after me. At first I had enjoyed his lingering glances," she starts to cry. The priest says nothing. "He had forced himself onto me. I was not strong enough to overpower him. I fell limp and waited."

The vicar says nothing.

Again, Nora falls limp and waits.

He clears his throat. "Adultery is a mortal sin. You have given something away that which does not belong to you. You must be cleansed in the eyes of the Lord. Remove your clothes and step outside of the confessional," he orders.

Nora does as she was told. She steps outside into the muffled light of the church and waits for her whipping. The dust motes sparkle in the suffused, stained light.

...

He tells her to call him on Saturday. She does. It goes straight to voicemail, which relieves her because then she can call again without him knowing she had called in the first place. So she calls again. And again. Finally, after two hours, she leaves a text. Did you skip town? Fall into a manhole? Die and come back without any thumbs? Then she keeps her phone close. Too close.

The phone is an umbilical cord between her and Jake, necessary then useless.

...

d. Nora drops her head. She raises her hand to the brim of her bonnet, making sure no hair is showing. A nervous tick she's developed. "Mistress," she curtseys. Then immediately starts peeling potatoes again.

Her untouchable, fair-haired mistress stays, towers over her like a Titaness, her privileged jaw clenched from the gravamina of rejection. She eyes Nora from sooty bonnet to greasy foot. Then gives a sigh of disgust.

"Did you honestly think you'd get away with it, you little slut? I know what happened and I'll make sure of it that you'll never see him again."

Nora looks up, meeting her gaze now. The Titaness, now a quivering cuckqueen, spits on her face and tells her to leave at once.

. . .

"There is no reason to lie. No. Reason. You can tell me that you have a girlfriend. That's always been our thing. I like it that way! I probably would even help you get laid! Other girls don't bother me. But lying does. Why, WHY wouldn't you just say you were on a date? Instead, you give me some bullshit about studying, cancelling *our plans*, to go on a fucking date with some random skank! I don't understand! I'm okay with you seeing other people, just don't fucking lie! I tell you when I'm seeing someone. I always have! But you! Oh no, it's always been different with you. *Stranger*. What the *fuck*, Jake? Seriously. What. The. Fuck? I mean are you even going to fucking say anything? *Ugh!*"

And so his fair maiden waits…

. . .

e. With his velvet coat folded over his arm, the Baron waltzes through the mirrored French doors into the salon. He throws his coat over the edge of a chair and admires himself in the mirrors. He straightens his silk cravat and clears his throat. The Countess is seated at her desk, writing a letter. She doesn't look up from the paper until her quill has dried of its ink. "Jacob," she says, dipping her wick, "To what do I owe this unexpected delight?"

"Madame," he bows, begins. "I was—"

150

"If you don't mind, I'm in the middle of a letter to the Earl," she says, her milky white breasts heaving as she pants through her tightly laced torso.

"Oh please, do give him my regards. Tell him I look forward to a stroll inside his garden. I hear it's lovely this time of year."

Her servant leaves, bows as he shuts the doors.

"You must leave at once!" She rises, looking to the glass doors, to her sometimes eavesdropping servants. Jake stops her at what could only be described as a fainting couch. He places his hand upon hers, she pulls away.

"Surely, the world is large enough to hold both he and me," he points to himself, posing.

"Stop being so dreadfully stupid. It's unbecoming."

"I am only here to procure what is rightly owed to my personage. If you hadn't wished to be in my pocket you shouldn't have come seeking my services. I am a man that always collects, no matter the cost, and you Madame, are no different than the tart I dipped my own wick into just last night. This is thy divinity which stirs within me, look unto it," he says, pointing to his erection.

His unceremonious manners and frank speech are unwelcomed, and though Nora has half of mind to ring the bell, the complexity of her passions sought otherwise, and when a mind is cleft in twain as such, the body goes one way while the mind goes another. Within seconds he is upon her, ruffling her skirts, kissing her rouged lips with an ardent desire that could only be described as irascible.

As her breasts spill out of their confines, she lets a melancholic sigh, and her pride, escape her ravished mouth. Her body cannot be used as payment when she wills it to be such.

. . .

There, in the parking lot, long after dusk, they're about to pass a little boy of about seven. He's alone, his

151

back is to them, and he's stooped over, seemingly looking at something intensely. Nora lets go of Jake's arm.

"Hello?" she says, meaning it, but also inquiring in case the boy is either lost or afraid. She bends her knees and lowers her head, bringing herself down to his level before she walks around to see his face. "Whatcha got there?"

The boy drops his stick.

A pigeon. It's not moving but looks as if it should. The boy seems embarrassed that he was poking it, prodding it, trying to bring it back to life.

"It's dead," the boy says.

"Sometimes that happens," she says, slackening her mouth into a half-smile that curves slightly downward, a frown, but a friendly frown, a frown for an other, a frown full of warmth.

"Sometimes it's not always sad," the boy says.

Nora pulls back, disquieted but impressed. "You're right," she says, "it's not always sad."

Jake looks uncomfortable. "You shouldn't touch that," he says. To whom? To her? The little boy? "It's full of diseases." Then he adds, "Rats with wings," something everybody says. Nora wants to pretend that she couldn't hear it, wishes she didn't hear it, and tries to speak over him: "Your parents are around here, right? You're not lost."

No, the boy's not lost but he kicks his stick and runs away all the same.

Jake shakes something free of his body, something metaphorical, or invisible, like germs.

With her elbows on her knees, squatting still, "I'm afraid to die," Nora says, in sudden need for a cigarette. She picks up the stick.

"Put that down! It's filthy! Filled with all sorts of diseases! Blech! Come on, let's go."

"Hold on a sec," she says and pokes once, twice, at its mighty hollow chest, its still heart, rocking the dead, seemingly stuffed, taxidermic bird.

"God damn it, Nora."

. . .

"I'm on my period."

"I don't care," he says, getting up, pushing her back on the couch. She's coy, feels gross, unclean, and this seems sudden, but somehow devoid of sweeping passion. It seems domestic and clinical. Oppressively sober. He must sense this through her balking, so he pushes her again. She hits the back of her head on the couch's wooden backing. Instinctually, she grabs her head and sucks at the air through her teeth. He lifts her dress up, over her head, leaving it there, so he can see her body but not her face. Kissing, licking, massaging, venerating her underwear, the sanctified veil between them. Playing in the shadows, biting along the edges of her panties, pulling at their strings with his teeth, pressing the other side painfully into her, pinching her, ripping into her skin, until the elastic snaps in his mouth and the velour hangs limply at her sides. He tugs at her tampon strings. She wipes her dress away from her eyes to see him throw the bloodied wad of cotton across the room. He runs his fingers across her face, stroking her cheek, then covers it again. She lets him take her sight, save for the small particles peeking through the fibers of her black dress. Blood rushes up and down, into her legs, her sex, down her thigh, weighing her arms, prickling her face, escapes from her mouth, in spattering moans she bucks, creams before him, onto him, into him, he laps it up, like a tiger, clawing at her veins. In a movement of anguish and nostalgia, he inserts one

153

finger, two, three, his entire hand, stretching her, splitting her, he puts his hand over her mouth, she can smell herself, the cotton dress still in between them. She bites it. He lets her. He grunts, she cums. She has no way to know what he's doing, no way to see without disobeying him. Just movement and light. And then he dives, a moment of white death and a cruel, undeniable, borderless tongue, flicking, kicking her down to the edges of where she is willing to go, down to the moments before she had known all that she knows now, a moment of passion sparked between two kids with rollerskates strapped to their feet. "You're a fucking goddess," this bloodthirsty god of war sings into her cunt before he bites down on her labia, mixing blood with honey and terror and lust he bites at her clitoris. She screams, screams. Live tears streaming down her face, "No more," she begs, he drinks, and drinks, kissing her, licking the inside of her, a nucleus knotted to Hell, only for him. "Only for you!" she yells. He asks her to repeat it. To repeat it again and again. "You're mine," he says, unzipping his pants, he pulls her dress away to look at her tear-stained face, blood on his lips, "Mine," he ravishes her, one, two, three, four, five, six times without a condom. He covers her face again, pulls out, and cums all over her stomach, her pretty black dress, a long black veil. Bruised, moved, she feels lightheaded, as though she were about to faint.

He licks along her throat, nibbling, teasing, sussing, he opens his mouth wider and presses his sharp teeth to her pulse, breaking the skin like puncturing a hymen, severing an artery, he drinks. Her eyes roll back, flicker white, she quivers, trembles, blood hemorrhaging, she raises her hand to pull him away, to breathe, he clasps it and twists it around her back and thrusts his other hand back inside of her. She blacks out, dies.

154

···

Come to our All Hallow's Eve party! Five dollar cover, but ladies are on the house!

Was that a mass text or a personal invite?

Ha!

I know, I know. It's a frat party, but it's also Halloween, you can pretend to be whomever you like. For instance, someone that attends frat parties.

She opens her closet, finds a box of older linens that she can't bear to throw away, just in case she ever owns an extra-long twin mattress again. She wraps herself in a white sheet stiffened from bleach and time, a sheet that has cradled his soma as he dreamt beside her those three nights in her dorm room. Inhaling, tingling, wrapping, tying, enveloping herself in a series of moments, skin on skin, coital night sweats, the crack in her curtains, a sliver of morning's light as he whispers, "Good night," kissing her forehead then walking out the door, only to have Anna burst in a few hours later, plopping down to her computer, opening AIM. The incessant tapping and typing. Nora would pull this sheet over her head, thinking of last night, squeezing her legs together, playing with her raw labia, queasy from cheap alcohol. She twists her hair into knots then pins ten plastic snakes into them with over a hundred bobby-pins. She stains her arms, her bust, and her face green, an alienating glow, creating a sort of ceremonial mask. She paints her lips the color of menstrual blood and uses false eyelashes to accentuate her eyes. She looks at herself in the mirror, these eyes will penetrate Jake, petrify him.

When she looks at him, with her dramatic basilisk eyes, when he looks at her, with his enigmatic thalassic eyes, they stare for too many seconds, too many prolonged, luxurious heart beats. Everything else becomes background. This is not what was supposed to happen. He was supposed to turn to stone. Become a concretized memory. A relic. An abject spoil of war. She wants to take him home to her back porch, place him next to the pigeon's nest, look at him out her back window every day, let the rain fall on him.

Like always, he's the first to break the gaze. Standing in a suit made up of question marks, he covers his eyes with his forearm and hisses. Then his cock bends toward vacancy. Calling Rainbow Brite, who appears, who giggles, who takes him by the arm and nuzzles her sparkling nose into his mooning face. He smiles uxoriously and nuzzles his crinkled nose in response. She grabs him by the cheeks, smooshing his face into itself, and kisses him. Their kiss is long, wet, and sloppy, and leaves his mouth dusted with glitter. Nora can't look away.

Jake raises his drink to her in valediction, as if she were just another girl who attends fraternity parties. He then turns away, his arm around his blonde honey pot. Nora looks to the sunny girl in the rainbow striped socks who isn't Nora. Her dress is much shorter than the real Rainbow Brite's and lined with a fluffy white trim. She has nice legs. In fact, she's nearly all legs, spindly legs made for spreading. When she bends over her rainbow panties command the attention of everyone around her. Twice, already, Nora has seen Jake slip his hand to touch them, to feel the crack betwixt her flat derrière. The first time, she stubs her cigarette out on an armchair. The second time, she lights another just as Superman walks by with a plate of Jell-O shots. She grabs two. He tells her that'll be five bucks. She gives him a ten and takes two more.

The party continues. Everyone drinks warm beer out of red, plastic cups. Nora argues with the adamant Tweedle Dee and Tweedle Dum about *Reservoir Dogs* being a love story. One of them calls her a whore. The other

156

defends her. A fist fight ensues. Cameras everywhere begin flashing.

```
    I'm leaving.
        Wait!  I'll  send  her  on  a  fool's
        errand. Give me ten minutes!!!!
    This whole night has been a fool's errand.
        WAIT!!!!!!!!!!!!
```

Downing her fourth watery, piss-warm beer, she sees Ms. Brite's spindly leg pop as she kisses her boyfriend on the cheek. "I'll be right back!" she says. "I'll get you something special!" Their kiss is a long production staged for her friend, a dumpy Raggedy-Anne, who looks as jealous as Nora feels. As Rainbow Brite walks out the door, she turns to her grossly unfaithful boyfriend and waves emphatically. Both Nora and Jake are watching her. When the door shuts, they look at one another. He nods upstairs.

They meet in the bathroom.

"You look like you blew a fairy."

He looks in the mirror, wipes off his mouth. Most of the glitter remains.

"I had no idea Angela would come tonight," he says into the mirror.

She rolls her eyes, looks back at him through the mirror. "I didn't even know you were still dating Angela! Why did you even invite me? If she hadn't have come, at the very least this party is probably crawling with her sisters! Why did I even come?" This last line she says while looking at herself.

He kisses her. Salty, carbonated, glitter kissing. Some of her green paint stains his collar, gets on his face. This is all she'll get tonight. One of her snakes falls into the toilet. She leaves it, and him, as he washes his face.

> A day to blame her actions on a pseudonym,
> to be somebody else.

She promptly leaves, walks to Gabe's, meets Jiji, Lej, and everyone else. She ends up going home with one of Lej's roommates. Frankenstein. He's painted green too! They Match!

"Morticia" freshly written on her green forehead, she wipes ███████ with her wrist ███████ ████████████ off spit, ████████ too drunk for this to matter. ██████████ onto the bed, impatient, ████████ tearing ████████ the stitches pop, come undone. ██████████ lolls her head to the side. ████████████████████ spinning. ████ her panties off. She's ██████ undone. He's undoing her. He unzips ████████ ████████. The whole room smells like latex. even more. ████████████████████████ Vodka and cranberry juice. Sex on the Beach with a shot of cream, the cloying ████████ the roof of her mouth, ████████ ████████████ on her stomach. "Hold the Beach!" Takes her from behind. Tequila. ████████ ████████ salt shaker, throwing it across the room for ████████ kicked out of ████████ wonders if the bouncer will remember ████████ ████████ only the slap against her ass. ████████ the way the Bailey's curdles in the Guiness. ████████ fakes an orgasm. ████████████████ He throws up beside the ████ pale and yellow ████████ vaguely like pizza ████. She then immediately follows suit.

The next morning she wakes up completely naked, still green, still with "Morticia" written on her forehead. She throws up, this time consciously. Her sheet is crumpled in a corner, stained with green make-up, sweat, lubricant, mud, and vomit. Her phone blinks inside her purse.

4:13am: The Eagle has left the nest. I repeat, The Eagle has left the nest.

...

7pm she writes, Are we still on for tonight?

7:13pm, 10 o'clock, on the dot.

She naps. She cleans, showers, shaves, dances, smokes, spritzes, lingers, stares, eats an apple.

9:30pm, he writes, 1 hour, maybe just a little bit more.

A little bit could be the length of a cigarette, half a drink, another hour, a day, or even a month, knowing him.

10pm, she situates herself on the couch, *Melancholy of Anatomy* in tow.

At midnight, she rereads all of the messages, again, for the fourteenth time. Including the one from the night before, Tomorrow. Including the saved texts, sexts, sects from months passed. I jerk off to you in your Catholic school girl skirt at least once a month. When I look at you I see a hotter version of myself.

She presses the side button on her phone every ten minutes or so. She knows it hasn't beeped or blinked—the phone's been next to her the whole time—but the action is beyond her control.

My Achilles heel…

1:25am. She thinks of the possible excuses he'll have for being so very late and makes a list, thinks of giving it to him, having it framed.

She thinks of Dorothy Parker's *A Telephone Call*.

She counts to five hundred by fives. Attempts to do it backwards.

She falls asleep, wakes to the noise of the garbage truck. Grabs her phone. 7:13am. Her heart submerges, descends into the depressing sunlight of rejection.

...

3:22pm: I'm sorry I didn't make it last night. I came across Larry.

Which means he came across some cocaine.

...

Anger feels like stillness; the world is calm in comparison. When the rug is ripped beneath her, when she feels as if she's been harpooned in the chest and her skin becomes constricting, self-destruction becomes desirable, necessary for Nora, as if she didn't engage in something unsafe then she'd be unsure of her ontological existence. Turning toward an invisible dream, a God, a goal, feels counter-productive. It's the call for drama, but a private chaos, instability, self-indulgence. Wallowing has its place, is the obverse side of the coin, but the other, for a moment, for the duration of the cigarette, or the high, her nails into her wrist, the razor's drag across her inner thigh, while the ravenous lust consumes, Nora feels alive. She oscillates. Is ambivalent. Her love for Jake is cowardly, vanquishing, but it's also fortifying and distinguishing. False strength, she coughs.

I broke up with Angela, you know, he tells her.

It takes her all her strength to not respond. All. So she eats half a spinach pizza, two cupcakes, and smokes four bowls and sixteen cigarettes.

...

That night, Nora dreams Saturn falls from the sky. Just falls, as if gravity were partial. This terrifies her.

...

She asks Jiji for a favor, the kind of favor Jiji relishes in accepting.

"Good afternoon, Mister…Noyes. Yes. This is Jezebel from the Emma Goldman Clinic. We are just calling to inform you that one of our patients has contracted Chlamydia and Hepatitis C, and that she had placed you down as one of her recent sexual partners. We would like for you to stop by, either here, or a clinic of your choice, to get tested at your earliest convenience. Thank you."

...

In an instant, with him buried deep inside her, a vagina dentata fantasy. The sideways teeth of a piranha. The grin of a cat. She wants to devour this cock. Rip its delicate skin, the skin as soft as the inside of an elbow, softer. Skin stretched clumsily thin over imaginary steel. She wants both. Both skin and bone. The perfect boner. To pull it off and never return it. Not because she feels full with it inside her, as if this penis, his penis, a penis, completes her. Not because she thinks of it as an innocent fetus. His dick, inside of her, a *raison d'être*, unbelievable. This crazy creature, an uncontrollable child, wriggling, obeying her hips, disobeying her heart. This dick gallops for others. Led by the balls. Exposes itself wherever desire is reciprocal. Separate from the mind that wills it, separate from him, a mind of its own. *Separate him from it.* Take him by surprise. She wants him to suffer. Both the pain of the tear, the red-hot needles of phantom dick, and the humiliation, the terror of castration. She wants him to feel worse than a woman—how he defines a woman. She imagines her womb full of acid. And this cock, his cock, bubbling, bulging, sizzling, melting, disappearing. Doing the world a favor. She imagines the act altruistic.

...

Then she meets Brent. An artist, a painter, he looks at Nora as though he's drawing her. She watches him sketch on bar napkins or with the tip of his cigarette in the air, all but drooling over his inimitably chiseled jaw line, his sculpted forearms, the passage from his thumb to his forefinger.

He's much older than Jake, out of college even. A degree in verisimilitude, he speaks in maxims and holophrases. It's as though she's always known him.

"Over educated and under-employed," he says, "living the Iowa City dream."

His penis is the most beautiful penis Nora has ever seen. When she kneels before it, choirs of angels sing and a golden light emanates from his lap, kindling her hard clitoris, she can't not suck this holy gilded cock, and when she does, she sucks with a purpose, from a passion deep within. A guttural yearning for amends, for transfiguration. For unadulterated carnality.

A desire so desirable it's painful.

To console the disconsolate. Stretching a gloved hand to the ceiling, she rocks her hips into a coerced coexistence, pulling at the stars, pulling him into her, she touches his face only feeling his stubble poke through satin.

Her dulcet virtuoso, this candied surrogate fucks her with a practical desire. Pragmatic finesse, fire without flame. As if he had made a rational decision to let passion grip him by the balls.

"I'm not looking for a thing right now," he says.

Unknowably, Nora wants to recreate a past she does not understand.

"To be thingless is good; keeps things fresh," she says.

She likes him though. She likes being around him. She likes his scent of Turpentine and sanded Oak.

Lather. Rinse. Repeat.

She likes watching him dress.

"I should go though, got *things* to do in the morning."

162

"I'm not a whore," she says, at which he pauses for a second, leaving his shirt over his face, elbows bent and stretching the cotton fabric, still exposing his rippled abs contorted from the act of pulling his shirt on, and finally over his head, tousling his hair.

"And I did not imply that you were."

"I'm just saying." Just saying, just words, just like before, like an idiot speaking before thinking.

"Okay," he says with a slight inflection. "Good to know."

He wraps his watch around his hairy wrist, taking his time to fasten the buckle, which he pulls toward his body with his teeth. He then grabs his money clip, some random papers, sketches, and a couple of toothpicks, then he puts it all in their respective pockets. He scoops the coins off her dresser then tosses them onto a white coffee table at the side of her bed. "For your trouble," he says. "For your hospitality."

She throws her Teddy Bear at him, breasts flopping from the leverage.

"I'll call you," he says.

Then he does, four days later, around 7pm, to make plans for the next day, at 9pm.

When Christmas Break rolls around Nora misses him terribly, but never says so. She doesn't even mind when he didn't get her anything, and instead of making a fool of herself, she leaves his present, *Wittgenstein's Mistress*, wrapped in her closet. He would've loved it.

. . .

Jiji looks up from Sartre's *Imaginary*. "Knock. Knock," she says.

Nora looks up from *Nausea*, they're in the same class, but they could write about either text for the term paper. "Who's there?" she asks, without breaking her

163

thoughts, as if her thoughts had already included Jiji, as if they already included an independent joke outside of the text she was just inhabiting.

They are high, after all.

"Philip Glass," Jiji says, then adds, "You haven't heard this one?"

Nora shakes her head, says "Philip Glass who?" Excited for the punch line.

"Knock. Knock." Jiji says. Eyes excited for the punch line.

"Who's there?"

"Philip Glass."

"Philip Glass who?"

"Knock. Knock."

This goes on for three more rounds, becoming funnier each time, laughing harder the more they look at each other's face. Anticipating their next line, happy to deliver, caught in a rhythm, a cadence. They laugh and laugh then Jiji says, "Orange you glad I didn't say banana?"

To which Nora responds, "I feel sick."

"Roquentin," Jiji then says in a French accent, forcing drool to fall to her chin, wiping away the tears from so much happiness, so much laughter, something— the girls have learned—that is necessary when one reads too much Sartre or Beckett. They then also insist on watching *Return of the Jedi*. Right now. They insist on Ewoks. And purple potatoes, and simmering strawberries in cream. Jiji sings *God Only Knows* in a French accent too loud for apartment living at 4am. Playing in the colorful mist of a moment that repeats itself, knits itself into others. Is weightless, immortal, recreated. Like a meme, only personal. An inside joke. Only better. Because there is also cheese.

. . .

Jake invites her over, at the beginning of the night. "Like a real date," he says. She arrives in a black dress, not exactly sure what to expect. He gives her flowers, tells her that they have reservations, that she looks gorgeous. He kisses her cheek.

Something's tepid.

His restraint unnerves her. So she jumps him.

Her legs wrap around his waist. Impossible to tell where she ends and he begins. They are one glob of flesh, moving, breathing as flesh does, but with every breath, every exhalation, they let out steam, shared smoke from their mutual organs.

The solidity, the guts, the opacity drains out of their bodies. Their shadows disappear, their blood evaporates.

Flesh of my flesh, blood of my blood.

They become pencil drawings, mere sketches of their figures, their forms.

They look like a tangled ball of black string. The static from a cableless television, just making out the figures from the Pay-Per-View channel.

Like Nora's dress trapped in the closet.

Moving in obstructed circles, at an alarming rate, like the hands on a broken clock in a cartoon, her laughter peels off the carpet.

At their conjoined heart three ellipses move, one point of light on each of the ovals, and it moves around and around its track. Like the symbol for nuclear energy. With a star in the middle, at its center, its core, its nucleus.

As she moves her hand across his chest his stomach swallows it. It was as if her hand was never there. As if she didn't have a hand or a forearm. Their bodies were fusing as they disappeared.

And then they stop. Two bodies, melded into one. Without skin, without hair, without teeth. A ball of black string. Stiff, soaked in glue. Glutinous.

They were the perfect chameleons. If they stood in front of the door they splintered, if they lied on the rug they scratched each other with their fibers. If they ran through cement they would feel their skin flaking off.

She imagines a field of wildflowers, and as he slithers through her petals and leaves she screams in ecstasy, calling his name, regressing to a little girl inside of a mansion with no furniture, screaming and screaming until he runs into the room, lifts her up over his shoulders, carrying her home to safety.

Sweat streams down her neck, she gets on top, bucks with a barbarous thirst, her tits, her maniacal tits, bounce, shake with the sudden weight of the earth, the weight of his cock, rising, pressing into her abdomen, deeper than he's ever felt to her before. She can't stop, it's beyond her control. Pressing. Pushing. Fucking.

Then, an explosion. Of barometric proportions. Of thunder and lightning and hazy pink. A scorching firewall that rips through parched trees. The green eyes of tornados as chaos breeds futility in their quake. The wet swoons of a tsunami slapping against the empty brick houses.

The explosion is beyond words, an unnamable force, a full spectrum, pure wet heat.

They flop onto his roommate's futon, both catching their breath, fumbling for cigarettes.

For a minute they are too impressed with their feat that they say nothing. Then, they speak of nothing else. And miss their reservation.

She excuses herself to the restroom, there, she begins to weep, then wail, forgetting herself, forgetting her place. She wipes her face and returns to his room.

"I should go," she says.

"You sure? I thought, maybe, you could stay tonight, like old times."

"No, I really should go. I've got so much to do."

"All right? You sure?"

"Yes."

On her way home, he texts her. Happy Valentine's Day! Have a wonderful walk home. She looks at it sideways. *What?*

Then again, My heart is bursting with love.
I sent you two emails to make up for the loss. They await your immanent arrival, my kitten.

They will wait for two more days.

She wants to give him the shiny red ball of power, [*Here! Take it! Take it! Take it! Pleeeease!*], she wants to signify that she misses the chase, that this has become too easy. That he's becoming almost sappy, cloyingly so. Saccharine. Unmanly.

Where is the Jake that loved her but didn't know he loved her.

The Jake that wouldn't love her.

She seduces to capture, but when he submits she's repulsed. Nothing she writes satisfies her anymore. Words are no longer her own. She steals, she plagiarizes.

He writes, tells her that the last time he saw her she looked like a photograph taken from far, far away.

Something is uncanny.
Both of us, two black and white silhouettes, covering one another's eyes, standing outside in the rain at a bus stop, chewing fingers to the bone, smoking cigarettes to their filters.

. . .

Brent likes to sleep for a little while after sex. Clenching her, he clenches his teeth. He moans and sweats then usually leaves early in the morning, way before she gets up, leaving his change on the white coffee table, kissing her good day. He's both jockish and mawkish, a performing jester and a reticent artist. He'll go into the bathroom happy, content, and come out with a saturnine temper. Then they'll bicker. They argue about whether or not gray is a color. Whether or not Socrates wanted to die. They argue in their underwear, in hallways, at gas stations. After any uncompromising argument, he leaves, stomping away from Nora, still yelling his point. "Wile E. Coyote NEVER caught the Roadrunner! Ever! It's against the rules! *Preposterous* to think they broke the commandments *just for* viewer gratification. Then the show would die! Roadrunner would be no more! Wile E. Coyote would have nothing to chase! Nothing! It's like breaking the sexual tension!"

"Like Leela fucking Fry?"

"Yes! Wait, no! God damn it, I hate you."

Nora called him crazy once. He left her at the bar without paying his tab. When Maryanne came to visit, Nora found him at that same bar, and when she introduced him to her he glanced from over his shoulder, nodded, "Sup?" keeping one eye on the game. They also have never done anything besides drink and fuck. She's met his friends, which she takes as a good sign, but not enough to quell her insecurities. He's a lot like Jake, not in personality, but in prototype. This is why some nights are for Brent, some are for Frankenstein, and some are still for Jake.

. . .

You are dust and unto dust you shall return.

. . .

Jake, 1:13am: My coquettish kitten. What are you doing this holy evening?

Jake, 1:25am: I have something you want. It's in your best interest to call me…

Brent, 1:31am: Just finishing this last round. I've got to win my money back! Just another hour or so, I swear.

But the bars are closing now.

Her, to Brent, 1:33am: You wouldn't happen to be playing with a guy named Ben would you?

NORAAAAAaaaaaa……

Okay, she gives in, I'll be by in fifteen. But you must supply tequila!

Done! Jake says.

He opens the door, "Ugh! Go wash your face," she says to the cross, or rather, the smudge, on his forehead. He reeks of desperation and a noxious mixture of hard alcohol. She walks past, clomping into his apartment, flattening him with her stilettos.

"No."

"Then I'm leaving."

"Are you serious? You're serious?"

"Yes! Get that death shroud away from me."

"Oooh a text!" she exclaims.

No. Why?

"Who is it?" Jake asks.

"Death shroud!" she points.

"I'm not washing it off because you're uncomfortable. I thought hippies were supposed to be tolerant."

"Should I answer him? Or make him jealous? You're an expert at being a dick. Do dicks like dicketry?"

"What? Who are you talking to?" His ears turn pink, he crosses his arms, uncrosses them.

No reason, she types. I once dated a local Action Jackson.

"Should I have said *loved* instead of *dated*? Does it really matter? It must! But I mean how much did you ever read into my texts? Wait, you go to church?" she says.

"Sometimes I—"

"Blech! Human sacrifice death shroud!"

"Who the fuck was that?!" Jake demands.

"I can't take you seriously until you wash that shit off!"

He walks to the bathroom and turns on the faucet.

"Don't act all high and mighty! I've got evidence you participated in these Lenten festivities," Jake yells from the bathroom.

"What?"

Nora's phone vibrates. Her hopes are immediately dashed. Sluuuuuut! Come to Nick's, it's better than whatever you're doing!

With a clean forehead and brushed teeth Jake returns. He smiles broadly, folds his fists onto his hips, and tilts his chin in triumph. Super Jake. He then lays a couple of photographs onto his glass coffee table. A couple of photographs of a topless Nora making out with Maryanne. Their naked breasts pressed into each another, flattened against one another.

"I swiped these from Chris. I know he still has the negatives but he promised me—"

Nora laughs, "Where did you get these? Were you there last night? Oh my God! We had so much fun last night! We got so many beads we had to rake them off of each other! We even went home and made a deposit, so we could collect more. My neck is still stiff! But, *fuck!* I do have better tits than her. She may have a better body, but I'd take my tits any day!"

"Nora, these were passed all around the house!"

"Actually, I like my body. I mean it has its—"

"NORA!"

170

"What? Did somebody recognize me? I'm sure you settled that debate when you became all protective and took the pictures away! Why are you so jealous?"

"Nora, you need to be more careful. Who knows how many others of these pictures there are! Don't you care?"

"Would I have done it in the first place if I cared? I was in such a lezzy mood last night. But not for Maryanne—I know her too well. Besides, she's too skinny. I like 'em curvy, or more masculine looking. Oh! There's this girl in my Animal Bio class! I have SUCH a crush on her! She was out last night too. *Christ!* What I would have given for a cock, or at least some balls! Ha!"

"How come you didn't call me?"

"Not your cock! My own! What do you think? Do you think my tits are better than hers?"

"Did you go home with somebody last night? Did you and her go home with somebody together? Nora, why are you torturing me?"

"Why do you keep saying my name? Are you trying to make me human? Humanize the whore? Dude! You didn't answer my question!"

"Yes, Nora, I like your tits—"

"Excellent! Now bring forth the tequila! And get us a hooker! Or a text message! Whichever arrives first!"

What is this quintessence of dust?

He leaves the room. She checks her phone. Still nothing.

When Jake comes back to her, he sits down, too close. She can smell his fresh mouth. Spearmint toothpaste and alcohol. He lunges toward her. This makes her miss Ben.

"You know what? Don't," she says with her palm in between them.

171

She gets up, he follows.

One hand on the wall, with a stale tongue, he speaks bluntly. "Be my girlfriend."

BAHAHAHAHAHAHAHAHA!

"Where's the tequila?"

There is no tequila.

His chest is sagging. He may or may not be struggling to breathe; it looks as though he has gas. Acid reflux. He hiccoughs, "You know we're meant to be."

"In another life! Star-crossed lovers!" She's hysterical.

"Nor, I'm serious."

Her forehead indents, wrinkles. She sees couch sharing, hand holding, candlelit dinners, movie nights, Prime Time television. She scans his apartment. His white walls are bare save for a framed Pink Floyd poster, the one with all their album covers painted on women's butts. His television is larger than Nora's arm span. He has cable, and a glass coffee table, always polished with Windex, clean and uncluttered. Four coasters, stacked, two remotes, side by side, one for the cable and one for the television, and two new, unlit, scented vanilla bean candles. Underneath are towers of Maxim and Playboy. She balks. She can't live like this. He can't become boring. He is a character, her character.

"You are my confidence and conflict. My *confidant*," she says, trying to sound French.

"Cut the bullshit, Nora."

"But the turbulence!" She affectively sighs, thrusts her hand between her thighs, allows herself this moment to play their montage, then she comes to. "I won't stand for this!" She hears a buzz, thinks it's her phone, glances her bag, to see if it's alight, but alas, it's not. She sits back down, rounds her shoulders. Reaches for her cigarettes.

"I've finally come to appreciate you," he says, "You're the only girl that can level me with a glance."

No! Yes! The light! IT RINGS! She bolts into his kitchen, away from him. She doesn't want him to see the giddiness, the blushing, the hair twirling. But he does. Because she wants him to. He watches her through the reflection in his living room window. She's on television.

"I'm at an after-hours party," she smiles.

"Ten minutes," she says. "Yeah, I'm only like a block away. I'll be right there… Totally!" She hangs up the phone then turns to Jake. "Umm… Bye!"

"You used to smile like that for me," Jake says.

"Oh, Jake, don't get all soft on me now!" She says playfully, channeling her inner Miss Piggy.

"What?"

"I've got to go! Brent called!" She says as she spritzes the air to twirl through a mist of perfume.

"He called for a fuck, Nora, an easy lay. He's using you. Don't just give in like that."

"What the fuck is the difference between you and him then? Stop raining on this here parade."

"I want things to be different."

"No, you don't. And I've got to go." She can't stop beaming.

"Apparently," he says, taking her phone from her hand.

"Don't do this," she says, her tone now more austere than sweet.

She taps her toe with impatience.

"Then stay."

"You've got hoards of women. Go call one of them," she says, no less severe.

"I don't have hoards of women! Why do you always think that? But we're talking about you and your voice switching just now. You were openly flirting. To torment me? It wasn't even just flirting! It's beyond! You're smitten!"

"So?"

"So, stay. I'm here pouring my heart out to you—"

"You're all sorts of too late." She waves her hand around his face.

"I deserve more," he says, refusing to back down.

She laughs. "I deserve more!"

"You do! Oh, Nora, you do."

"Then take me on a date."

"Where? When?"

"Plan it. Call me. Set everything up. We'll go on a date like a normal couple."

"So you're staying?"

"What's all this?" She reaches into a box full of Halloween costumes near his front door and pulls out a mesh pink cowboy hat.

"Can I have this?" she asks, rhetorically, hat in hand, plucking her phone from his palm. *"Yoink!"*

He doesn't say anything. His silence blooms, it spirals. Like a rose, red and radiant, ripe past fecundity, climacteric, so full of itself it, so open, so vulnerable and proud, his silence droops, wilts, ever so slightly into decomposition.

"Mister," she says, doffing the hat, turning the knob.

"Wait," he says.

A command and a question.

Wait? Don't go. Not with him. Not tonight. Stay with me? Stay here. Stay close?

Not a chance. She removes the hat, brings it to her heart, and bows. "Adieu," she says.

As she's halfway down the stairs he runs to the railing. She looks up, puts her hand on her head, to prevent the hat from falling off.

"I love you," he yells through the symbolically germane metal bars, "but I fucking hate you!"

In thirty minutes she'll be riding Brent with Jake's hat still on her head, scuffing the walls with her cowboy boots, shouting, "Yippee ki-yay mother-fucker!"

Justice.

A pile, a mound of metallic-colored plastic Mardi Gras beads sparkle in the corner of her bedroom. Scarlet reds, deep purples, royal blues, rich gold. Fern, emerald, and lime greens. Pomegranates, currants, and oranges. Reflecting the sun's rising rays in a panoply of light and shadow.

...

Okay, she writes, at 6pm, I'm sorry I stole your hat.

He doesn't respond for six hours:
Fuck you, YOU fucking CUNT.

Then, thirty-one hours later, Come over. Let's talk. I need to talk to you.

Thirty-one hours and seventeen minutes later, I heard you that night. I heard you, Nora! There's no mistaking your voice. Not like that, not ever.

Thirty-one hours and nineteen minutes later, You broke my heart.

Thirty-one hours and forty-six minutes later, Come over...

She knows exactly what is within his ellipsis. Not every omission is sexual. Sometimes, the trauma cycle. Repetition compulsion. Lather. Rinse. Repeat. Dot. Dot. Dot. Sometimes an apology. Sometimes, a plea. Come over [I'm sorry].[I love you].[Come back].

I miss the mystery, she writes in her journal. *I miss the pain.*

I don't understand you anymore, she texts him back, forty-seven hours after the fact.

...

He says he's not mad at her anymore, that he probably deserved it.

Probably.

But for some reason, she doesn't want to talk about their relationship, which is strange, considering she loves talking about feelings, definitions, barriers, deconstructions. Jake.

She makes note of this, but, feeling protective, distant, an island unto herself, she moves on to literature, the only true antidote.

1984 is still his favorite novel, and though Nora concedes that it is a very important novel, she deems the book plain. He becomes angry, pink in the ears. A look Nora rarely sees, but has now seen twice in one week. He says it's a stroke of brilliance, then chides her for fearing its auguries. Nora merely doesn't like post-apocalyptic stories, but she enjoys his anger, so she presses, comparing capitalism to communism to fascism. Then the conversation takes a hard right into the war, and the towers, and terrorism. The culture of fear.

"I thinks America has a death wish, much like our own death drives."

"I don't even know you anymore!"

She thinks, *Do you know me?*

Who am I?
Who are you?

As he sucks back the joint, as the cherry stretches and sputters, she regrets offering him any. He inhales deeply, then holds the smoke inside, blackening his lungs, making these guttural noises, like he's suppressing a sneeze, like it's a contest. She's disgusted. Already, he's annoying. Now he'll be different. Bug-eyed, obvious, giddy with affection. He stands up, shakes his hands like he's shaking off the rain, but continues their conversation, saying that there is a difference between Bukowski's poems and his prose. "It's like the difference between Miller Lite and Bud Lite." Which, he insists, is a huge difference.

"They both taste like shit."

He prattles on.

Like a friend would.

This moment feels very platonic to Nora, boring and beside the point. She'd rather to talk to Jiji, so she texts her.

"Maybe, *maybe*, you can compare him to Anaïs, but you *cannot* compare Bukowski with Djuna Barnes. I mean, if Bukowski were Joyce then—"

He doesn't even know who Djuna Barnes is. He's going off of what Nora says.

Jiji's with Lej, a far superior manbrain to Jake. They invite Nora but this will only depress her.

Jake grabs two books off the shelf: *Women* and *The Days Run Away Like Wild Horses Over the Hills*. Keeps on talking. Wildly, with more animation than five minutes ago. This is a conversation they've had before. She feels her heartbeat slip into her wrists where it slows to an arrhythmic gallop. Feeling her heartbeat frightens her. Its irregularities, its delays, terrify her. She prefers it when she pretends it isn't there. But now she can't avoid it, her own mortality. He notices that she is elsewhere. "No, no," she says, "I'm listening. Go on."

Go on, he does. And on. Trying to convince her of something she's made up her mind not to listen to, now and the next time.

"It's completely without editing. Straight from the heart."

The heart, she thinks. *His heart. Her heart.* Dub-blub. Faster. Dub-blub. Dub-blub.

Their heart.

As their heart weakens, thickens, stiff from a lacy web of yellowing plaque, she presses two fingers into her neck, counts her pulse. One-two-one-two-one-two-one-two-one-two-one-two-one-two-one-two—

She thinks she's doing this with subtlety. That he doesn't notice.

One-two-one-two-one-two-one-two-one-two-one-two-one-two-one-two-one-two—

"I'm having an anxiety attack," she says, betraying herself.

His face splits in two, as if he had just caught the paranoia himself, and was fighting it.

I'm having an anxiety attack. A ghost sentence. Naked, elided, hovering.

The space in between his eyebrows crinkles, folds into the face he'll have when he's old. She can see it. She tells him so. He pushes her, playfully, but she can see the fissure. He doesn't like thinking about himself as an aged man, as aging. She wants to leave, insists they need more wine.

Something burns underneath her, irritates her, like a network of mosquito bites. Internal rugburn.

Heavy with drink, she lets him make love to her. She feels as if her limbs were leaden with sand. Removed, on her back, dry, she watches him shove, pump, ram. She counts: one-two-one-two-one-two-one-two-one-two-one-two-one-two—

The rubber chafes her vaginal walls. She watches his face change, like the baby in the ocean from *Solaris*. She shuts her eyes, practices her Kegels: one-two-one-two-one-two-one-two-one-two-one-two-one-two—

"*Ooh*, I like that."

One-two-one-two-one-two-one-two-one-two-one-two-one-two-one-two-one-two-one-two-one-two-one-two-one-two-one-two-one-two—

"Oh God!"

He wants to cuddle. They never cuddle. She hardens, lights another joint, removes part of herself from the situation, returns to seduction. Bedroom eyes. Smoke in mirrors.

He wants her to sleep over.

If he were to spoon her, fall asleep clutching her, his cock would disappear. He would become useless, as horrifying as an insistent irregular heartbeat.

"Sleeping is too intimate," she says.

Lying under the blanket she had given him, he pulls her back into bed, embraces her, becomes infantile. He asks if they can just lay there.

Here, on the stiff, cum stained mauve sheets.

Their legs braid, her leg stubble abrading his skin. His arms are around her. Meaning she is lying on his right arm, cutting off its circulation, while his left arm clings ever tighter to her back, pulling her into him, as close as they can be. Cradling, hugging, cuddling.

In these moments she feels farthest away from him. Unlike sex, where their consciousnesses could transcend their bodies, and unlike deep, metaphysical conversations where she imagined their words dancing, intertwining, making love overhead, in these moments of pacific hugging and holding she feels infinity between them. Darkness. Nothingness.

When she first opens her eyes Jake appears to her at the far end of a tunnel. Gradually, as her eyes adjust to the light, he comes closer, advances, intensifies. But before she opens her eyes, before the pin prick of light, before scintillas and sanctimony, the gulf, the blackness between them is a materialization (as much as blackness can be) of the expanding, cooling distance between them.

She may know his patterns, but she cannot know what he's really thinking, what his anxiety feels like, how it approaches. He will never know the ferocity of her headaches, what pain feels like to her, just as she can't know what her pain feels like to him, what he imagines. She knows he enjoys causing her pain, creating an absence, an incision, an abscess in her flesh.

She enjoys the pain of his absence. She finds it fertile, sumptuous. Pain and absence are part of their repertoire.

In Catholicism, pain is absence.

Absence of God, not Jake.

When Jake is not there Nora feels the presence, the redolence of his absence. She evokes him, the qualities of him that she likes, into a fantasy. She regenerates him, imbuing her mind with him, an analogon of him, a vestigial whisper blows through her from eyes to cunt.

She has nothing to be ashamed of when he's gone, nothing to hide, nothing to try and articulate. When he isn't with her, it's just him and her inside of her, him as she creates him, as she understands him, as she translates him, as she desires him. A man qua fetus. Love qua fetus.

But here, in his arms, pressed against his chest, smelling him (what he cannot smell), she is so far away. Farther than a dream, farther than her own consciousness, her own ego. There is an infinite distance between them. Already in between their utterances, he must translate her words, her thoughts. She cannot see this internal action. She can never walk through its fluctuating terrains. And yet he holds her, thinks their hearts are beating as one *Dub-*

blub, Dub-blub thinks they are collapsing time and space together, on this mauve bed.

And with this she cries. He thinks she is crying sweet tears of happiness. He sees her as a tender object, pondering temporality, so full of love for him. She cannot tell him how absent she feels, how empty and alone.

She smiles gingerly, he misinterprets, begins fumbling through the sheets, fondling her breasts.

The never satisfied void of physical desire is easier to deal with than the void of isolation.

He wants to make love to her again. She wants to fuck.

> The difference between a Schumann sonata
> and a symphony by Shostakovich.

His tenderness is foreign, saccharine.

Awkward. Distilled. Maudlin.

When he finishes she couldn't be farther from orgasm. Her eyes are wide open, counting the cracks in the ceiling, depressed from the motion.

As his breathing deepens, she runs the satin across her lips as she used to when she was a child. Stretching her toes into the soft blue, she wishes she could take this blanket back, undo the moment when she had been so vulnerable. Seeing him curled up in her childhood, she buries her face in the wool to muffle the thought. It doesn't even smell like her anymore. She imagines other women's genitals, in an attempt to conjure jealousy. But the feeling is fleeting, doesn't seem real, doesn't matter. She loves them, those happy cunts. An unavoidable kinship.

He loves me, she thinks. He sleeps.

Replacing her figure with Frumpy, she tip-toes out the door.

. . .

In the morning, she falls into mourning. Jake is both remote and dead, dead at least as she loved him. He calls her a couple of times, texts her a couple of times, but she doesn't answer, doesn't respond.

Then, silence. Sweet, eclipsing, edifying silence.

To drown it out she blasts Leoncavello's *Pagliacci*.

Silence that will be heard. Silence that reiterates the in/significance of it all. She deletes all the texts that she had saved in her inbox. (But keeps one voicemail.)

Her muse is dead and gone.

She changes his name in her phone to Douchebag.

Because to utter a name is a form of love.

Because douches are bad for vaginas.

She then attempts normalcy: studying, writing, washing the dishes, but all this makes her anxious. She checks her phone, the same device, still a portal to his world, but now it lies mute, motionless, trivial, deadly. Cheap gray plastic, secreting radiation. Considered now a carcinogenic hazard.

. . .

Brent suggests that maybe they stop doing what they're doing. The karmic, superstitious part of her feels as though she deserves this. If she must lose Jake, she must really lose him, all back-up files, all reincarnations, all talismans. But she can't, not all.

To repeat history, to reclaim it, she steals Brent's hat, sleeps with it for awhile. He never comes back to claim it. To compensate, she sleeps with Frankenstein, whose name is Todd, and Ben as well, for old time's sake, for fuck's sake, which soon leads to a Dan whose tongue is sewn too closely to the underside of his mouth. He says the inability to blow raspberries made his childhood extremely difficult, and now he's insecure about his cunnilingus abilities. He's not bad, she assures him, not great, but she keeps that to herself. She's certainly had worse. Then one night Brent calls in a drunken haze. She takes advantage of it and all else he's willing to offer.

Yet something still nags, snags.

. . .

Memories, rewinding them, playing with the tapes of reminiscence. A memory cannot think for itself, cannot act of its own will. Jake is as she thinks him, he moves as she wills him, as she remembers. In her mind, she controls him, plays with his body, his emotions, his reactions. She alters history, creates fictions. When she senses too much artistry, which is inevitable, she rereads letters, listens to that one saved voicemail, but these images are predictable, tired, stale. They're dull phantoms. Without luster. Only an eidetic trace of their original intention, and what little is left is drained by the monotony of repetition.

She plays the message again, falls into its waters. "Nora, Nora." He speaks her name with a short o, sometimes accentuating *nor*. Sometimes just *or*. But always ending in an abrupt *a*. It's his Chicago accent.

"How the hell are you? I suppose it wasn't that long ago this time, but still, nonetheless," he stretches the s's, laughs, then inflects, "*irregardless*, I think we had plans for tonight. I'm looking at my planner and it certainly says 'Chat Noir.'" He says 'chat' with a hard ch, like in 'church,' not the soft, feline, French 'sh' that Nora's screen name intends. "That could only be you. So, I know I have no right to inquire, but as you are late, and as this is most unlike you, allow me the simple question: Where *are* you? I do worry, you know."

It is no longer him speaking, he left this message over a year ago, the text is speaking, the phone is speaking. His image fades away, becomes a bloodless voice in the phone, a voice without its pneuma. Unable to answer questions, it creates questions. This voice is the disappearance of Jake. This slight, nebulous, yet monumental voice is all she has.

An alienated voice that shouldn't be.

These words should drift off, fade, float up, up, and away the second they were uttered.

He's gone,

and yet,

she listens.

She tries to imagine him saying other things, moving the letters around, forming other phonemes, a general syntax, but she is fusing his voice with the voice through the telephone, in the telephone. A cognitive dissonance intrinsic to their lover's discourse.

. . .

Hand in hand with Dan, walking home from a bar, One Eyed Jake's, in fact, because it was somebody's twenty-first birthday, a friend of Dan's, who, like everybody else, wanted those twenty one pitchers for twenty one dollars.

Walking down Burlington Street, out of the corner of her eye she thinks she sees Jake, but then again, out of the corner of her eye she always thinks she sees Jake. Except this time, she's right. She lets go of Dan's hand.

Evanescent eye contact, slack mouth, she strains her eyes away, anywhere, away.

She doesn't know why she turns her head and pretends to be engrossed in whatever Dan is saying, something on somebody cheating him out of ten dollars or rather. She doesn't know why she isn't acknowledging Jake, because it's not like Dan has any idea who Jake is, or why they would be nodding, or smiling, or even having a brief conversation. He could be an old fried, some guy from class, or even a fond dalliance, why not? Dan wouldn't care, at least she doesn't think so.

But still, she walks past.

Receding back into a secretive,
evocative imbroglio.

A familiar flutter. A disturbance in the Force. A madness that is absolute goodness.

Her arm is yanked, hard, a burning stretch, whipping her around, stopping time with a toe. She pirouettes into his arms. He dips her back, locks her in, and kisses her deeply. Nora is in shock.

Infernal, passionate, acquiescing shock.

Dan pulls her away.

"Yeah, it's like that," Jake says, dropping Nora, who, because Dan is slow, because of the exhilarating, alleviating, scintillating shock, falls to the pavement.

"What the fuck?" Dan yells to Jake's sprinting silhouette. "Come back here and fight like a man, you chicken shit asshole!"

Nora rolls over onto her stomach and laughs. "I don't know who the fuck that was!"

Dan doesn't believe her.

She doesn't care.

. . .

He had written:
Tuesday. I'm coming over on Tuesday.

Joy explodes in the reflection. Her reflection in the mirror, the sun's refraction through the blue vase casting a blue shadow across her blond dresser. The purest blue. Thalassic, unequivocal, lissome, cavernous, divine. Its neck is long and slender like a swan's while its base is bulbous and sturdy. Its beauty mesmerizes her to a frenzy of consumption. She plunges the vase deep between her legs, she thinks of that indefinable, chimerical, ephemeral smile, the glass suctions her cervix, its mouth corrugates against her urethra sponge.

Incurvatus in se ipsum.

Viscous lava collects in the bottle, falls about her hand, saturates the carpet, sparkles in the sunlight. This is the only time she has ever successfully made herself ejaculate. Now she feels like celebrating.

Mirror, Mirror
        Fucking you is like fucking a mirror.
    A limpid mirror of their senses.
            Unclouded. Unspoken. Deliquescent.

Re: Mirror, Mirror
        Fucking a mirror would be painful. Chards of glass cutting your vulva, cutting my eyes. You castrate me, Nora. But sometimes you make my dick bigger than it ever was or could ever be… Swollen with the blood that boils only for you; this massive cock still trembles at the very thought of you. So if I saw you in the mirror, whenever I looked at one, there would be nothing left of it. Broken, ground-up glass powder. I would lose you forever, or spend an eternity gluing the pieces back together just to fuck them again. And I'd repeat the whole process as long as I could.

Re: Re: Mirror, Mirror
        I am in that mirror. Look. Go. Right now, look. You'll see yourself through my eyes. I'm not the one in the reflection. I'm the one looking.
                    ...

The rich blackness of the velvet, as if she were wrapped in the night, carries enough of a moonlit, televisionlit sheen to nourish the bed of crimson roses embroidered along the curves of her breasts. A shrill scream shifts Nora's gaze from her lover to a woman covering her mouth as a zombie eats her beloved. She scans for the remote, to no avail. She clamps her eyes shut. Wishes it were a vampire movie instead.

186

Black and red. Ink and blood. These two colors mark the mood of passion, they are an ambiance in and of themselves, both feared and loved. The colors of Dis, of anger and lust. The cold onyx throne Hades strokes his bats upon combined with the ruby juice streaked down Persephone's white arms from the pomegranates she devours. Like blood seeping into the night, flooding the streets and the all too solid hearts of the forlorn. This is why sex is a sort of *danse macabre*, a miniature death, coveting the moments of danger that can squeeze breath back into a corpse. Tortuous and contorted, sometimes it's hard to tell the difference between a face red with pleasure or one writhing in agony. Both bubble with sanguine heat and read like a paperback novel.

Both belong to the realm of the unnamable.

Word as bound flesh.

Tuesday is an act of love, a wholesome dinner with warm meats and crisp vegetables. Nora only wants sex. Not dinner, not daylight, she just wants to get fucked.

She opens her eyes and by the blue light of the television sees a dissonance flashing in his appearance. He looks like pure light, a child of the morning twisted into the night. He belongs in the sun with a fertile woman, one who walks through the fields barefoot. He needs the opposite of Nora, he needs a mother, her allegorical mother, Demeter.

And they both know this, even now, as she comes toward him, unpinning her hair, forcing a moment as far away from this domestic scene as she can. He meets her half-way, burying his head under her chin, in her collarbone. She gropes for his sex as he kisses her chest, allowing the futility of the moment simply to exist without exerting itself.

And it was all fine, just fine. Nice, even. A formulaic, proscribed, eidetic trace of their original intention, but just fine.

Mitosis? Meiosis? Let's call the whole thing off.

...

`I'll be by in fifteen minutes.`

Unshaven, dirty, Nora grabs the bottle of Captain Morgan's, turns on Madonna's *Immaculate Collection*, and dolls herself up in a happy flurry of fantastic anxiety. She fastens the stockings to the belt of her corset and ties the ribbons with serpentine prowess. Accessorizing with stilettos and a black satin robe, she feels like an adult, the mistress of someone important, someone powerful. She opens the door, invites him in. He slams her against the wall, kissing, fumbling, laughing subsides into irritation then ire. "Next time you're artificially euphoric call one of your strumpets, you fucking coke head!"

The wind from slamming the door pulls her robe into the door's clutches, and rather than risk seeing him confused, limp, pathetic, she slips out of her confines, leaving the robe stuck in the door, and makes herself a hotdog.

...

Concentrating, with his neck bent down, thumb on the keypad tapping and moving in jagged diagonals, he looks to his phone, positioned at his chest, alighting his face, flashing his chatoyant, iridescent eyes from across the bar Nora watches, tapping a folded Jackson in the direction of the bartender. In this dark bar, his face is a magnetic beacon of blue light, attracting attention, like a peacock's feather; texting is now a mating ritual. The cellular telephone is a tool, a spotlight, signaling to Nora that Jake is wanted, desired in one way or another someone else is vying after his attention, splitting it, seeping into her night, the kind of night she's coveted for some time now, a night where they start the night together. The bartender points at Nora. "Go," he says. She leans onto the bar.

"Two Blue Moons, three shots of Patrón, and a couple of lemon wedges."

The bartender takes out three glasses and pours the tequila across the row, spilling a little as he does. "Lemon?" he asks, yells. Nora assents. He grabs a handful of lemon wedges and places them on a paper napkin next to a salt shaker. Nora glances back to Jake, whose brow is still knit into his phone, and drinks one of the shots with a quick tilt of the neck. She makes a face of pain and disgust then grabs a lemon wedge and sucks its juices until the taste of the liquor washes out of her tongue.

The bartender returns with two pint glasses garnished with orange slices and says, "Fifteen even."

Nora leaves the twenty and walks away, hoping he'll remember her next time so she doesn't have to wait in line for six minutes. She returns to Jake without any change, which he doesn't seem to notice, or doesn't care, but he does briefly look up from his phone and say, "What? They ran out of limes?"

"You go up there and wait."

"Fuck it, it's almost Last Call. And Tuba just sent me the address to a party. Want to go?" he asks.

She shrugs.

Flippy Cup, Bean Bag Toss, Asshole, Circle of Death, Bull Shit. Various games teenagers use to avoid meaningful conversations. Irksome and younger than Nora's tastes. She crosses her arms, gets into an argument about truth being an illusion. That life is essentially meaningless and those who conjure a God are too afraid of their own potential, that they desire perpetual enslavement, that they're weak minded. Some guy threatens to punch her. She finds his rage hilarious.

"We should go," Jake says.

The guy stammers, "Jake, I didn't know she was with you."

Nora flips him off as Jake pulls her by the bicep to a cab out front.

"*Jesus!* You're hurting me."

"You're embarrassing me!" he says.

She laughs. "In front of those imbeciles? Those Philistines?"

"Why do you have to be such a snob?" Jake asks, but then his phone rings. He silences it.

"Who was that? A *girl*? A *little lamb*?" she teases. "Another chimp?"

"I know you don't even believe everything you say. You're just regurgitating."

"Does that make you feel better? Help you sleep at night?"

"Stop being a fucking bitch or I'll give you something to whine about." He spanks her hard. She creams.

At his place, another round of gin. She swirls it around in a jelly jar, looks at herself in the window he once watched her fawn over Brent through, which makes her debate texting him, but then decides she's too drunk, too sloppy. So she texts Ben, then Todd. Then Jake's phone rings again, or rather, it vibrates across the table.

"You should answer. I know what that's like, and it sucks. I can call her." She wants him to hit her again.

He turns on the television and up the stereo. He walks over to one of the speakers, calls her. "Jenny!" he says, walking in circles. He says he's still at the party, he says he can't hear her, that someone is trying to get his attention, then he assures her that he isn't going to stay out much longer. He'll call her later, he says.

After he hangs up, he apologizes and turns down the stereo.

Nora clicks the television off. "Who's Jenny?"

"My girlfriend."

Nora's labia is now throbbing. Tomorrow, when she's sober, she'll think about this inappropriate response to his overly casual missive. She'll try to think about why she's only turned on when he's lying to her, when he's better than her.

But now, everything's changed.

"I doubt *Jenny* feels any better," she says, liking the sound of her name in her mouth. *I bet I'd like fucking her*, she thinks then unbuttons her jeans and brings her hand to her wet vagina. Jake doesn't move. He takes a drag off his cigarette and watches. This is what she wants. *To perform.*

"I want to fuck your girlfriend," she says. "Will you share her with me? Can I fuck your girlfriend?"

"You can do whatever you like to her," he says.

Moving her finger in small circles, around and around. "Can I eat her pussy?" She pants.

"I don't know," he says. "Do you deserve it?"

Then,

There's a knock at the door.

And just like that, everything changes again.

His eyes bulge and he raises his index finger to his lips. "*Shhhh*," he whispers, just barely.

He turns up the stereo. Nora checks her phone. 4:42am, no response from Todd or Ben.

Knocking to pounding to kicking. "I know you're fucking in there! I can hear you!"

"Shit," Jake says through clenched teeth.

The knock, her heartbeat, morphs into a clobber.

"We're not fucking in here or anything. Let her in," Nora says.

"*Shhhh!!!*"

He runs to his bedroom. Trapped. No less jittery, Nora lights another cigarette. Jenny hammers on the door, ceaseless, threateningly. "Ted fucking Danson!" she says. "*Cheers*? At a party? At this hour?? I will fucking kill you! Open this door!"

Jake doesn't come back. Nora walks to his room, past the menacing door, where he is making a make-shift rope, as if in a cartoon, tying together three sets of sheets.

"No! No way in the world!" she hisses.

He gives her a pleading look. And then there's a different kind of smoke, thicker, blacker, the smell of camping, of burning wood.

Jenny has lit the door on fire.

Jake runs to tend, grabbing the fire extinguisher.

The door, the proverbial threshold. Pandora's boxed plywood. Up in flames. Like a phoenix.

Then the pervasive, screeching fire alarm pulses. Jake pulls the fire extinguisher, sprays white foam all over the foyer. Once the bottle is empty, he opens the door.

ENGH! ENGH! ENGH! ENGH! ENGH! ENGH!

She punches him in the face and steps inside. "You fucking piece of shit, mother fucker!"

ENGH! ENGH! ENGH! ENGH! ENGH! ENGH! ENGH! ENGH! ENGH!

Jenny is huge, not fat, but big, like a Roller Derby Girl, clad with striped socks and a wicked sneer. She reaches up and rips the smoke detector from the ceiling. Plaster falls all over the floor and into their hair.

With her mouth agape, Nora watches her berate Jake, agreeing with nearly everything she's saying. She should be moving, running, apologizing, *something*, not dumbly staring at this woman who just punched down a guy, then pulled a bolted smoke detector from the ceiling. Jenny looks to Nora. "And *YOU*, you fucking slut!"

Nora opens her mouth wider to speak, but catches sight of Jake shaking his head. For himself? For her? She isn't sure, but she did decide in a blink that he was probably right, for whatever reason.

Nora tips her jelly jar to this behemoth of a woman, to her heroine, "I've always wanted to do that," she says, which was the wrong thing to say.

Jenny inhales.

"I cannot believe *you* have the *balls*—"

Nora, without thinking, corrects, "The ovarian fortitude," then immediately regrets it.

"YOU FUCKING GOD DAMNED SLUT FROM—"

"You know? I'm gonna go," Nora says.

Then she does, straight out the blackened door, down the steps, and into the rosy-fingered dawn.

. . .

slut |slət|

Dirty, slovenly, untidy habits or appearance. The rise of Chlamydia, Cervical Cancer. The slut's light burns unsteadily, flickers, like the guttering of a candle. A foul slattern. Wet and stormy. Opposed to one's desired course, the one being male. A troublesome or awkward creature. Neurotic, often low self-esteem. A woman of a low or loose character, the scarlet letter emblazoned on her breast. A bold or impudent girl. Aphrodite. A hussy, a harlot, a whore. The jade whose jade flower opens for any son. A female dog: a bitch. Two of the most overly used feminine insults, cunt being unforgivable. A piece of cloth dipped in lard or fat and used as a light. A corner left unclean, after

all the stones have been turned. To act as a drudge. Cinderella, slutting about in loose fitting cottons. To behave as a woman of loose morals. Uncorseted. A tart. A ho. Very different from prostitution because money isn't exchanged, only pleasure.

ORIGIN Middle English : of patriarchal origin.

...

A mistress causes tiny ripples in space. She is responsible for the destruction of galaxies, for chaos. She isn't a wife and she isn't a girlfriend. She isn't the better half, her parts don't even add up to a balanced fraction. She is what she is not. She is an excess, a lack. She is defined as an action, encapsulated in a moment, in a cloud of steam, the gray, misty air of the sea. She is defined as her own. The title is only uttered in a whisper streamlined into an ear behind a cupped hand. Sometimes she evokes pity, sometimes, though rarely, she evokes obeisance, but mostly she evokes scorn. Most women don't identify with Jolene, they identify with Dolly. Jolene is young, she's beautiful, she wears diamond chandelier earrings and slinky red dresses, sometimes with thick black sunglasses standing a respectable distance from her lover's funeral, a long black veil obscuring her identity, haunting the procession like a ghost of his deception. She is mysterious and luminous. Pure sex. She can have high or low self-esteem and she isn't always afraid of commitment. Sometimes she does it just for the money. Sometimes, because she cannot be with him any other way. In Nora's case, she does it to defy propriety, to defy God.

Mistress. May stress. My stress.

...

Nora thinks of love. Of eternal return. Of the proverbial boomerang.

Jake loves *something* about her.

194

He oscillates between loving her and loving her availability. Her openness. He loves tying her to the headboard, covering her eyes. Shibari ropes digging into her wrists, how long she can hold her breath. That she can take a lick.

...

O Period, Period! wherefore art thou, Period?

...

Smile at the cashier act happy and she won't judge you she won't tilt her psoriasis head down to the lucent red circle encircling a little cross stamped on your forehead like a brand upon the brain *unholy* unholy dirty slut, slattern, lady of the night in a scarlet dress sad that her panties remain unspotted, unstained, clean, immaculately white. *Smile! Your Mother was Pro-Life!* Smile, look excited, hand over your credit card, not the one your father pays for. Good luck she says she thinks you're married you've won, you've psyched her out, clutching the see-through plastic handles knuckles white nails indenting unholy palms guilty of the sin of forgetting your canvas bag, now everyone can see, is looking, watching, laughing, no more shadows, no more desk tops to crawl under *no more alone*. Hand to belly cramping and dry as the martini you drank when you thought it was okay because you were on your period, like a bun already in the oven, overcooked, he boiled and poached your eggs scrambling your brains you kicked the corner of his coffee table and the ashtray fell on the floor spilling dirty ash of varying shades of gray. Sandals slapping against soles the meat tears from the shins as you sprint, walking as though someone were following you *someone is following you* as though you had something important to do, somewhere to be the bag slaps against a

195

prickled thigh the cardboard corner poking through threadbare corduroy.

No one's home yet the bathroom door is shut, the knob's outtie belly-button is pressed in where it sticks making a clicking sound signifying a secret or an act too impolite for prying eyes you read the pink cardboard box again *simple* too simple one pink line if it's a yes two if not stomach in knots. Two would be bad, so bad, colossally bad. You already made up your mind to abort *duh* you knew that five years ago you knew that as he licked your cunt and poked himself in between the curtains back behind center stage. Right from stage-left flames licking her saintly toes she screams SLUT! Fuckface you fucking cunt fucking his face! She could've been there, she could know that too, that inside her a parasite wriggles, fingers popping out of unholy palms, touching its forehead, lamenting its lineage *How could you be so stupid?* The diseases crawling in your cunt secreting juices that couldn't be human but some bacterial strand of a virus leaking from your unblinking eye staring into his face that launches a thousand tender kisses and vows of celibacy just this one last time I'm sorry, Jenny, I'm sorry *but I knew him first* I saw him first. I loved him before you. Before the awful acrid offal thought budding into fleshy fruition of terror, a little bundle of scapegrace burning inside in between crowned prince and carrier of blood, the blood of his first-born, the unexpurgated, unclaimed, illegitimate son from a woman who was never supposed to be a mother, not to him *Not to you!*

My baby my darling my light my life my universe kicking as babies do sucking thumbs holding onto feet rocking back on a crinkling plastic mattress and giggling white powder dusts his alien body like snow like love *I love you so much I can't even remember life before you.*

But you can't share him. He that is already halved, already two, fused in him and you. This baby laughter is evidence, innocent evidence of an unholy alliance, a match that should've never been, that almost never was but now cannot be denied. Everyone will laugh everyone will know you grip your stomach and hate it you hate your very entrails cramping and piercing and bubbling blubbering you haven't shat in days you can't shit even as you suck back your cigarette so quiet it crackles you drop it into the toilet where it sizzles where you piss clear onto a white stick and a little on your hand. The warmth nauseates you feels like insects, worms and maggots, under your skin, formication in your belly, in your vagina, millions of wriggling sperm swimming about having a party conversing about how comedies just aren't funny anymore, but one of them says, What about *Super Troopers*? I guess so *It's today's Office Space* he chews on the pink walls of your womb. You have been invaded, and in secret. He came on your face, on your tits, not inside of you, but maybe a little, pre-ejaculation, a teardrop's worth, *myriad homunculi, tiny yous, with your acerbic smiles and insincere gesticulations of exaggeration, beckoning, tricking, sinister, chewing and lying as you already knew and couldn't care that I'm already out twenty-six dollars and ninety-nine cents plus tax that I can't ask you for that I wouldn't dare, not now, not after that charade, you know I don't have two hundred dollars for an operation.*

Feet stick to the linoleum, lift suck slap lift suck slap. The stick's on the counter, dripping urine, you want to clean it up, erase the moment, already forget it, like a suppressed trauma that never suppresses, how can you suppress an abortion? An abomination? How could you even think it *if your grandmother only knew* she who only votes on one issue *Every fetus is a life!* Every life is worth something *worth fighting for* except yours as your vague dreams of solitude flash before you like stereoscopic scenes from Hell, mocking and mangling any freedom you think you have over your own body, that vessel, the vassal pulsating vascular sentiments of lust convincing yourself that it isn't love, that you hate him you really hate him that his child would be an abomination that you wouldn't have a choice that you couldn't have him in your life forever, pretending, or worse marrying, uniting, sitting next to him as he cuts his toe nails on the bed and you dream of sleeping on them digging into your back his waste like feces digging into you as you sleep you wake up screaming and you're late for work, he's showering, packing a sacked lunch, asking you whether or not Chinese food containers can be recycled. How about chopsticks? *Chopsticks…*

The orange shower curtain gives the shower a red glow like you're showering inside a womb, or inside a hellish tomb where you can walk around and soak yourself under scalding water. Strangely though, you can't cry. Head craned past the first curtain, the white mildew flecked one, past the second striped orange and red and yellow, ninety degrees, the light feels like the sun you really need to replace these fluorescent bulbs, but you think it'll make you a bad hippie if you do. The stick sits there, it lies there, no longer dripping, probably registered, fate sealed, but like a cat in a box, both dead and alive, there is both a baby and nothing inside of you. You hope for nothing, black bile, the stomach flu, anything but his child that cannot be. Dripping, soapy, sudsy, doesn't matter, the mat feels squishy under your curling toes ONE PINK LINE. *Nothing.* You just felt fat, had gas, couldn't poop. Stress from finals kept you from bleeding, maybe that one day you were spotting when the toilet paper had the faintest bit of pink on it like when you brush your teeth too hard and spit in the sink. Back in the shower you rinse your hair, brush your teeth, spit onto the drain the pink swirls, fractures, lands on your leg in spatters like one pink line of FREEDOM from secrecy, from abdominal pain, from the nagging fear of telling your parents, or your friends, asking someone to drive you to a Planned Parenthood, where you didn't plan, where you wish you could have a semblance of peace as you felt the pill dissolve into a part of him, dismembering him, disfiguring him, not your baby, your beautiful baby boy that couldn't be, that gasps for air, for mother *Mommy!* that he could never know about, that he would want to love. Even from a distance that disgusts you. How could you fuck someone you wouldn't want around your children? How could you be so stupid? So selfish? So slutty? Fucking without purpose? Bareback and raw, bloody and carnal? *Let this be your warning.* You are officially warned.

. . .

She visits an installation that Jiji made. Circular mirrors hanging from the ceiling, in a sort of mobile, always swaying from the wind. The words BACK or FORTH are written on each mirror. The dance of seduction, a necessary dance, but a discreet dance, a *danse macabre*. Fort/Da. A give and take. The chase is dying. He asks her to be open to anything. She is taken for a prostitute, her body is an illusory escape, the terrain on which he can map out his fantasies. But it's too blunt. Mind games have crossed into perversions. Explicit pornography disgusts her. She wakes to a picture of his dick, he asks her what she thinks. Immediately she deletes it saying, Every lady worth her salt enjoys waking up to a stiff cock. He says that her sarcasm isn't appreciated.

. . .

She develops eyes for another man, someone in her Augustine, Anselm, and Aquinas class. When he first spoke to her he compared their class on God to staring into the sun for an hour.

...

A pause, a breath, a period.

...

To forget about the sun, to hide from its rays, gaze, to smoke cigarettes and slug coffee, she is reading Sartre's book on emotions at the Deadwood. She doesn't see him come in.

"Therefore, we shall call emotion an abrupt drop of consciousness into the magical. Or, if one prefers, there is emotion when the world of instruments abruptly vanishes and the magical world appears in its place."

Jake sits down. Asks her if it's any good. Before she can answer the waitress appears. He orders a Heineken then grabs Nora's hand, strokes her fingers, her knuckles. She closes her eyes for a second. Indulges in the way that makes her body ache to be in roller skates. He pulls her Claddagh ring off. Looks at it as if it held all her secrets. When he places the ring back on her finger he turns it around, turns the tip of the heart inward, toward her chest, the way a married woman wears it. The ring feels differently, misshapen. While she stares at it, the waitress returns, sets the beer on the table. He tips her too much, pokes her rear end with his eyeballs.

"I think I'm going to start dating someone real soon," she says.

"Do you think of yourself as a serial monogamist?" he asks. She thinks.

"It's more that I live in a suburb of monogamy."

He laughs, "I like that," he says, fucking quaffing his beer. "I like that. I guess I live in a suburb of monogamy too."

200

"I guess so," she says, turning her ring back around.

"Aw," he says, "Come on. Humor me."

"*Suburb*," she says. "Not the city itself."

...

At Jake's apartment, while he is in the bathroom, Nora sees a photo album on the table. It's the kind of cheap, translucent plastic photo album one gets for free when they open a checking account, just big enough for one roll of film. She picks it up, flips through it. First, a picture of a sunset, then a tent, then him and Jenny floating down the river in a set of innertubes.

Jenny.

The same Jenny that punched him in the face, that kisses him on the cheek and shows off her volleyball body in a pink bikini. He looks happy, untroubled, like someone who wouldn't keep a mistress. Jenny is either pretending that all is well, or that they've talked things through. Maybe she no longer even worries about Nora. Maybe she doesn't even know what Nora really is to him. Maybe Nora actually means very little to her, she was explained away as an ex or a home-wrecker *in potentia*. And yet, here she sits, flipping, listening to something as intimate as him releasing his bowels. Though, he had turned the water on in an effort to mask the noises, but it only calls attention to the act.

Nora masochistically keeps looking. More pictures from which she is excluded. Never has he taken her camping. Could she have had this? Camping trips are not for mistresses. He sees them as a family function, a requisite for respite. She comes to a photograph of him: laughing, drinking beer with a yellow coozy. A friend stands behind him, drapes his arm around Jake's shoulder. Nora pilfers the photo, puts it in her purse, then slides the

201

album across the floor. "Why don't we go on a trip? Like to Minneapolis or Wisconsin? Hell, I'd even go to Mexico with you."

"There's no way I could get away with it."

She looks to those two unlit, vanilla bean scented candles.

"Say it's a boys thing, a secret fraternity thing."

"It doesn't work like that, Babe."

He never calls her Babe. She wonders if that's his pet name for Jenny, then lights the two candles.

"I hate the name *Babe*. It's so generic, and ugly."

He flushes, opens the door.

"Apologies, Chopsticks."

"I can't see you anymore," she says.

"What?"

"My body cannot be your graveyard!"

"Wait. What? Why did you light my candles?"

. . .

Alone, with a photo of her lover
as she's never known him.
As a friend.

. . .

loquela
     This word, borrowed from Ignatius of Loyola, designates the flux of languages through which the subject tirelessly rehashes the effects of a wound or the consequences of an action: an emphatic form of the lover's discourse.

     – Roland Barthes. *A Lover's Discourse: Fragments.*

5.
Three years later.

A postcard, to her parents' address, postmarked from Arizona. *Arearea AKA Joyousness.* Gauguin. Two women. One bare-breasted in purple, looking down, away, playing the flute or a pipe of some sort. The other looking ahead, straight ahead, at the viewer, at Nora, almost daring her to comment, to speak now, or forever hold her peace. Her breasts are covered and she's wearing white. A dog sniffs the land at their feet. Three women are in the background, looking as though worshipping a large-headed deity.

I'm in love! (But I do still think of you from time to time.)

White supremacist male chauvinism disguised as a misplaced desire for primitive nostalgia filtered through Post-Impressionism and entitled colonialism. A return to a time and a place where women knew their place.

Nora fucking hates Gauguin.

There is no return address.

...

Nora now lives with Jiji.

Jiji's sadness is different from Nora's, it's more ubiquitous, heavier. Two years ago she had an abortion. Two years ago she lost her and Lej's child. Then a year later, she lost Lej, or rather, Lej lost her. Her body, at once a vessel for both life and death, couldn't cry enough. Her tears homogenized into a new body, an endless body of water as dense, as distant, as mystified as the sea herself. Nora can still sometimes hear her cry, though it's much softer now, like water sloshing around in the bath. And she sympathizes, she listens, but she doesn't understand. She can't empathize, not really, not enough. She looks into Jiji's art; loss tantamount to grief bleeding into guilt dominating over the canvases, reigning over the graphic colors that tremble before the emotions they live to represent, raining into the viewer, onto the viewer, Nora cries Jiji's tears. She can't help it, she loves her so.

The el train roars past their apartment every ten minutes, only letting up from 4am-5:30am. If she wanted to, she could open her window and touch the tracks. The first night she slept there, sometime during REM sleep, her heart rate increased, blood pressure rising, vulva aching, rib cage splitting, cracking, parting for the monorail that spreads her arms into a cruciform span, palms turned up, back arched, throat exposed, head back, as if she were receiving divine light, giving birth to the el from her heart. She wakes with a sweaty start, clutching her chest and clawing for breath. Twice she's been caught naked by a stalled train. This satisfied the exhibitionist in her, but it didn't come without embarrassment. For a while she blocked the sun, and the ~~Sear's~~ Willis Tower, shading herself with a sign that read: "That is a brown line train."

. . .

Chicago, all grown up and nostalgic for bathtub gin and flapper dresses. But Al Capone is dead. Dion O'Banion is dead. Bugs Moran is dead. John Dillinger, and his huge cock, are dead, betrayed by a woman dressed all in red, who is also dead.

. . .

She lets the word "atheist" fall off her lips.
Nihilism gets caught in her throat.

. . .

"I live in the city now with Lindsay."
The sentence rolls off his tongue, like water slipping through sore and flaky fingers.
"I thought you were in Arizona," she says.

"Oh no," he says. "Are you dating anyone?"

"Yes, his name's Brian. We've been together for about two years now." She doesn't tell him that Brian is currently living in South America.

"We should have dinner, catch up."

"Okay," she says, because that's what people say when they're asked to a hypothetical dinner.

. . .

She writes on her torso, backwards letters in purple lipstick, while looking in the mirror: **I WILL NEVER EAT DINNER WITH YOU**. She takes a picture, sends it to him in the morning, when she knows he'll be at work.

. . .

He's older, noticeably older, much older than her, though he never seemed so before. He's wearing a baby blue sweater. He smells like high school. Like Hugo Boss. Like Ford upholstery and mentholated cigarettes. Like suede, cedar, and moss. Ground coffee beans and cracked black pepper.

He smiles at her.

That indefinable, chimerical, ephemeral smile.

"Did you drive your truck?" she asks, not for the answer, but for the memory.

No, he did not, that car's been long dead. The carburetor. Besides, they're just in Wicker Park. He took a cab.

"You look fantastic," he says. He looks tired, calcified, both weathered and polished.

Pale, almost violet-tinged, she looks as though she hasn't seen the sun for months. One of her eyes twitches the slightest bit. She curls her frozen toes inside her boots, fidgets with an oversized ring, a Bakelite red rose.

"Why did you call me?" she asks.

206

"Why did you call me?" he says, inflecting differently.

He's gained weight. In his face, around his middle. He looks as if he's been living off of pasta.

"I wanted to see how you are," she says.

"You felt vulnerable and wanted to fuck me."

"Now, Jacob," she says, as calmly and as slowly as she can, "I'm not even through with my first drink. Let's save the debauchery for our fourth shot of tequila."

He flags down the waitress, orders eight shots of Patrón and two Blue Moons.

"You're switching to beer," he says. "I don't want you getting sloppy and ridiculous."

"I don't get ridiculous. I get honest."

"Honesty is a form of ridiculousness."

She sips her dirty martini, laments that it isn't dirty enough, that she can still taste the sting, the hair of the vodka. She picks up her cocktail skewer, sucks at her olive, looks him over. He doesn't smile, he lets her look at him, at his face, the face that she can't place, the face she endlessly places. That face that isn't his, or rather, his face that isn't hers.

"You have a girlfriend," she says.

"When has that ever stopped you?"

"You told me you were in love."

"She means a lot to me."

Nora takes out a cigarette. He's quick to light it. Their alcohol and a salt shaker is laid down on the table, along with four limes. She doesn't even flinch to take out her wallet. "Oh, and two lemons, dear. The lady hates lime."

Nora excuses herself to the bathroom, bringing her cigarette.

In the bathroom, she doesn't lock herself in a stall, she doesn't even need to pee, though the sudden licentious nudge did stimulate her digestive nerves, did give her a powerful urge to masturbate. She looks in the mirror, watches herself smoke, exhaling slightly, inhaling through her nostril, exhaling again against the glass. She watches the cool gray escape from her vivid blood lips. She's watching herself, pretending she isn't there, that she's back, sitting across from him, crossing and uncrossing her legs, pupils immense and glossy, though, she wishes they could shrink back into slits, preferably horizontal slits, cold, incalculable slits.

She shakes herself out of fantasy then looks again. She too has gained weight. Looks a little older than she once was. A little sadder. A little sullen, sturdier, weighted by time and by Brian. She puts her cigarette out in a toilet, enjoying the sound of the brief fizzle.

"I said we lived together," he says as she sits down.

"You said you were in love."

"No, I said we lived together. Why did you wear red lipstick? You know I hate red lipstick."

"Oh, don't act like you didn't send that postcard!"

He laughs, heartily, apparently he has forgotten all about that. He's a business man now, selling medical equipment, defibrillators and stethoscopes to hospitals from behind a desk, from a prominent company. He convinces for a living, wears a suit everyday. He rides the el and reads the paper, sometimes he brings a book, some Bret Easton Ellis or Jonathan Franzen, Nora assumes then suggests the Marquis de Sade. He's never heard of him, writes it on a napkin. Spells it wrong.

He lights a cigarette, holds it differently from before, with slight affectation, between his thumb and middle finger. Pensive inside the cynical shadows of noir, like he's up to his knees in conspiracy. This is when Nora wonders if he really sells medical equipment. He hands her a business card with thermographic lettering.

He has a new watch on too. All the gears are visible and gold. The hands are silver and the band is made out of brown leather. She doesn't ask him about it, instead she imagines it belonged to his grandfather, a World War II vet. Jake was his favorite grandchild, the one with the most potential.

Nora resolves never to ask him mundane, diurnal questions about his life, about what exactly it is that he does with his time. He wouldn't tell the truth if she did, so she drops truth. She abandons, neglects, reshapes, mishandles truth. But she speaks with candor, about them, about desire. She lets fiction override reality. She thinks in polychrome. Sees him as powerful, as rich, with minions, lackeys to do his bidding, behind a bar made out of steel and blue embedded lights, pouring Scotch from crystal decanters. She's always seen him as blue, like the ocean, like cold metal, able to slice through a moment, whether she wills it or not. He asks her questions, questions that pertain to a mystery, one that has him chasing her, fighting for her, something, in other circumstances she wouldn't imagine him doing, but here, she's fantasizing, she looks up, hasn't been listening. She brings the conversation back to where she wants it, back where it was.

"And what about *Les Desmoiselles D'Avignon*, where you told me you 'were undeserving of such a gift,'" she makes quotation marks with her hands, "Probably because you felt bad for ignoring me on the bridge after you fucked me for the first time. You knew, you knew even then—"

"Ignoring you? Do you remember how freezing it was outside?"

Nora remembers black garbage bags, two teenagers kicking rocks and plastic bar bracelets in the gutter. And that she wanted so badly for him to tell her that he loved her.

He takes back one of the shots, without salt, but does suck the lime.

She resists the shot, but does light another cigarette.

"I feel so stupid telling you this," he says. "I was so insecure there. I was looking up at you. I mean, I was looking up *to* you. I felt like a child. You looked so tall, so sure of yourself. It was as if you were untouchable, like a goddess, just radiating pure beauty. I knew I would never be good enough for you."

She looks down, at the table, their tools. Setting the cigarette in the clean ash tray, in one of the resting slots, she licks her hand, not in a sexual way, but in a practical way. Desperately hoping he doesn't notice, she shakes a little as she pours the salt over where she licked. Tiny crystalline particles spill, bounce onto the table. Then, she drinks, slamming her head back, popping out her throat for a quick second.

"That's not what I had thought," she says, making a face, her teeth in a lemon, her cigarette back in her hand, inhaling, exhaling, obscuring herself, then ashing her cigarette methodically, as a distraction. She wants to throw up.

"Clearly," he says.

She stands up too fast, the blood rushes to her head. "I'm getting a water. Do you want one?"

He nods. She turns her back to him, walks over to the bar, rounds the corner, disappears for a second, to blush, to smile, to order two waters and a couple more lemon wedges. *Don't be a fool, Nora. He's playing you.*

"Come with me to the bathroom," he says.

"What?"

"Or should I say: Come with me in the bathroom?"

"We've only had half of our shots."

He slams the next one, just like that, again without salt but sucks on the lime. He doesn't break eye contact.

"Dude! I'm not even a quarter done with my martini! What the fuck? Slow down. Did you just call me to fuck with me? There used to be artistry to our courtship! Fucking A, are you engaged or something?"

"Why would I be engaged?"

"I don't know. A final hurrah or some shit? I haven't seen you in nearly three years!"

"Nora, I've missed you, and I know you've missed me, that's all. You're gorgeous, every bit as stunning as you once were—"

"Oh, well now I know—" she interrupts, is interrupted.

"I don't know why we've gone this long without seeing each other. I masturbate to you all the time, just thinking of that little Catholic school girl skirt," he shivers, maybe notices her eyes, and certainly her pupils, are wide, though feigning incredulity. "Am I being too forward? I thought you liked when I was forward?"

"I don't know what I like, and I don't know who you like! It's been forever. What's going on with you and Lindsay?"

"There are things I just can't do with Lindsay. She's not like you. I'm just not cut out for monogamy, I prefer its suburb," he winks. "Monogamy is not how humans are meant to live. It isn't natural; it's an *unnatural* constraint on sexuality."

"Save your canned moan for your senator."

"I thought you would be on my side."

"You assumed a lot coming here tonight."

"I just wanted to see you."

"The veiled veneer of vague verbosity," she says.

"That's good. You just come up with that?"

"Fuck you."

"My little wordsmith, let's start over," he says, putting his hand upon hers.

"That's impossible."

"Look: *Nora*! It's been so long! You look incredible! Exactly the same—no, better! Come here."

And then he kisses her.

"That's it," she says. "That's all you're getting. I've got to think about this."

"Speaking of," he says, "not tonight. I was only able to get away until eleven. We'll have to reschedule for another time. And this next time, don't pretend to bring any sanctimonious baggage with you."

Three months then slip through the sieve of desertion.

. . .

Against Jiji's counseling, Nora texts him: Meet me at Cloud Gate.

Disembodied, fluid, luminous, as if it had fallen from the sky, as if God had meticulously placed it there, as if at any moment it could collapse into a puddle of mercury.

A sister to *2001: a Space Oddessey*'s proud black rectangle, giving the illusion of wholeness, pushing people to the brink of greatness, at the edge of what humanity can do, pulling it back, breaking bones with bones, bread with hands, wiping away the seams of past and present, merging, bending the primal duality of genitalia, of sky and earth.

It, like Chicago, thrives on tension, the tension between progression and regression, the tension between

212

the lingam and the yoni, between black and white, or black and white and red and blue. But the usual tensions, the tensions between races and classes appears in the sculpture itself, renews itself daily, in the individuals, the ones stupidly pressing their fingers against the welded steel taking photographs of themselves besides themselves, or above themselves, reaching out to themselves as if they were both God and Adam.

Nora has taken one of those photos.

. . .

Tchaikovsky's *Romeo and Juliet* won't do. Not because it's inadequate, but inaccurate. Jake does not smile that smile to the overture. He and Nora don't float toward one another. There is never any slow motion running through a field.

Their moment is quick and sharp, sentimental only for a second. "I thought you were never going to call," he says.

She brought a wedge of *Coeur de Chèvre*, wrapped in a chestnut leaf, a French loaf of bread, and some perfectly ripened strawberries.

He brought a Frisbee.

It's sunny, beautiful, crowded. They sit with their feet in the shallow pool, watching the two glass towers change faces, puckering, parting their lips, as if they were about to spit onto the crowd, but it's only April, the water hasn't been turned on yet, though the children still run and wait anxiously, yearning for life to begin, staring up at these fifty foot tall people, these gods and goddesses of Chicago, blinking slowly, as if in pain, as if in sorrow, as if in penance.

He throws the disk, it spins, rotates, planetary revolutions around itself, appears to be coming straight at her, she looks up, holds her hands up, she's ready, almost, but then it curves, slightly, to the left, makes a J in the sky, and already she's betrayed her façade, so she lets it curve to the left, without diving, or moving her hand slightly, it lands, sunny-side up.

"Go get it," he says, shooing her with both hands, telling her to go and fetch, like a dog, pushing her farther away from him already, as if Lindsay were riding her bicycle along Monroe Street.

This offends her but she makes a petulant grunt and does as she's told.

The disk is blue but purple in spots from her hands' shadows. She grips the Frisbee's lip, rubs her thumb along its plastic cords.

Then she hurls, whirls it at him, lets it go, hoping this time it will come back, like a boomerang, right into her arms, without effort, without accentuating her athletic incompetence.

And it does.

This time she runs to catch it, to touch it again, to feel the weight of its disposability. She catches it and feels like someone else.

She throws it back to him, toward him. He runs, jumps into the air, flexing his muscles. Catches it.

He throws.
She catches.

Home.

She throws.

Away.

He catches. He throws.

Home.

Away.

Home.

Away.

Home.

Away.

"I have to get back to work."

"I know."

...

Laced on Vicodin and marijuana, the girls cannot sit still through *Back to the Future*. Not at all a reflection on the film, but on Nora's mood. She's anxious, her leg bounces. She checks her phone, checks the time, knows that he won't be texting anymore.

They pause a lot, to let the train roar by, to talk about time travel and the impossibility of not immediately recognizing the uncanny resemblance to yourself in your future son. Jiji looks at Nora check her phone.

"Do you know where he lives?" Jiji asks.

Nora does, but she's never been there, only ridden her bike past. Jiji smiles puckishly, ecstatically, like a teenager. She gets up and leaves the living room. Nora yells after her but her voice was muffled. Another train sped past.

Too lazy, too nihilistic to get up, she waits.

Jiji comes back with two wigs, one long and blonde, the other ratted up into a pink beehive. She says, "Hear me out."

Nora doesn't need to. She shakes her head vehemently, *No!* laughing, *No way in the world!* betraying herself with body language.

"Why not?"

"For one, what if they're home?"

"Don't be daft, that's the point."

"He'll *so* recognize us. This is something he'll expect from me."

"Why on *earth* would he expect you to wear a pink beehive wig and spy into his bedroom window from a parking lot's worth away on a Tuesday? And he's never even seen me before! I'll be your shield. And besides, I am DYING to see what he looks like."

"Absolutely not."

"It's happening."

"No!"

Jiji runs away again, singing, "We even have binoculars!"

Nora looks to the wigs, situates one atop her head.

"So what if you get caught?" Jiji says. "Seriously, so what. That dickhead expects WAY too much from you. He's not even worried you'll tell Lindsay. Maybe this'll make him sweat a little. He deserves it."

"I don't want to get caught! That's not what we're like. I don't want anything more from him. I like this. I just don't like when he suddenly stops texting or stands me up, but this arrangement works for me. And I don't want to hurt Lindsay! It's not fair of me to—"

"Okay. Okay. We'll just drive up there, sit in the car, and spy a little."

. . .

Though Jiji doesn't need a disguise, Nora's assuming she's doing it out of camaraderie, for the sake of the anecdote. For fun. And at the moment, everything's funny. They riff off one another. Laughing (so hard that Nora's begun to cackle) at the enigma, the persistence of pragmatics. When Jiji says "du chien," Nora cites dogma. "And I stood upon the sand of the sea, and saw a beast rise up out of the sea, having seven heads and ten horns…"

"You can't teach an old dogma new tricks!"

"…and upon his horns ten crowns, and upon his heads the name of blasphemy!"

"Curb your dogma!"

"Maybe if I count to one hundred by fives," Nora cites Parker.

"Then he'll call!" Jiji says.

"You can bring a whore to culture but you can't make her think!"

"In the garden of earthly delights."

"If friends were flowers I'd pick you."

Jiji can't sit up straight and wear her wig in the car at the same time. She slouches in the passenger seat and ashes her cigarette into an empty pop can. Her eyes are drawn out like a cat's, painted thickly with black liquid eyeliner and smoked with the tip of a match, but still, she's wearing a hoodie.

It's almost as if they have forgotten where they're going.

Even when the treasure is forgotten, the adrenaline, the anticipation is more potent than the drugs now winding down in their system.

Nora's wig is itchy but bearable. She had glossed her lips pink and frosted her eyelids. She can't help but toss repeated glances at herself in the rearview mirror, admiring her striking eyebrows juxtaposed with the long flaxen hair of a princess cascading into cashmere argyle, a sweater Maryanne had recently left at her apartment that miraculously fit her.

They arrive at his building close to midnight. A brownstone, four flights. All the lights are out, except for two unblinking rectangles on the third floor. The blinds pulled partway. They look like eyes. She sees yellow and a black blob, the Hawkeye's logo, a flag, tacked above a denim colored couch. White walls. Picture frames, big smiles, no doubt, captured inside them. A flickering television. Yellow flowers. Real, not silk. (She can tell because one is drooping, wilting.) Nora wants to look in as long as she can. She wants to map everything inside these rectangles, make immediate sense of him, of him and her, of him and her and herself.

"Look," says Jiji, "The Hawkeyes."

"Jesus Christ, it's as bright as the tip of the sun's dick!"

"Who uses overhead lighting anymore? It's awful."

"There's not a single lamp in there. Do you see one? I told you he was aesthetically challenged."

"I thought she would've done the decorating."

"Maybe she did," Nora says.

She. She really is Nora's opposite, so Nora now thinks, as she looks into the apartment, from across the street in a blonde wig the color of Lindsay's hair. Jiji has the binoculars, she peers into their living room. Nora turns off her car's lights, puts on sunglasses, slumps in her seat. "What are they watching?"

"Those sunglasses don't look conspicuous or anything," Jiji says, immediately, but then, "I see a woman on a couch."

"Lindsay?"

"How the fuck should I know? But no, in the television. No one's on the couch. Why are the lights on if

218

they're not in there? Why is the television on? Don't they know we're in the middle of an energy crisis?"

"Wait, why the fuck do you have the binoculars? Give 'em here."

"No, you've got to switch seats with me. You can't have the driver looking dead into their front windows. It looks hella suspicious."

Nora squints, makes out an Apple computer and Carrie Bradshaw. "*Ew!* Too bad, it's *Sex and the City.*"

"That really is too bad."

"I'm getting in back." Nora unbuckles herself then dives into the backseat, nearly kicking Jiji in the hair. "Get back here too. That makes more sense. If the cops come, it'll just seem like we're making out. Give me the binoculars!"

"Might as well; they're a bitch with glasses. But I want to see him!"

"No, you don't."

The metal feels foreign against her skin. Her eyelashes bat against the glass. Holding onto the antique barrels, she adjusts the wheel in the center with her index finger, sharpening the image, honing in on the yellow flowers blossoming into daffodils on the counter separating the kitchen from the living room. They have a print framed of a tomato, above it reads, "Pomodoro." The people in the picture frames are smiling. Nora thinks she makes out Jake in one of them, holding a fish, but it could just as easily be his brother, or her father, or his.

Neither one of them are in the living room, but, at least, someone is home.

Nora looks to the bedroom, a lone black window to the left of the living room.

"I think I see movement in the bedroom! Look!" A blur of silver, of white.

"I have night blindness. I can't see shit in there," Jiji says.

A calf, an ankle struck by the moonlight. A toe pointed to the ceiling, shadows playing on the wall. One knee bent. Jake's ass, pale, pumping, flexing, holding onto her calf, pulling up the other, squeezing them, propping them, so he can access, so he can sink, into her, in the dark, Nora squints, claws, kicked to the stomach, blood rushes to her face, her clitoris, her lungs deflate. The tiniest sound escapes from her mouth.

A gasp of shock, of ripe pain. A squeak diluted with hot breath.

"Can you see them? Are they home?"

Nora's has about a couple seconds to answer. Yes, or lie, no, one of those small lies, one that doesn't, shouldn't matter in the scheme of things, as Jiji could really care less whether or not Jake was inside, pulling out of his girlfriend, leaving a string of prosaic drops of cum on their white bed. This would be about Nora, about her being vulnerable, honest with someone, with herself, about her feelings toward Jake. She shushes Jiji, making her decision, rejecting the terms.

Handing over the binoculars she says, scrunching her nose, smiling impishly, "Dude, I think they're fucking."

"Holy shit!" Jiji climbs to the front, turns the car on then honks the horn to the tune of *Shave and a Haircut.* For a while Nora's quiet in the passenger seat until Jiji sings, "We'll eat again. Don't know where. Don't know when! But I know we'll eat again some sunny day!"

Then she chimes in.

. . .

When they get home they make a small feast of cheese and bread and Nutella and strawberries and bananas.

220

When Jiji gets up to refill their water Nora grabs a banana and smashes it into the floor, slowly, consolingly, irrationally, digging her fingers into the forbidden fruit, its mushy guts creeping under her fingernails and into the grains of wood.

Seeing Nora grab the banana, thinking that she's going to eat it, from the kitchen Jiji yells, "Dude, don't even. You're pissed off." Then adds, almost to herself: "I know I would be."

. . .

Jiji leaves town, goes home for a week, to see her mother. Nora shuts down, shutting her phone down, for once, because even if. *She couldn't*. She doesn't trust herself.

She leaves the apartment only to buy cigarettes, then smokes way too many because she has back up, because Jiji's not home to complain.

In bed, her lungs feel heavy, a metallic taste settles on the back of her tongue. She coughs, frightening herself, thinking about the inevitability, the inertia of an ending. How she's speeding things up smoking like this, how huge the apartment feels without Jiji. She calls Rufus, clicking her tongue, making kissy noises to the air. A train goes by, Rufus does not emerge. She gets up, goes to the window, looks at her reflection, imagines Jake on the train. She stares at the tiny windows roaring past, the tiny heads, wondering what exactly is romantic about a beautiful body colliding with a dirty train, a train full of people, all now inconvenienced and groaning. Such a bourgeois way to die.

The rain has stopped. The clouds have dissipated, scattered. The moon outside is perfect, gigantic, bright yellow, so close, so terrifying. She turns her phone back on.

One missed text. It's only midnight.

. . .

The bar drenches Nora's thoughts in disorientation. It's the music. Euphoric to some, discordant to her. The way it enters the chest, pulses with the blood, consumes everything it touches. Never a symphony of sound, just a sexual thump, a cacophony. Theme music for the bar's clientele.

Jake is easy to spot. He is so very drunk, dancing at his table. His table of three pretty women and one nondescript guy, whose arm is claiming one of the girls. Jake grabs Nora's arms and attempts to pull her into the center sludge, where no one is dancing. His eyes are glazed and he has a goofy grin on his face: his drunken grin. Nora hates that grin. That grin disintegrates his intelligence. That grin absolves him of anything he wants to be absolved of. That grin splits his personality and stores them both within itself, where they have a drunken brawl. Right now she has no patience for the mud, the blood, and the beers within that grin.

"I want more than this. I'm sick of being the other woman," she says. "I want to date you. I want to get it over with. You know it will fail. We'll last about a week. I'll piss you off, destroy the magic with a mud mask or a fart. And you'll irritate me with television and shit. We would never work. Let's fail. Let's get over each other." Logorrhea, before she can stop herself.

He blinks a few times. "Hello to you too," he says, then starts dancing again. Nora persists, circumventing everything she just said with different nouns and adjectives. She's careful to speak slowly, and loudly. She's competing with Ludacris.

Ludacris is winning.

He can't dance, but extends his ass towards the crowd. His back is nearly at a forty-five degree angle. He has to look up to talk to Nora. "I'm waiting for you to break up my family."

"That's not funny!" she snaps. Jake turns.

"I don't want you over me," he says taking another drink of something clear, something strong. He says it without looking at her, but without pain. He says it to signify that the conversation is over.

She can pretend that that ass wasn't his, that she didn't just see him make love to his girlfriend, possibly even, someday, most likely, his wife. Jake goes up to the bar and orders two shots of tequila. "You look like Scarlett Johansson," one of the girls says.

"Thanks," Nora says, flattered, but looking nothing like Scarlett Johansson.

When the shots arrive Nora takes them both.

Jake cheers, then licks her cheek.

The Lethe River streams through the bar, streams between the ponds of sensory memory and short term memory, leaving people forcing polluted, convoluted fragments into their long term memory banks. The in between of these fragments are devoid of all light. Blackouts. Amnesia bestows libations. Jake and Nora offer this moment up to her.

Just like they used to.

Then, they drink. Nora doesn't have any trouble catching up…

"Last call! Last call, for alcohol. You don't have to go home, but GET THE FUCK OUT!"

It's already 3:30am. Lindsay must be wondering. She must be angry.

"Come over," Nora says. "Jiji's out of town."

"I can't," Jake says.

She grabs his hand then runs through the bar, snaking through the crowd, bumping into some arms and some purses. She has no idea if he's running as smooth a job, but she doesn't care. At the back there's the bathrooms, where she can buy some more time. She pulls him into the guys' bathroom. Two men are peeing. Neither notices. She pushes him into the stall, locks it shut, then drops to her knees.

She unzips his pants and takes out his penis. His familiar, particular, circumcised, astonishing penis. It hardens, lengthens against her cheek. Water flushes, streaming through, sloshing against the porcelain. Shoes stepping in puddles. Taking him in her mouth, she puts a question to him, biting down on the tallest bit, she's giving a prelude to what hasn't been, not for so long. She's being difficult, only going half-way, wounding the decision, playing unfairly…

At her apartment there is a glass door that opens onto another locked glass door. Nora calls it the Glass Elevator, as it's about the same size of an elevator. She can stand in the middle of that room and touch both doors. Once she unlocks the first door, Jake sits down, says he can't go upstairs because she deserves better.

"That's a lie," Nora says. He plays with his shoe-laces. She opens her mouth to say, "Lindsay doesn't deserve this," but instead says: "I'm obsessed with you."

"*That's* a lie."

Nora slides down the wall, when she sits her hair is still above her, as if she were still sliding.

"It will never work," he says.

"That's what I want."

They're both looking straight ahead, at the row of ribbed silver mailboxes. Meaning, neither is looking at the other. It's as if they're thinking, assessing, as if the scene were stylized. Nora notices every finger smudge, every chink in the metal, every scuff of railroad tar, every hint of dirt smeared into the wallpaper. After a minute he stands up, puts his hand on the wall, then extends it to her.

She doesn't take it; pushing herself up from the floor, pressing her palm into the tar.

"I want you to see me doing laundry, making quinoa, wearing unflattering pajamas." He shakes his head. No, no, no. "Because then you wouldn't love me," she says, "and I wouldn't be on reserve to inflate your ego. Because then it wouldn't be *us*. Because then I would go away."

"You've already gone away," Jake says.

"I'm here now. It's like nothing's changed. Nothing ever changes between us. It's dreadfully boring. I'm sick of being your preferred mistress."

"You're my only mistress."

"Bullshit."

"Jesus Christ," he puts his hands on his head. "You're not even my mistress!"

"Oh, not that again. All right, Jake, we can call it whatever you want—"

He grabs Nora by the shoulders and shakes her violently. "You're *Her*," he says. He looks as if he's about to let go, but doesn't, he tightens his grip, holding her, keeping her arms' length away. He's nervous.

Then he slides one hand around her neck and slams her against the mailboxes. The metal corner cuts deep into her shoulder, right at the bone. Her head rings from its collision.

> Cold agony. Warm blood, turgid shoulder, staining her shirt, staining her sweater.
> She doesn't even flinch, but blinks a lot, to hide her dizziness, to not cry from pain, from sentiment.

225

"I love you," he says. He brings his other hand up and clutches her face, pushing in her cheeks, puckering her mouth, making her look like a fish. He forces her back again, against the mailboxes, hitting another spot, a different spot, though it feels the same. "I love you." The words point like a gun.

He says this not to hear her answer, but to say it. As if it were not a question. He lets her go.

Breathless, molten air, she responds anyway, crying, barely, from the pain, her voice cracked, parched. "I love you too."

The wound is so big, it gapes, it weeps,

it stimulates.

Her statement follows his as if it depended on it. As if it were variegated. As if she could doodle it inside a notebook. As if she hadn't already. But she's still careful to deconstruct all the connotations, all the history, all the *herstory*. Still careful to mean it.

Here, in the Glass Elevator, their words, given so often to others, make Nora feel like a fraud, a charlatan. Like they could erupt through the roof. Fly far, far away from here.

"I'm going home," he says. "I'm going home and I will call you tomorrow."

She nods, lets him leave. But as soon as he's out of sight she texts: You be him and I'll be her. Then I'll put on my pink pillbox hat and shoot you in the fucking head.

. . .

He does not call the next day. Nor the day after that. Nor the day after that.

In the interim, her bruise changed from purple, black, and blue to green and gray and pink. A constellation of popped blood vessels still dapple the wound, but the gash had closed up, precariously, with the kind of scab that doesn't induce the desire to pick at it.

...

On her bicycle, Nora gets lost in the rhythm of the city, especially when she rides without purpose. Straying from CVS, she pulls off Damen Street, by Jake's apartment. This time, glaring in front of his building, begging for her to stop, touch, write, she sees the forbidden yellow tape, the warning flags: an empty patch of wet cement. Like a child, she's drawn to its permanence. Its concreteness. She cannot resist.

She pulls over, drops her bike on its handlebars, lets the wheels spin themselves to stagnation. She searches for a stick, one blunt enough to withstand half-dried cement. She squats near the edge of the sidewalk and writes, **I LOVE YOU ANYWAY**. She writes it on the underside of the curb. Hoping one day as he walks home from her apartment, he'll see from across the street and recognize that this is a letter to him.

Back on the bicycle, she pedals into perversion. Placing her feet on the handlebars, she imagines herself young, eleven, the she that dropped the indefinite article. Nor in overalls embroidered with neon fruit. Immodest Nora, a little girl in a tulle skirt, cutting Barbies' hair and making them kiss. Nor, a conjunction, an adverb, a reference to herself in the negative, always split in two. Like her hair. In pigtails, bouncing. Running to daddy with a scraped knee. In this way she thinks of Jake as a father.

"Daddy! Daddy, someone hurt me!"

Daddy bends down and kisses her booboo. Tells her she's beautiful. And watches her ass bounce away.

...

The story is tired, as though she were parroting herself, Nora soaks herself in the cycle of monocarpic desire. The cycle of every time being their last. Enjoying the paphian ritual of preparing her body for sacrifice. They are to meet up at a bar of her choice. Idiotic excitement. Then. She waits. An hour ticks by. He texts. He's at another bar, with a friend. He wants her to come. Already drawn with eyeliner and bored from the metronomic click-clack of her heels pacing the floor, at the spark of a syphilitic idea, she concedes to give up, to give into this now corroded evening.

All dressed up and no where to go but *into*.

She wants to punish, to maim.

When she arrives, she looks at his mooning face from across the bar. He looks dumb and plain. Even the man, the usurper he is sitting with looks disinterested in his company. On the other side of this horseshoe bar, away from them, Nora sits down and orders a dirty martini. She asks the bartender to send Jake's friend a shot. The bartender sets it down in front of him, "Blowjob from the lady," he says, her request.

Jake recognizes this.

Both in stiff cotton collars, they simultaneously look up. Jake smiles then tries to take the drink from his friend, who won't give it up, but still, he raises his own pint of beer in salute, and sends some Patrón her way, garnished, of course, with lemon.

Before Nora shoots her clashing shot, both boys come to her.

"I'm so glad you came," Jake says, wrapping his arms around Nora in an awkward sort of way. Not as though he was claiming her, though maybe, but because she is sitting down, the effect had the look of a mother bent in discomfiture, hugging her protesting child.

"Nora," she nods to the man she had just offered fellatio.

"Aaron," he says. "And thanks for the shot."

"*My* shot, he means," Jake says, his eyes were puffy and purple, like a gamer's in winter. Like Nosferatu.

"Anytime," Nora says.

Nora is immediately attracted to Aaron, aware that this attraction is partly from inspiration, partly from fetishizing a fetish, and partly because he's tall, slender, sarcastic, bearded, and has crow's feet around his unpretentious eyes. He looks like a man next to Jake: calm, easy to swallow, easy to take, like a humid breeze in August. He reads Dostoevsky and owns an original Dr. Seuss print. Nora feels like a promiscuous teenager talking with Aaron, caught between his gaze and Jake's, whose peering ventures on leering venturing on glaring.

"We were just talking about opening a restaurant," Aaron says.

"Is that so?" Nora asks. "I didn't know you cared about the culinary arts."

"Do you?" Aaron asks.

"I love to eat! But I'm more into the written word, particularly conceptualism. When I saw Joseph Kosuth's *One and Three Chairs* at the Art Institute in high school it slayed me."

"Really? I think I remember that exhibit." Aaron says.

Jake might have said something as well.

"My friend and I own a gallery. We're really into art that emulates philosophy or theory. I like when the ideas claim all the power. The tools, the medium, the texture are all secondary affairs, an afterthought."

"Doesn't all art start with an idea?" Aaron asks.

"For a great many people aesthetics are far more important."

"You can't judge a book by its cover," Jake says.

"Well, but Jake, the printed page never claimed to be more aesthetically pleasing than the font it's encased in," Aaron says.

"I'll encase you in my font any day," Nora says, then adding, "but I wouldn't say never. In fact, no. Literature is far more—"

"Feeling a little bold, Nora?" Jake asks, a little late to the punch.

"Merely italicized, but not nearly enough. Get me another drink, *will ya, babe?*"

Ignoring her, Jake says, "I always liked Impressionism," then pressing his hand to his chest.

"Study nature then brood on it and treasure the creation which will result, which is the only way to ascend towards God."

"Yes, I remember you having a particular affinity for Gauguin. Apt, no doubt. But do you know why Gauguin desperately needed to seek shelter in the primitive—and let's not forget, prepubescent—bush? Because his grandmother was one of the founders of modern feminism, which at the time—and still, even now to some—frightens the hell out of men. And like all men with frustrated, pent-up Oedipal anxiety, castration anxiety, identity and existential *and midlife* crises, he violently turned on women and tried to heal his bruised and pummeled self-esteem by fucking bright-eyed girls who validated his manhood, who dutifully submitted and cooked an elaborate meal afterward. He wanted to turn away from everything 'artificial and conventional,' he said; this included the unnatural act of a woman thinking for herself. So poor Gauguin left Europe, fucked little girls, painted, became God, got Syphilis and died. Fuck Gauguin."

"I think the lady doesn't like Gauguin," Aaron says.

"God damn right. Now where is my fucking drink?" she says, thrusting her empty martini glass into Jake's chest.

"Chill out, Chopsticks. What's with the sand in your vagina?" Jake says before walking away, toward the bar, past the bar, then into the bathroom.

"What's your poison?" Aaron asks.

"Catholicism," she answers.

"'Your poison' means your drink. Haven't you ever seen *The Breakfast Club*?"

"Oh, right! I should probably switch to beer. I get drunk really easily these days. How about a Blue Moon? Or 312, if they have it!"

"I like you," Aaron says.

"I know," she says, "you're strangely, oddly falling in love with me this very moment. It's captivating."

"Oh yeah? And how can you tell?"

"You have honest eyes."

"How do you know Jake?"

"I'm his mistress."

"Are you serious?"

"Are you kidding? We've known each other since high school. Get me a drink and I'll give you my number."

"Sold," he says.

Feeling as though she were being filmed, being studied, sucking on her cigarette with smug satisfaction, hidden behind a brume of smoke, reminiscent of a mosquito net, she doesn't see Jake approaching, empty handed as it were, save for a single Jameson on the rocks for himself.

"What the fuck are you doing?"

"We had plans," she hisses.

"He's my boss, Nora. I couldn't just ditch him."

"You could have lied. You're good at that."

"Oh like you: *My friend and I own an art gallery*," he says the last part in high-pitched mimicry.

"We do. In a way. All the art we make in our apartment is for sale. Not like you'd know. When it comes to our personal lives neither of us is the expert on the other."

(Life is always the product of the decomposition of life.)

This is when Nora fantasizes that she's on television. *Lover, look at me!* Jake is unable to change the channel, his narrow eyes refusing to pull the plug, knowing that if they were to look away Nora would pounce like a panther, smearing her cunt all over Aaron's unsuspecting body. Anesthesia grips him by the shoulder and whispers, blowing a fast and furious swarm of hairy botflies into his ear, where they lay their eggs, burrowing deep into his itchy, splitting skin, hatching, munching, beating their virescent wings, plucking his vocal chords, tickling his prick.

This is when Nora bends over the pool table, her breasts grazing the green felt, bare clavicle flushed from the static electricity, she reaches, feels that warming tickle on her belly as her shirt rises, as she stretches toward the cube of blue chalk a finger traces the lace waistband of her neon pink panties, slips underneath the elastic, sending ripples of blooming, incandescent pleasure throughout her body. Assuming it's Jake, she backs up into a thicker erection, she slowly erects herself in breathy fricatives, backing into Aaron's broad, hardened, flexing pectorals. Jake is across the table, gripping his cue, glued to channel Nora, who licks her lips as she presses her ass into Aaron's cock.

"Your shot, Jake," Nora says, peeling herself away.

"Three ball in the corner pocket."

Nora jazzes her hands while still gripping her bottle of 312. Jake makes the shot. Aaron slaps Nora's ass and says, "I'm going to the bar. Anyone want?"

"Get me another Jack and Coke."

"Another, dude? Already?"

"*Yeah.* Do you need money?"

Aaron waves him off then vanishes.

At this Nora starts singing Madonna: "*You put this in me. So now what? So now what? Wanting. Needing. Waiting. For you, to Justify my love. My love—*"

"You better stop this shit, Nora."

"Or else what?"

"He's my fucking boss! And he's a nice guy! He's a serious monogamist. He wants to get married, settle down, have kids. He falls in love really easily. You can't do this to him."

"Maybe I really like him."

"Stop acting like a cunt," he raises his voice. "You like me. You're addicted to me. I can't fuck you if you're sleeping with him—"

"You can't fuck me now!"

"You don't know how badly I want to."

"How badly?" She says in her low, raspy, vampish voice, walking toward him, daring him.

He takes a step back. She takes another forward, forcing him into a corner. "He'll be right back," Jake says.

Nora turns to the bar and scans for Aaron's rusted head of hair. "I don't see him. Do you see him? I'm sure he's in the bathroom choking his bishop."

"You have to knock this shit off!"

"You could've had this. You could've had all of this. I know what you like, Jake. I know what you want. You go home and titty-fuck Lindsay tonight. You give her another pearl necklace to drape around her soft, white neck. You tell her you love her with the satisfaction—and the relief—that tonight you don't have to wash off my perfume in the sink, you don't have to wonder whether or not she can smell me in your hair. You go home thankful that you were a good little boy tonight. The ever-faithful husband! A chaste testament to your love. That's why you brought him, isn't it? To keep yourself in check? To throw an obstacle in front of your temptation. Well, bravo! Let's keep building this wall. Brick by fucking brick," she says, lips so close all he had to do was lean forward, take her. She would leave with him. She would leave Aaron in the bathroom, beers in hand, wandering around the bar looking for them, for her.

"It's too late," Jake says.

"It's never too late," Nora says.

She grabs his dick, can feel its bulging veins through his slacks. "I'm so wet and swollen you could just slide your cock into me, let me wrap myself around you, suck you into my soul, like a thousand tongues gliding, kissing, sucking. Total bedlam. Impale me with your madness. Claim me as your own. Or suffer the consequences. You have about a minute to decide. Maybe more, maybe less."

"He just came out of the bathroom."

She leans into his ear, whispers, "Remember, this is all your fault."

"Is this revenge?" he asks.

She laughs loudly. Loud enough to diffuse the heat of their exchange.

"What's so funny?" Aaron asks with drinks for everyone. With trembling fingers Jake takes his Jack and Coke and gulps down half of it while Nora tells a joke. "Why *do* the ladies love Jesus?" she asks Aaron.

"I don't know," he says.

"Because he's hung like this!" Nora stretches out her arms and nearly whacks some stranger in the head with her beer. She starts laughing again, puts her hand on Aaron's chest. "I thought I was going to piss myself when he said it. You should've seen the look on that girl's face." She points to a woman with a high-collared dress, then spills a little of her beer on her pants. "Ope!" she says.

"Some joke," Aaron says to Jake. "I've never heard you tell that one around the office."

"I don't want to offend anyone," Jake says.

"Yes, you're always so worried about what everybody else thinks," Aaron nudges Nora in the chest.

"What does that mean?" Nora asks.

"Well, let's just say, Jake's has no problem dipping into company ink."

"Oooh! Scandal! What about your blushing bride?"

"Aaron…"

Aaron holds his palms up, "I'm just saying! And dude, we're in good company, if Nora saw Becky she'd be proud of you too."

"So proud," Nora says. "My little boy's all growed up." She pinches his cheek but he turns sharply away.

"Does anyone else feel like going to the Green Mill?" Aaron asks.

"What an excellent idea!" Nora exclaims.

"Maybe I should go home," Jake says.

"You sure? Oh, come on!"

"Let him get home to his wifey."

"Yeah," Jake says, spirits returning. "Lindsay is expecting me. Whenever you and I go out, she says you always keep me out way too late."

"All right. She'll be so proud of you. Tell her you finally found me a girl worth meeting her."

"Oh, yes. Tell her, Jake."

"You two lovebirds have a goodnight," Jake says.

"But not too good," he says to Aaron. "Let's keep Ms. Childers an honest woman. You wouldn't want to upset her boyfriend."

Aaron looks to Nora, not angrily, not shocked, but slightly confused. "He's right," Nora says. "My boyfriend's huge and mean and super jealous, especially of successful, good-looking men. We should watch it. He has a habit of spying on me. We'll have to be super careful."

"Let him see! I want the world to know of our love!"

"We musn't!" Nora says, pressing up against him.

"Aaron," Jake says, fist out. Aaron repeats the gesture, then they bump fists, just like Nora's seen on television. Jake then runs his fingers throughout Nora's hair, mussing it up, yanking it a little. "Goodnight, Nora," he says with droopy, glassy eyes, pleas popping from his irises, he yanks at her heart, bubbling her stomach, unsure, for the first time tonight, if she had gone too far.

Fuck it.

...

2:10am: Meet me 2 blocks down in 10.

2:13am: Bukowski says it better than I could: In that drunken place/you would/like to hand your heart to her/and say/touch it/but then/give it back.

2:16am: Nora, I should've just met you tonight. I'm sorry. I didn't think you'd mind. Next time we'll meet wherever you want. At your place even. I get it now.

2:19am: I want you, I do. I've always wanted you. It's always been you. You made your point tonight. Don't go home with him. Please.

2:24am: I'm leaving with or without you.

2:35am: Fuck.You.

2:57am: Are you with him right now? Did you go home with him?!?!?

236

3:33am: You are UNFUCKING believable!!!!
This is a new low.

...

Hungover. Elated. Ashamed. A note on her dresser: "You've won me over, and you have my shirt. ♥ Aaron." Nora curls into a ball. Throws up. Puts an icepack to her temples. She takes the battery out of her phone, throws it into the toilet. Jiji takes a picture of it, then gets an idea. They throw an old cellular phone in the toilet, take a picture, then print it out on their black and white jalopy printer. After writing, **Ooops!** in red lipstick along the top, they tape it to their living room wall next to the other pieces they've painted/constructed, each with a price sticker next to it. This one is currently priced at twenty dollars.

...

"You said it was just a high school fling. I don't need to know any details." This he says casually, like he means it, as if a sentence could be a shrug. He thinks of Nora like a fresh diary page. He doesn't want to know her proclivities. He doesn't want to think of her with another man, especially one he knows, someone he works with.

Relief. Stress. Distrust. A sort of miasmic soup. He won't let her purify herself, or the beginning of their relationship. All the same. This relationship is pure— *unadulterated pollution*—smut. Yet she likes him, she really likes him and this gnaws at her intestines.

...

Aaron and Nora date like any other jejune couple would. They have enough in common to sustain a perfectly average inchoate affair, one based on complementary qualities as opposed to fire. They go to the movies. They go out to dinner. They have drinks afterwards. They both like salmon, Peggy Lee, and quiet bars. He's more conventional than she is, preferring his spaces glossy as opposed to gritty, but it's no difference. Nora's mother likes him. It's all fine, this is how people meet, through friends, she justifies, and besides, they consider themselves casual. He's getting over a long relationship and she may be moving out of state for graduate school. On the weekends, she waitresses. Sometimes they meet up afterwards at the Green Mill, the jazz bar with a tunnel that Al Capone used to sneak through. Nora doesn't know what he does in his spare time. She doesn't ask. She doesn't care. She's a filler, a girl he fucks while he finds himself, something white men in their twenties are always losing. But Aaron is in his thirties, and though he says he's been through the necessary psychic expeditions, there's still something about him that seems undercooked to Nora. It's not that he seems in his twenties—there's a great deal about him skirting the knife's edge of middled aged—it's more of a reticence to fully mature. She doesn't know the details of his psychogenic baggage, and she doesn't care to. This is perfect for her. He doesn't interfere with her art, her reading, her nights with Jiji. She sees him twice a week, at most. Any more and it would be too much.

. . .

Why can't he be you?
      When he lays me on my stomach, spreads my legs, my buttocks, he licks my cunt and I look at my desk, to my desk chair where I imagine you're sitting, of your own volition, though flashes of you bound at the wrists, hands tied behind the back of the chair, watching me, watching him stick his tongue up my ass, lay it flat against my labia, he lifts my hips and inserts himself. I grip the edge of the mattress and grunt, looking into your eyes, water leaks from them. I don't belong to you. Oh, but I do! Watch him fuck me. Without touching yourself. Watch me wish it was you. My leg in the air, draped over his shoulder, you're hypnotized by his clenched buttocks, blocking your sight of me.

You move, come to the side of the bed. Take my
hand. Let me press yours against my lips, caressing
that space in between your fingers. Get him off of
me, Jacob. Get this imposter off of me. Take his
place. Come inside me. I miss you. Come! But you
can't. You're impotent. You're afraid. This makes
you angry. You take pleasure in my pain. In the
pain he causes me. You want him to push faster,
harder. You want him to tear my cunt and smack me
across the mouth. You want him to rape me in half.
But he can't do that. He doesn't have it in him.
But you do.

...

"Maybe you went too far this time," Jiji says.

"What is that supposed to mean?"

"A person can only take so much. Maybe you
alienated him beyond repair this time. You fucked with his
life, *with his work.* Could you imagine if he fucked with your
work? If he had taken away, or somehow messed with your
Elaine Scarry book, like he just removed fifty pages? Your
notes? Your marginalia? Or, somehow papers—*topics*—
were just off limits? Like your Dante paper: what if you
couldn't write that anymore? What if he just took that
away? You'd flip out."

"First, his job is stupid, not the same at all—"

"I'm not saying they're comparable," Jiji says,
holding up her hands, palms facing Nora.

"Second, he's practically engaged to Lindsay. He
has no right. Why is who I sleep with a much bigger deal
than who he sleeps with. In high school we all knew
everybody. So, he slept with people I was friends with and
I blew a friend of his, none of it mattered. And why are
you all on his side? He's a complete douche bag."

"I'm just saying, he's a person nonetheless, and you
treat him like shit. Granted, he treats you badly too, but
you both deserve what you get. You may or may not be in
love with him—I think you are—I think you're whole

dating life has revolved around moments that Jake gave you. I'm not saying he's not in love with you—I'm sure he is. But in a different way. Albeit a fucked up way, but you can't punish someone for what you already knew! It's like you're suddenly changing the rules."

"Things are different now. Lindsay is serious, she's really in love with him—she's planning a life with him! I feel awful about her. You know that. And I don't think it's fair. But we both know it's not just me. He's a whore. A total whore."

"I only know what you tell me."

"Do you know how many women he's slept with? Like sixty seven!"

"Does that make you jealous?"

"I'm not jealous of Lindsay, not really, and I didn't used to get jealous of the others. I knew I was his bottom bitch, *the preferred mistress*; I knew above all he wanted me." She pauses, thinks of the unknown bitches, she imagines them much more beautiful than she is, in a cliché sort of way: blonde, leggy, perfect skin, flawless, hairless, fair: his type. "Sometimes I get jealous," she says.

"Like you said, things are different now. The stakes are higher. And now you've gone and dragged Aaron into this. He's falling in love with you."

"He is not."

"He could be. And you could give a shit about him too! You can't treat human beings that way! It's a horrible thing to do! Do you even understand what Lindsay is going through? The pain? The suspicion? Paranoid that your lover loves another more than you? You're torturing that poor girl!"

Nora's blood presses into her chest, rushes to her face, her ears. Tinnitus. She clenches her jaw. The fight or flight hormones have taken over, for both of them.

"What exactly are you angry about? Me? My life style? Is this about you and Lej?"

"God fucking damn it, Nora. Get over yourself!" she says, then leaves the room.

Nora is left with $8^{1}/_{2}$ on pause and a bowl of half eaten popcorn. The high completely gone. Another train goes by. She throws the remote against the wall. It breaks, and frightens the hell out of Rufus.

. . .

"We aren't friends anymore," Aaron says. "Not that I care. I mean, how can he even be mad at me? He's engaged to Lindsay."

The record scratches, the earth stops, its core flutters, arrhythmically.

Act aloof. Disinterested. Nonplussed. Just nod.

She can't. Her eyes look funny, like the muscles are straining.

"Really? When did that happen?"

What a stupid thing to ask. When shouldn't matter.

"Before we met. Odd. You didn't know? That poor girl. I mean, the asshole cheats on her all the time. She doesn't deserve it. She probably doesn't know, but if she does, she doesn't show it. She's so classy, a regular Jackie O. But he's no JFK, always bragging about this chick or that chick, some of the stories are just gross too. I don't know what you ever saw in the guy."

Aaron comes to her with slander. Things *she should know about Jake*. Most things she already knows. He's a pervert. A fetishist. Nobody at the office likes him or trusts him. He pretends to be a swinger. He meets women on the internet, "women two shades away from hookers," *whatever the fuck that means*. He fucks them in uncomfortable ways then never calls them again.

241

Nora listens. Each word, each phrase, is an insult to her. An insult by proxy. Aaron's disparaging her love, the one that she chose to love, her decision, a small part of herself. Within this gossip, Jake's name, his originality, is taken away. She is reminded of high school, things Salo would say.

Aaron is attempting to reduce Jake, to render him bloodless, a common surrogate. He is only what Aaron says he is: a sexual deviant, a monster. Nora does not understand. She cannot minimize Jake, who, for her, is always filled out, full, a fully fleshed character safely tucked away in her imagination. Aaron is telling her that he has written Jake off. He suggests she does the same, if she hasn't already. Has she?

"Yes. You know that," she says.

Aaron is telling her these things for his own mental health. A new piece for her mind, for his peace of mind. Revenge. His words fall limp. He cannot win Nora over. She looks out the window, a pretense for depth. She sleeps with him from her dysthymic haze. Every one of her orgasms is unfaithful.

...

Re: Why can't he be you?
When you shave it's like plucked chicken skin. Lumpy and protesting, it stings you and betrays your desire for perfection. It only calls attention to the violence you'll endure to make your beastliness alluring. I prefer your chaos. Slick, black curls, like the thorny brambles guarding a sleeping princess, protecting your soft, velvety interior, your shapeless lips, a vast ocean between your legs, a disgusting mess, bleeding and soupy. It ensnares me. You ensnare me. I'm tangled.

...

"I've got a headache," Nora tells Aaron, weighing her options of pain relief.

"You get a lot of headaches," he says.

"Could you just get me an aspirin?" She says, deciding on skipping the Vicodin, ergo, skipping the adjacent lecture she is sure Aaron would deliver again. She'll see how the aspirin goes, and when that inevitably fails to mitigate any pain, she'll pop a Vicodin in secret, hoping that it's not too late, hoping she won't have to sacrifice the rest of the evening to Imitrex. Hoping Aaron won't see her in such a vulnerable state of agony.

Though she's not terribly hungry, she's chopping carrots. And her hands are wet.

He goes to her bedroom. She doesn't direct him. He should know where her pill bottles are.

After a minute, he comes back and hands her a round, white pill.

Its inscription reads, I - 2, but just barely, so has it been eroded.

She sticks her tongue out, as if she were ready to receive communion.

"I found this one in your jewelry box," he says.

She abruptly shuts her mouth. It makes a clicking noise. "Not that one!"

Aaron doesn't understand her panic. She makes sure her hands are dry, then takes the pill into them, cupping it as loosely as possible. Reading its scuffs and smudges as if they could predict the future.

"What the fuck is wrong with you?" he asks.

From her trance, she looks up, befuddled, lies. "Oh, this was in my grandmother's purse. It's a sentimental thing. Like the last thing she gave me before she died or something…" She trails off.

This generic Ibuprofen, this special, magical, metaphorical pill has sat with her, has traveled with her, undigested, for nearly ten years. Because the pill reads I-2, it was as if it crystallized, articulated what she was already, back then, beginning to think. That he was her *other*. That because of him she had to create a second self, another I, the dark, courtesan side of her.

That he was going to cause her a world of pain.

This Ibuprofen, a generic gesture, inverted by her into inviolable love. One pill from a bottle of fifty. But a gift meant more to her than a mere four hours of temporary pain relief. She endured the headache, even pretended to take the pill. So when he wasn't looking she put the pill in the front pocket of her jeans, the small useless pocket inside the pocket, thinking that someday she'll have to take this pill because of him. That this pill would alleviate any suffering, any wound Jake would cause. Now it has grown into something more. She thinks of it like a suicide pill. Once consumed, there's no turning back. Once ingested, her and Jake would be over.

Thinking Nora misses her grandmother, Aaron mutters something like sympathy then leaves her to her thoughts, her grief, and goes to fetch an actual aspirin.

The snow finally begins melting.

. . .

"Oh, what the fuck?" Nora asks, backing away from them, backing herself into a corner, near the juke box. They smile enthusiastically. They laugh and continue their game of Buck Hunter. She feels foolish, displayed. Aaron squints one eye and pulls the trigger of his blue plastic gun.

Jake approaches her. He's wearing glasses with thick, black rims. They don't look like him. He looks sensitive and nerdy. He takes her arm and pulls her into him. He hugs her. "It's good to see you, Norabora."

"I like your glasses," she says. "Now you'd finally fit in at the Deadwood."

"I'm still wearing a collared shirt," he says.

"Ah! But you could be doing so *ironically*!"

"Your go," Aaron says, looking to Jake then to Nora, whom he hugs and beckons to the nearly deserted bar. There's only one other group of people here. They're boisterous but don't give the impression of good friends, more like office buddies, sharing an awkward happy hour. Five guys and two girls, one of which seems very bored. They give off the air that they're leaving soon.

"I thought we were going to the movies," she says when out of earshot.

"He wanted to see you."

"I thought you and he weren't friends."

"I just thought we should all…" at this he shuts his eyes and playfully shakes his head, "clear the air."

"You're acting strange. I don't like it."

"You said wanted a sadist."

"No, I said I was more masochistic, and that I couldn't date another masochist because I didn't want to compete for sexual attention. I think you have a hard time understanding me."

"What do you expect? I only have a quarter of the details."

"You never asked."

"I'm asking now, sweetheart!"

"Ugh!" Nora takes her martini and walks to a table where she can set her things down, collect her thoughts, and smoke a cigarette. The table is barely cleaned, covered in carvings and graffiti, and merely wiped with a wet rag that has been soaking for hours in a dirty bucket of bleach water. There's mold in the corners and splashes of dried beer on the walls. It smells musty, like an ashtray in a bathhouse and the tiled floor recently given a once-over with evergreen scented cleaning products is painfully assaulting to her burgeoning headache. An unforgiving golden light bathes the bar in an Edward Hopper glow replete with alienating shadows and the overwhelming feeling of premature autumn. Her phone vibrates. From Douchbag: `Sero te amavi`.

She writes Jiji: `Quick, go to Google, translate: Sero te amavi`.

"You're going to hurt him, you know." Jake sits down next to her, nods to Aaron whose seated at the bar wearing a four hundred yard stare.

"This is all so annoying. What do you want?"

"I want you."

"Knock it off."

"I've always wanted you."

"Why are you here? Does he know about the emails? Does he know about us?"

"I haven't told him anything."

"Why am I asking *you*?" she says, widening her eyes and looking at an imaginary person to her left. As if his chicanery just dawned on her. Then her phone vibrates.

`So late have I loved thee.`

"Oh God damn it."

"Who are you writing?"

"Jiji. I'm asking her to come down here."

"You need back-up? Can't handle us boys on your own again? Come on, Nora, I know you can take us. I know you can take both of us at once, with both arms tied behind your back."

"Is that what this is? You want to fuck Aaron under some pretense of a threesome with me? By all means, have at him! He's kind of vanilla for your tastes, but knock yourself out. Don't let me get in the way."

"If that's the only way I can be with you—"

"And what are we discussing?" Aaron asks.

"Wittgenstein," says Nora.

"You," says Jake.

"Dare I say, Wittgenstein is the more interesting subject," Aaron says. "Can I bum one of those, darling? We can leave for a movie right after this drink."

"Don't you know Nora at all? Once she's had a drink she has to keep drinking to ward off the migraine. You'd think he'd know this," Jake says the last line looking exclusively at Nora.

As she sits here, Nora is nothing but a throbbing labia to either of them. A trophy, a vagina to be won. A vagina that gets migraines.

"Migraines are a myth, one of her many yarns. Just take an aspirin and get over yourself," Aaron says.

"Ope! Now you've pissed her off!" Jake says.

"Migraines are a disease, *Fuckface*! And you hate smoking," Nora says to Aaron.

"There's always a first time for everything."

"Here! Here!" Jake says.

"Indeed. Look at the sparks between you two!" Aaron says. "It's hypnotic to watch."

"Stop acting like an idiot," Nora snaps. "Both of you!"

Aaron's grin becomes clownish, manipulative. He enjoys exposing her. He enjoys the conviviality of the moment and orders a round of lemon drop shots.

"Nora hates lemon drops," Jake says.

"But I love 'em. You can have hers."

"What's mine is yours," Nora gestures to Jake. She takes out her phone, texts. Too soon did I love thee.

Jake doesn't reach into his pocket. She admires his restraint, always has.

She then gets up and goes to the juke box. Just like that, Aaron can no longer see her; he and her are back to back, which means her backside is directly facing Jake. She inserts one dollar and flips the CDs, watching the spectrum of light play on the laser disks. Until she finds something she likes, something she can use, something from the past. She presses 0871, The Cowboy Junkies, *Sweet Jane,* from *Natural Born Killers,* one of their early dates. She lays her elbows, her forearms, her palms flat on the glass. She begins circling her hips in a figure eight, dancing a lemniskate to the adagio, methodic melody.

. . .

The lemniskate. The symbol. The emotional linchpin.
Shaped like a figure 8, or a knot, or the bow of a ribbon.
Unboundedness.
The infinite, an unbound limit.
Forever and ever and ever and ever and ever and ever.
Around and around and around and around and around.
The twelve senses of the lemniskate, starting at the top,
then snaking down and around then back: Sense of
hearing; Sense of speech or word; Sense of thought; Sense
of touch; Sense of being; Sense of motion; Sense of
balance; Sense of smell; Sense of taste;
Sense of self or "I"; Sense of vision; Sense of heat.
The lemniskate as a numerical, real, definable increment,
growing beyond any assigned value.
An unbound universe. An unbound woman.
An unbound flood.

. . .

The woman inside the juke box sings softly, sultrily, like dark chocolate. The combination is like slowly making love. She knows Jake is watching her. She can feel him through her plaid pants. *I love you, Mickey!* The back of her knees tingle, a parade of gooseflesh breaks out. This is how she wants him to love her: slowly, rhythmically, infinitely. Without being able to. Perpetual anticipation.

Like metal poured into a glass, opaque, unattainable.

When he used to touch her he was always so rough, so angry, so desperate. He takes, he owns, he conquers. When he watches her, he's forced to relinquish control. Right now, he's subject to her tempo. Like a cat, she tortures. Obliterating everything that matters to him. His friend. His job. His fiancée.

"Why would I bring the woman I live with around the woman I want to sleep with? It's insulting," Jake says, as Nora sits back down at the table.

> The glass has been broken, windows shattered from a torrential soprano. They are all seated within the secret, its breath quickens from the intrusion, like the protesting cunt of a virgin, its muscles strain from the invasion. It's looking for a way out. A way to be left alone.

"Hey! Hey! This is ridiculous—"

"Shush. The men are talking," Aaron says.

"That's it," Nora says.

"Stop being so sensitive. We're all friends here. We're just having a friendly conversation, that I, for one, am terribly interested in," Aaron says. "I mean, aren't you? The guy is about to pour his heart out to you. Maybe you guys can finally consummate the relationship."

A quick laugh, "Okay, Aaron. Let's clear the air! Jake and I have known each other for years—"

"And I've wanted her from the second I laid eyes on her, but I never had the courage to tell her how I really felt," Jake says.

"You've got to be kidding!" Nora says.

"Nora," Jake takes her hand. She pulls it away.

Aaron tisks his tongue and shakes his head. "Are you saying the feelings aren't mutual?" he asks. "Aren't you

249

even curious? I wouldn't mind if you two would like to experiment. I give you my full permission."

"I don't need your permission for anything."

"I didn't mean to imply that, my dove. I simply meant that I wouldn't break up with you."

"Have you asked her about Brian?" Jake says.

"Who's Brian?" Aaron asks, all smiles, as if he were on a game show.

"I lost my virginity to Brian. And you know what they say, you never quite get over your first love."

"I heard it was your second," Jake says.

"Who was your second love?" Aaron asks.

"Fuck this Spanish Inquisition!"

"Thou shalt not suffer a witch to live!" Aaron says with vigor, in a foreign, robust tone; an imitation of Jake's virile humor, Nora thinks.

"Fuck you," she points to Aaron. "And fuck you too!" she says to Jake. "I'm leaving."

"Okay. Okay. Okay. We'll stop. We'll stop," Aaron laughs. "Come here." He wraps his arm around her, pulling her close, and kisses the top of her head. She can smell his aftershave, it reminds her of her father. "Let's just hang out, with or without Lindsay—"

"And with or without Jiji," Jake offers.

"With or without Lindsay, *or* Jiji, and have a good time. A round of tequila, on me!" Aaron gets up and goes to the bar.

"God, you're beautiful."

"Why are you making this so hard on me?" she asks.

"Why are you making this so hard on *me*? I told you I was sorry. I told you he was unstable. I told you I wanted you. What more do you want? What proof do you need?"

"I told you we can't do this anymore. That we needed to date, get it out of our system. I want this charade to end. I want you out of my life."

"No, you don't," Jake says without hesitation.

"You're the one who needs me."

"I need you like I need a hole in the head."

"All right then, it's settled."

"But I want you like I want a hole in the head."

"I get it. I'm your death drive, your cigarette, your heroin. I get it—" Nora says.

"You and I both want the same things. We want the white picket fence, the two-point-five kids and a dog—or in your case—cat. We want the family, the career, the calm, placid life of American success. But we also want the danger. Lust so powerful it steals your breath and ices your veins. If we were together we would implode in an orgy of savage hedonism."

"That's not what I want! I want to be rid of you! I want to love you up close so I can tire of you! So I can demystify you."

"Together we can have it all," he says. "Your choice."

"Well, they're all the same, but what the hell." Aaron bends at the knee to give Nora first pick of tequila shots.

"Hold on one second, I'll be right back," Jake says.

"Are you mad at me?" Aaron asks.

"Aaron, I don't understand. Why did you want to *clear the air*? Why didn't you just ask me? I would've told you anything."

"I just wanted to be sure. He told me he was in love with you, that he was always in love with you from a distance, and that you and I together is killing him."

"And you believe him?"

"Why wouldn't I? I know we have our differences, but he's a good guy, Nora."

"For one, you told me he wasn't. With all the internet fucking and the what-not. For two, he's engaged! He's already in love. For three, why the fuck do his feelings matter? You're prevaricating."

"He forgot the lemons," Jake says, sitting back down.

"My humble apologies, my dove."

Nora digs her nails into her wrists.

"To friendship!" Aaron says, glass in the air. Nora licks that fleshy place between her thumb and index finger, the side of her clenched fist, and then pours salt on the moistened skin.

"Here's mud in your eye while I look at your girl," Jake says, winking at Nora.

"Here's to women's kisses, and to whiskey, amber clear; not as sweet as a woman's kiss, but a whole lot more sincere!" Aaron yells with that same virility then downs his shot. Jake and Nora follow, neither of the boys wince, but Nora does. This is only her second drink of the night. She looks around for something to chase, a dirty martini being the least appetizing, she grabs the nearest beer, Jake's beer, out of habit. Out of sincerity.

"Let's do another, shall we?"

"No! Give me at least ten minutes," Nora says, as she puts a cigarette in her mouth. Jake is quick to light it.

"Oh, bartender!" Aaron yells. "Another round!"

A man rolls in a giant piece of equipment and begins setting up the karaoke machine. Night has arrived, and so have the customers, bringing new scents of perfumes, sweat, and sunblock. Because of Jake's charisma, coupled with Aaron's newfound careless confidence, their table has taken on a group of sun-kissed Australians, each eager to share their traveling experiences. A friendly cloud of anecdotes mushrooms above them, dissolving the tension, leaving Nora free to swagger about the bar, martini glass in hand, seducing anyone who will talk to her. Chairs gathering around their table at obtuse angles, Aaron is swallowed by the charm of the Aussies. Jake keeps checking his phone, and responding to someone other than Nora, who currently is talking with a light-haired, American-born German man in his forties about the meaning of life, which is simply, according to him, live and let live, a motto surely in response to some tragedy that befell him years before, or maybe as an apology for, or just to distance himself from, national socialism. Nora feigns interest, nodding her head, accepting another drink, batting her eyes and asking questions.

"Love," the German says. "Love is the ultimate good."

"Can I borrow her for a second?" Jake asks.

"If the lady so desires," the German says.

"Excuse me," Nora politely says, as if she'll be right back.

"She's a smart one," the German says. "Sharp as a tack."

"Don't I know it," Jake says.

"That guy is too much of a hippie even for me! And condescending! Blech! Smart as a tack? *Asshole*!" Nora says when they're a safe distance away.

"Leave with me."

"Are you nuts?"

"He won't notice. Look at him. I think he's even taken a liking to one of the Aussies. I don't blame him. What man isn't a sucker for a supple blonde?" he says, then reaches into his pocket and sighs.

"Who's that? One of your supple blondes? Becky? Some other skank you picked up off the internet?"

"Hardly. Lindsay's pissed I'm here with you."

"How does she know that?"

"She called earlier, asked to talk to Aaron."

"What for?"

He doesn't respond right away. He's typing.

"I guess Aaron invited her out tonight over an email he sent today at work. He thought all four of us could get together. I had told her he and I were going out. I didn't say anything about you, which made her all curious that Aaron's girlfriend got to come but she couldn't. So I had to make something up, I said, I was out with a bunch of people from work and that you and Aaron weren't staying, but when he got on the phone with her, he asked her if she had ever heard of you before you and he started dating. She said she hadn't, and then she said she would call back."

"Did she?"

"No, but she sent this," he says, flashing her his phone. Have you slept with her?!?!?!?

"Jesus, you never told her about us?"

"Why the fuck would I? Do you tell your lovers?"

"I'm not engaged."

"I'm not either."

"What the fuck! Between you and him I don't know what to believe!"

"Believe this: leave with me now. I'll get us a hotel. I'll drive to Madison. I've got to have you tonight, Nora. It has to be tonight."

"Why? What's so special about tonight?"

Aaron steps in between the two of them. "So," he says. "So, I'm not supposed to let you two be alone. Direct orders."

"From who?" Nora asks.

"From Mrs. Noyes."

"Did she call you?" Jake asks.

"Yeah, I just got off the phone with her."

"God damn it. Excuse me," Jake says, walking away, phone pressed into his ear.

"Come on, let's go," Aaron says.

"I don't want to leave."

"No, why would you?"

"You're the one who invited him!" Nora hisses.

"Nora, I see the way you look at him. I see it. You look so happy when you talk to him. It's not right for me to get in the middle of such things."

"Such things?"

"If you want to be with me, leave with me."

"What about your Sheila?"

"What?" Aaron shakes his head. "I could've fallen in love with you."

"No, you couldn't have. You want to love someone. You just want to be in love."

"Doesn't everybody?"

"Is this guy bothering you?" the German interjects.

"What? No. He's my friend."

"Friend. Okay," Aaron says then walks away, to the man at the stage.

Nora sinks into her chair. Jake approaches her.

"God fucking damn it. Leave me alone."

"I called a taxi. It'll be on the corner two blocks down in ten minutes. Come away with me for the night, for the hour. I don't care. Just come with me."

"Jake, I can't."

"You can. I'll see you in ten minutes." He turns and walks away, walks right out of the door and into obscurity.

With unsteady hands she approaches the bar and orders a shot of Patrón then drinks it without any training wheels. Staring ahead, ignoring the noise around her as much as she can, she tries to think. Aaron has just become her executioner. Demanding a confession, trial by fire, Jake speaks as a voice from inside her, cooing her, lulling her. *Softly shall you sleep in my arms.* A fruitless act of cruelty. No one's learned anything. Not even Aaron, who's now French kissing one of the Australians. As if it were a sign, a key, a code. Pain for the sake of pain. She has failed. Meaninglessness chokes her. This whole experiment was a testament to sadism. She thought she could play both sides against the middle of herself, circumvent the deleterious force within her, protruding from her neck, pulling her by the hair. She can't believe she's crying. She looks to the door as it opens, her disobedient blood rushes to her face, leaks from her eyes, when she sees that it isn't him, she collapses, slamming her head up against the brass rail lining the bar. Her German friend appears again, "Are you all right?"

"Fuck!" she runs outside. Looks for him down the right side of the block, then runs left. Running, her bones pounding the pavement where her flesh deteriorates, she runs a tightrope, chasing the chase of needlessness, refusing to turn around, to confirm that he isn't following her. The bluebird flapping inside her heart transforms into a cawing raven. She rounds the corner and falls into the grass, skinning her knee, beating her palms against the earth like a madwoman. People walk by and whisper. She digs her nails into the dirt. Shaking, sobbing, she's an hemorrhage inside an excavation. Until she picks herself up, as if it were all an act, so embarrassed, she holds herself together, stitched with thick black thread and a fat needle. Like a doll, her seams are showing. She walks home and removes all her clothes. Nude to cover her nakedness. Hiding in plain sight. She turns off her phone and takes a shower. Hugging her teddy bear, she curls into a fetal position on top of her purple comforter, and spins herself to sleep.

Two texts follow an unwelcome alarm.

Douchebag 12:34am: I will always love you from afar.

Aaron 1:15am: I think we should see other people.

...

The following night, beginning at 1am...

HIM: I have the next three hours to myself. How should I spend them?

HER: Spend them however you like.

HIM: I asked you, and hurry, time is ticking down.

HER: I'm at home, sober, and in no mood for this.

HIM: Okay. I get it. I'm not drunk either. But I want to sleep with you. Now.

HER: Way to charm a lady.

HIM: I'm not trying to charm you right now. It's an instinct. Nothing changes if you say yes or no. I just had to let you know.

HER: I'd like to sleep with Jon Stewart. It's an instinct. I just wanted to let you know.

HIM: Forget it. You wanted honesty and now you mock me.

HER: I asked for honesty a long time ago. Now, I'm confused. I don't know what I want from you.

HIM: What's there to be confused about? I have two and half hours now. Do you want me to come over? I believe you do.

HER: I will hang out with you but I'm not going to fuck you because you feel carnal.

HIM: Then why would you fuck me tonight?

HER: If carnality is the only reason for this sudden rapture then forget it, but if you want to hang out then fine.

HIM: If you can tell me that there will ever be a time when we don't and won't physically want each other then you're right and I'm wrong.

HER: It's not so black and white. And don't bullshit me, you are clearly drunk.

HIM: We (Nora and Jake) are the best sexual relationship we'll EVER have with anyone. Care to deny that?

HIM: We are not getting married, so what is it?

HER: What is what?

HIM: Our relationship is purely sexual - half mind and half body.

HER: Whatever you love me.

HIM: (1 of 2) I'm going to ask you because I have just two and half hours left to myself. If you come to the door wearing nylon stockings and a garter belt with a flowery b

HIM: (2 of 2) ra and a robe over it all I'm so there.

HER: You said you wanted to come over. I'm not going to entice you now. What the hell is going on with you?

HIM: Entice and admit I'm right. If I come over I'm going straight for your pants.

HER: I don't hear back from you for months, then last night, now this. And you told me not to wear any pants. You're just all over the map.

HIM: Okay. I don't want to have sex, just make out, maybe oral if I'm lucky. This is way too planned. Can I just come over?

HER: No. This is all weird. Hang out with me tomorrow.

HIM: I can't. I have a wedding to go to, and I'm in the bridal party. It's tonight or bust. And. Time. Is. Ticking.

HER: I will not be rushed, or squeezed in for a dirty quickie before your curfew.

HIM: You're so sensitive lately. I'm going to bed. Goodnight Nora.

HER: What the fuck is wrong with you?

...

She sends him an email, 3:14am:

Dearest Jake,

My journal somehow seems suddenly insufficient to the power of dialogue, and this still lacks the essential dialectic, but it seems cleaner.

Every relationship I ever had was a recreation of Brian, a re-enactment of the traumatic experience relived, re-interpreted, and still grossly misunderstood. The boys. The Boyfriend: Archetype no1. Brian. Tony. Ben. Brent. Brian. Aaron. Picture your name slithering through the punctuation marks. Your name, scuffed and nicked all of them, after Brian.

When we first met we were both in love, with other people, with other people that we're still getting over. I took all the pain and suffering Brian caused me and threw it into your body. You caught it, swallowed it, and reciprocated. As I swallowed your cum, I became infected.

You saved me from the pain of Brian, only to replace it with perpetual yearning. You are bottled desire. We will never have one another. All we have are fleeting moments, impossibly fleeting. Space junk and electrons. You are immortality personified. To desire is to lack, and I love you when I lack you; and sometimes, when I'm with you, I desire you to disappear back into the folds of my mind.

You were always the constant *other*. You are a double other. You are my other, and you are their other. Whenever I sensed heartache, or mere rejection I fled to you. You have helped me build a glass barrier around my heart. I hid you from others because I was embarrassed. But I enjoy forbidden passion: fucking without arguments over the dishes.

I'm addicted to it.

But now, boyfriend archetype placed us in a room, watched us with that gaze that you initially watched over me and him with. He scrutinized us, criticized us. He's on to us. Or what do I know, your dynamic with him is so odd.

So here are the things I should never tell you, that shouldn't be written down, that you must promise to destroy, lock away, flush. I told him that whatever feelings I had for you were merely traces of a past that I haven't fully comprehended… I've been reflecting and recording. You cannot say that we are purely sexual, or at least I cannot admit that when you are a vessel storing my trauma. Our dialogues used to be saturated with double entendres, covered in metaphors and allusions, but now either you've become lazy or certain feelings have waned, though I'm inclined to say they have not. You miss me; you miss the times when you had the freedom to have me. The last time I saw you we were unable to consummate our contact. You could not touch me. We could not run away. There was no pocket we could tuck ourselves into.

But now. Oh, now. I hate you. I hate base descriptions of debaucheries. Without metaphor, without beauty, there is no passion. We cannot rely on a heated past to ignite the present. The past cannot sustain the present, that would be too ugly, and the sex would be awful.

In order for me to fall back into our old arabesque patterns you must relearn me. I am not the girl I was at eighteen. I have been ripped in half and stitched back together. I have had an existential crisis, a tragic love affair, and a creative epiphany. And so much I don't know about you. You fell in love as well. Your work has molded you into a different creature. Your goals, your aspirations have shifted. Your intentions with me also seem changed. And I will not live in denial. I will not falsely recreate something that has disintegrated, and I certainly will not recreate it cheaply or in haste. If you want that we will grab a dead pigeon and poke at it.

What I love about us is that our sexual relationship transcends the physical, but right now it is dehydrated. I am craving a night with you. A night that will go unscathed. Meet me, in both senses of the word.

With love, without love,
      Nora

                    ...

The doorbell rings. A man in a brown uniform hands her a box long enough to hide a rifle. She signs her name with an electronic pen on a small gray screen. Her signature is boxy and ugly; this bothers her. He hands her the box, she feels the object within slide, crinkling the tissue paper, striking the edge of the cardboard. She carefully removes the red ribbon, unearths a single black rose made of spiraled leather with a sharp, braided steel stem. Wrapped in red tissue paper, the image is both phallic and vaginal. Like a flower sprouting from a fist. Black for masochism, absence, exile, and futility. Its green felt leaves fall dull and limp. An imitation of life, an homage to infertility and illusion. To eroticism. He sent her a representation, a metaphor. Copying a copy, its bud will forever remain closed, tightly sealed, like a hymen. Something that is what it is not. The flower that isn't a flower with tough, durable leather petals and keen metal thorns.

The card is another postcard, Diego Velázquez's *Rokeby Venus*. Lying in bed, the goddess turns away from the viewer to admire herself in a mirror held up by Cupid, by the divine force of physical love. Through the mirror, as though she were looking from underwater, her gaze peers into herself and the viewer, into their soul, daring them to look back, to peel their eyes away, to interpret her. Soft, incandescent light and feathery brush strokes, Nora looks, she studies, compares the *Rokeby Venus* to *Olympia*. For the latter, her next lover, the viewer, is just another man, another customer. Her gaze is direct, confrontational.

261

There is no dance of seduction, just a body. Bone, flesh, and blood.

Tomorrow, my Goddess. I will see you tomorrow.

Incurvatus in se ipsum.
Fucking you is like fucking a mirror.

She runs the rose, this object of memory and death, across her lips, and deliberately pricks her thumb, drawing blood from one of its thorns.

...

Friday night, sprawled across the floor, escaping, drunk on Pullman's *The Subtle Knife*. At 9pm her phone beeps, it startles her. Hope twists into disappointment when she sees it's Maryanne. Jake's here! I even hugged him. It was weird!! I haven't seen him in years! I don't know if you cared, but I thought you'd might want to know. ;)

That lying son of a bitch.

Where are you?

    At Le Passage/the Drawing Room with Kevin.

Stay there. I'll be right over. But don't tell him I'm coming!! Nora writes.

    Why in the world would I do that?
    And: Yayayyy!! See you soon!

Rain pelts the taxi. Nora's hands are shaking, she's lighting one cigarette from another. Her eyes are darting. When they arrive she launches out of the car.

"Jiji! I didn't know you were coming!"

"Oh my God! You're glowing! Congratulations again!" Jiji says. The two girls embrace. Maryanne brandishes her diamond. The girls embrace again.

"Did he leave?" Nora asks, yells in Maryanne's direction.

"I don't know. It's packed," Maryanne says, gesturing all around her. A man with a ripped shirt and horrible body odor sits down next to them. He puts his cigarette out on his tongue. "Has that ever worked?!" Nora yells. He spits on the ground and walks away.

Nora opens yesterday's copy of the Tribune and pretends to be reading it. "Where did you get that?" Maryanne asks. "Did she bring it?"

Jiji shrugs.

"I know he's here," Nora says to Maryanne, to Jiji, to herself, to no one. "I can feel him."

"I'm going to go to the bar. Hang on a sec."

"Get me a Rum and Coke. And a shot of Patrón."

"I'll go with you," Jiji says, leaving Nora to her eccentricity.

She folds the newspaper methodically into an accordion file and then a fan. Her eyes flutter behind yesterday's news of Iraq, the combustion of a counterfeit jeans racket, and the trials and tribulations of Fois Gras. She creates her own breeze to calm the sweat beading around her hairline.

Maryanne returns with a Rum and Diet and a Rum and Coke. Jiji's holding two shots. Nora takes both shots from Jiji then drinks them both, one right after the other. They taste like poison.

> The overpowering, choking, noxious scent of alcohol as it sterilizes a putrid, rotting wound.

"Nora…" Jiji says.

"Which is which?" Nora says to Maryanne.

"The diet has the pink straw, yours is the green one," Maryanne says, sips, then makes a face. "No, no, this one is yours. Blech."

Nora takes the regular rum and coke and sucks half of it through the pink straw. The carbonation scrapes her tongue. It's deceptively warm.

"Come on," Nora says, grabbing Jiji's arm. Maryanne and Jiji exchange a look, but then Jiji with a quick gesture, wordlessly tells Maryanne that it's okay, that she's got her.

Jiji and Nora then go hunting.

There, behind a green potted plant, through a thick haze of smoke Nora sees him, recognizes him by the back of his head and the shape of his posture.

"Get down," she says, grabbing Jiji's arm, pulling her down with her, giving her no choice, so that they're both squatting on the floor amidst a sea of people. *A bottom feeder. I'm reduced to this.* A man standing next to them looks down, and smiles at Jiji. "Well isn't this suggestive?" he says.

"Go fuck yourself!" Nora says. He walks away, muttering, "Fucking ugly ass psychopath."

"Nora, are you okay?"

He didn't lie.

Nora sees the bride then three other women in black dresses fluttering and swiveling their hips. The bride then sits on her husband's lap, two pink shoes popping out of a world of tulle. Jake isn't moving. One of his hands is in pocket, the other is propping up his head. He's changed his hair, had it cut for tonight, or maybe he did it himself, maybe Lindsay did it. Either way, it's depressingly militant, boxy and tamed.

"I'm sending him a text," Nora says.

"Don't do that. Let's just go."

"I *need* to make him suffer!" She says, standing up, raising her fist in a gesture of justice, then begins texting.

"What are you saying?" Jiji pulls her back down to the stone floor. It's damp, cold, full of thin wet mud and beer. People are looking at them. She shuts her phone.

Fancy seeing you here.

"That's what you said? Did you guys have plans or something? Could you at least tell me what's going on?" Jiji now stands up.

Nora stands back up too. She wipes her hands on the back of her jeans, crinkles her nose, and waits. He doesn't reach into his pocket. His phone could be turned off. He could be incredibly patient, as usual. Maybe he doesn't get reception. Maybe she doesn't get reception and the message was never sent. She checks her phone. Check mark. Received. She waves the newspaper fan and stamps angrily. One of the women saunters away from the party. Dances straight toward them. Nora yelps, grabs Jiji and pulls her back down to the floor.

"We're more obvious down here than anywhere else!"

"*Shhhh!* That's Lindsay." Nora says in a whisper. She can't help but gawk at her. She looks like Jake, like their children would make sense. She's short, even in heels, she has to only come up to his ear lobes. As she sashays closer Nora desires to touch her, to feel her muscular legs, or even just the material of her dress, which looks as though it doesn't give her athletic body the room it needs to move, but portrait necklines always have a way of exhibiting a sophisticated stiffness, poised resolution. Lindsay's a package deal. Now, probably, even more than usual, she's got her own wedding beating on her brain. An outdoors event, in a garden surrounded by hundreds of vivid flowers in full bloom. She would dance with her father and cry, then happily kick off her shoes, put on a pair of sunglasses, and model for the camera in that live-action sort of way: tongues sticking out, lips puckered, arms in the air. A full blown celebration.

After she passes, Nora throws the newspaper to the floor.

"Let's go back to Maryanne and Kevin," Jiji says. Nora sighs. She's lost. The night is lost. Jake was telling the truth.

Nora cinches the belt on her coat a little tighter and slumps down on a bench near the exit sign, its red glow rouges her sallow skin. She lights another cigarette, blowing the smoke at her own reflection in the window. Melancholy has relaxed her posture and facial muscles. She looks so tired.

"What did you think was going to happen?"

"I don't know. I just had to see it. I had to be sure he was really at a wedding party."

"You guys have been seeing each other again?" Maryanne asks.

Chill out, Chopsticks, she repeats, like a mantra. *Chill out, Chopsticks.*

"If you could call it that. Jihad, do you have any Klonopin on you?"

Jiji shakes her head.

Nora can't concentrate on anything. She checks her phone every three or so minutes. Life continues around her. Jiji and Maryanne catch up. Jiji every so often putting her hand on Nora's leg. Maryanne every so often adoringly looking up at Kevin to steal a kiss.

Until the bride bursts through the crowd. She's got her hands in the air, while one of her bridesmaids carries her train.

Jake emerges with Lindsay on his arm and the rest of the wedding entourage behind them. He looks the same: pensive, rigid, truistic. A phallic monument of himself. Happy to a point of blandness. Lindsay breaks away and joins the bride, grabbing a piece of the dress, woo-hooing as they pass a cheering crowd of strangers. Nora lowers her head and shields her face with her hands, cupping her eyeballs and peaking through the cracks in her fingers like a child who's *It* counting out loud while everybody hides.

Jake is following Lindsay, but the rest of the soiree has past him. He is dawdling. Nora shifts in her seat. She takes her hands away, hears a harp playing in the background of her thoughts. His face is red, flushed with fear or anger or drink, or maybe, it too is just lit by the exit sign.

"I can feel his torment," Jiji whispers. Nora covers her eyes again. Total darkness.

If their eyes were to meet what would they meet her with? Hostility? Sympathy? Longing? If his gaze falls and his eyes widen saying, "I'm sorry. I'm sorry for everything. I'm sorry I can't talk to you right now. I'm sorry I love her and need her. I'm sorry I chose her."

And Amy. And Heather. And Jojo.

Then Nora would respond with hostility, fire around the pupils. *Do these ghosts swarm around your cock, Jacob? Do they tingle your balls with their butterfly kisses?*

But if he looks at her with hostility then she would look at him with sadness. Either way, glass would break.

But if Jake looks at Nora with longing, she has no idea what she will do.

But there was nothing. No looking of any kind. Not from him.

Nora watches closely, inspects for sweat, for anxiety, for some clue that he loves *her.*

She pictures him pleading: *God, if you let me get away with this I promise to never cheat again.*

She then watches the wedding party stand outside, each one of them decapitated by a neon Miller Lite beer sign. She watches his headless silhouette. He could have been anyone with a pompous gut, flicking his cigarette into the gutter. She watches him drape his jacket over Lindsay's shoulders. So sweetly, so lovingly. Lindsay then turns around, lifts her arms, undoubtedly around his neck. The tips of their shoes touching until she pops her leg, lifting one heel off the ground.

"I don't have any desire to interrupt this," Nora says, still looking out the window. "Today was her day."

She trails, then stares at their feet for a little while longer. Maybe he too looked down and saw her face illuminated by the neon gas. Maybe he too was looking at his own feet. Maybe he never knew she was there, although she doubts that very much.

. . .

Pain begins by being "not oneself" then ends with the elimination of all that is "not oneself."

The only productive pain is childbirth.

And Nora wants children.

She wants to grow up.

Just not with Jake.

. . .

The year Nora was born Theresa Hak Kyung Cha and Djuna Barnes both died. Djuna died a recluse, of old age and stubborn eccentricity. Nora's heard, or rather, read, that everyday Djuna still did her hair and makeup. She still wrote, scattering the pages around her bed, letting them fall to the floor like fat snowflakes. Theresa was raped and murdered on the streets of New York City. She was only a little older than Nora is now. In an indescribable tragedy, an act of severance, Theresa slipped into a category, a number. Melpomene even wept, just as she wept for Hecuba and Sappho, just as she weeps on behalf of apartheids and holocausts. She cries for her affixed mother who faces a mirror, not to see herself, but to see what is behind her, just like the Rokeby Venus, shivering from the cold, reaching for her fur. No one approaches her directly, not even Death. Images turn into memories which turn into descriptions which turn into words spoken from a slit in the face, a mouth wound. Catherine opens her mouth to speak but a canary comes out instead, flies into the cave, never to return. Like Philomela, like Theresa, cat got her mother tongue. But who is this cat? Sprawled, splayed as it were, so fluffy, so cute. So fluffy and cute Nora could just die. But he's dreaming. Once upon a time…when he caught that mouse, a muse, silently shrieking, no tongue and a stitched-up mouth, leaving only the tiniest of apertures for urine and menstrual blood. She can't breathe, the laces are too tight, her *stays* are cutting off her circulation, making her thin, pretty, *contained*. A corset is a line of demarcation, a border between life and death, between self and other. To improve posture. Induce the straight spine, a straight line, emphasis on straight. Atrophy, pain, reliance. Tight-lacing pushes the ribs in and up. Wandering organs. Elongated livers. Triangulated ribs. Constipation. Prolapsed uterus. Diminished lung capacity. Dyspnea. Hysteria. Yellow Wallpaper. She swoons where she stands. Falls on the spot, the clot of blood staining the sheets. She sleeps, dreams, her eyes roll behind delicate eyelids, they flitter open like shudders, shades meant to look like scrolls, hide, parchment, always pulled down, open, readable, blocking the light, forever dark in a prison cell, tongue turning silver, parched, Danaë stretches, welcomes the rain, but still, she wants out! Out of this womb! This tower! Out of this bed! She pulls the shade, it spins open, slaps itself like a reel of film, her eyes roll back, she's levitating. A sorceress! Night falls, Nyx is pushed off a cliff, offered as a sacrifice, her head splits on the rocks, just as Sappho's did, brains oozing into the water, Nora grips her head, presses the melting blue gelled ice pack to her left eye as it cracks open Athena bursts from the chasm, looking for her mother, all she sees is her father who looks at her adoringly, with twinkling orbs and conflicting passions. Mighty Athena, the straight line, the ray, the vestal. Always reaching outside herself, one step away from her body, cunt shunted. She clamps her eyes back shut and searches within. *This little light of mine. I'm gonna let it shine.* First her nerves, then her heart, then her blood. She lights up like a Christmas tree, incandescent like a hot pink glowworm, she spits silk, starts knitting herself a veil to drape over her face, her cunt, or like Baubo, whose face is her cunt, she pulls back the curtains and winks, smiling, beckoning, *Come in.* But with which mouth? Certainly not the one with teeth. *Still be more specific.* The one without the tongue. Neither has a tongue! Fine! The one that's bleeding. Philomela spits blood onto the dusty floor, it clots, just as Beatrix Kiddo spits blood on Bill's brother's face. But he retaliates with muck, brown waste, tobacco and saliva, the look and feel of diarrhea. She's stained, marked with excrement, with excess, with waste. She's paralyzed too! And bound, always bound. Hog-tied, the most hated animal, whose pink flesh apparently tastes like woman's. The pig roasts over a spit-fire with an apple in its mouth. Eve plucks the apple, passes it to Eris, who, scorned, hurt, jealous, rolls the apple down the aisle. *To the fairest*, its inscription reads. Hera, Athena, and Aphrodite pounce. *Who is the fairest one of all?* A man must answer. Naked, the goddesses stood before a trembling mortal whose painfully erect cock cums just at the thought of Helen. He hands Aphrodite the apple, who then gives it to Snow White's stepmother. *Mirror, mirror*, the queen begins. Morticia winks. She thinks she can see Sabina in her bowler hat hiding a sock. Shaking, red with rage, she must kill those blood red lips, but the huntsmen stops, falls impotent, is stilled by Snow White's beauty, her virginity. A pig's lungs and liver in her place, she hides in the forest, as her stepmother boils the organs in salt before she devours them. (She thinks she's consuming the child's beauty.) *Mirror, mirror...Motherfucker!* She returns with a corset. The flowing flesh must be disciplined, must undergo masculinization. *Cuirasse Ésthetique*, the classical male nude, a corset of muscles, naturally, invisibly corseted. A hard-bodied shell needs no protection, but a woman wears her organs on the outside. Her heart on her sleeve, her sex in her laces. She bites the apple and falls dead. They put her in a glass coffin, on display, she sleeps, cut off from her own scary body, she's guarded by brambles and enchanted forests, sleeping for one hundred years, a king stumbles upon her, putting his flag in her soil, he claims her. Hail Aurora! The sun also rises, her sheer curtains gently filtering the light but the guilt pierces like a fiery lance, like a gilded cock, heavy with meaning, too full of itself to ever become pregnant, it impregnates. Her body swells, it is no longer just hers (as if it ever was!), there is a tiny doll inside her, with its sex hidden she doesn't even know if she's carrying the sun or a daughter or the devil. Because she's Eve's daughter, she carries the weight of the world, the Word of God, inside her belly *Holy Mary Mother of God, pray for us sinners* resting on her bowels, tilting her uterus, serpentining her spine. She is not straight. Bisexual and curvy, amorphous and open, she can be read like a book *My vagina is a book! Read my lips: No More Tampax!* but only a book that she herself writes. *Interpret that!* She spits, he slaps her. *The failing heart of the world!* She can't win by brawn, she knows that, so she hides in the shadows, left alone to cry in the forest. She can't give up, Miss Midwest Midnight Check-Out Queen, not after she's come this far, she punches through the wood and crawls out of her own grave just as Persephone rises from the Underworld every spring, thanks to her mother's love she's reborn every year then dies again as the last leaf falls, returning to her lover, her master, her husband, *the King of Death*, and lies in bed with him, dies once again, then again and again. He kisses her with his forked tongue. So much has he missed her! He sucks at her labia, drinking her honeyed wine, spiked with venom, with passion, with life. As if he drank a gallon of mead, a drunken Hades sings her praises. *I would launch a thousand ships for you!* "You already did," she says. "Everybody died. You said you had never felt more alive." The moment his spear pierces the skin, pushes through, impaling his victim's resistant flesh, he feels the rush of their pleading life force run through his veins. *Empowering the already empowered.* A different kind of drunk. Nora wouldn't know. She's only killed insects and the instant she felt their life pass through her she wept, once, for killing a spider because she didn't get her right the first time. She suffered, felt hysterically guilty. Wore the mark of Cain, the mark of Rita, the mark of Hester Prynne. She knows lust *but a lust for life* if anyone died for her erotic pleasure it was going to be herself. But just as she pretends beef isn't cow, so she pretends her death wasn't killing Lindsay, Jenny, Angela, Heather, Amy. Hera takes on many forms, just like her husband she steals into the night and wishes to abolish any swans and their children. She wants to absolve Zeus of any impurity, wash the stains from his speedy feet. How can she though without destroying her own kind? Frailty isn't her name, she is the essence of despair, if she didn't dilute her ichor with heroin she would collapse into a puddle again, flood the earth once more, but this time more than a couple of unicorns would miss the arc's final boarding call. But she doesn't, instead she splits in two, yes, in a blue dress and a white dress, in a blue dress with a white stain and a white dress with a red stain, a brook of red, unclotted, shared between two, through a tube, her blue veins into her other's blue veins, her red blood mixing with her other's red blood, holding hands, sashaying toward Nora, dancing for her, rubbing her pussy on his thigh, slipping on a black dress, rouging her cheeks and her lips, kissing the window pane Nora lifts her white nightgown, gives him a taste, holding the scissors, playing a flute, painted so still, Nora wanted to keep him still, with just one look. Still, she wanted to love him from inside of him. He ate her to consume her beauty, so she was always with him, was him, looking at Lindsay, she can't look away. *Do it to Julia!* The walls of his chest echo, Termagant hisses as the snakes wriggle then strike her own heart, he holds up a mirror and she dissolves into a fiend, carrying children off in the night, bringing them to her tomb, she doesn't suspect he'd take her head, she only expected to receive head, but he strikes with the mighty hand of Thor. *Ding Dong the Wicked Witch is DEAD!* Burnt to cinders and ashes, her heart still beating on the floor of the pyre. This is when Nora snatches it back and locks it inside her desk. Dipping her quill in its blood, she always writes with *heart*, with grit and soul, signing off each email with a flourish, feeling so clever she was duped by a chain letter, writing him on their birthday, telling him, that tonight, of all nights, Jupiter was going to be so close the earth will look as though it has two moons! One for me, she writes, and one for Hera. *You should feel so lucky.* When he doesn't respond she throws herself into the sea. To end her suffering all she had to do was stab the prince and his bride, let his blood drip on her feet, but she couldn't. *She couldn't.* Like so many before her and so many after she sacrificed herself, for him, for mankind, replacing the world's failing heart with her own, she dies again and again and again and again and again, to wake up, just as one doesn't become an atheist but suddenly one day realizes they have always been one, the veil lifts and she kisses her bride, slipping in some tongue, beaming like the central body of a solar system.

...

"What took you so long?" Jake asks. He's waiting in her doorway, inside the Glass Elevator.

"I went to this amazing art exhibit. Here." She hands him a flyer. "Doesn't it kind of look like bones and lace? I mean lace and/or bones. Like nature and nurture. Bones as lace."

"Whatever you say," he says, dropping the flyer. She picks it back up, "Aw, come on," she says.

Once inside he doesn't say anything. He unties the strings around her neck, watches her dress fall away. He takes her breasts in his mouth then carries her to bed. She strips off his shirt, his belt, his pants, his boxers and begins kissing him. He fumbles through her drawer for a condom. "Are you sure?" she asks.

"Are you kidding?" he says. He tears off the paper, touches the condom to the end of his dick. It won't quite roll. His fingers keep slipping.

"What's wrong?" she asks.

"Nothing," he says.

And still, nothing happens. His fingers keep working away, trying to get the rubber up, over his limp, shriveled member.

Nora lights a cigarette, looks out the window. Waits. With a frustrated sigh of defeat, he takes one of her cigarettes. A train screeches past. He puts his boxers back on. The room smells like latex.

"Is it Lindsay or is it me?"

"What kind of a question is that?"

"An honest one."

"It's Lindsay."

"Then why the fuck did you come over?"

"I don't know, because I wanted to."

"But you don't anymore?"

"I do—I don't know," he says, dropping his cigarette onto the bed. "Shit!" he springs up. She smells burning fabric. They both spot the culprit at the same time. They both reach for it. He picks it up and she throws her hand onto the smoking bedspread, to stop the glowing hole from growing, all these tiny feathers rise up in a puff and flurry about all around them. For a minute it's as if they're stuck in a snow globe.

"Fucking God damn it," she says, blowing on her hand, making it worse.

"Sorry..." he says, brushing the feathers out of his hair.

"For what? Burning my comforter or your impotence?"

"You know I get enough shit from Lindsay I don't need you adding to it with your bullshit."

"My bullshit! Jesus. You shouldn't have come here. You can't handle this anymore."

"It isn't the same. Something's not right." He starts getting dressed.

"So it is me?"

"Nora..."

"No, this is good. This *is* right."

"I'm going to marry her..."

"You should probably go tend to that."

He gets up, walks out to the bathroom, and washes his flaccid cock in her sink.

"Where's Jiji tonight?" he yells to her, as if he weren't washing the sin off his failed dick—though he's probably just making it smell like condom laced patchouli with a faint hint of pussy.

Nora doesn't answer, she's thinking, fuming, at him, at herself. She shouldn't have left the gallery, she shouldn't have agreed to meet him again, she should have stood him up, but she never could. She had to see, had to know for sure, for absolute sure.

"I can't believe you don't have air conditioning. How do you stand it?"

His casual tone is unbearable.

He walks back into her doorway. "So it's going to be like that?" he asks.

She doesn't hide her nakedness from him. Sitting with her back against the wall and one knee bent to her chest, she stares past him to the train tracks.

"Nora," he says, meaning: *Stop it! Look at me!* She does, exhaling a plume of smoke at his face.

"I always loved you more than you loved me," she says.

"I know," he says.

"You should get back to your wife." She says, getting on all fours, reaching for the abalone shell on her nightstand, she stubs the butt of her cigarette out. She can feel him stare at her ass. She hopes he's conflicted. She lights another cigarette.

He yells, running, pressing his fingers through his thinning hair. "I'm going to go."

"Okay."

"You're pathetic. You don't even know what you want. Even now as you tell me: *This is over. Never again!* You still don't know! Because you never wanted me. You just want to be desired. To get *fucked*. You have no desire of your own! None. *That* is why you can't make yourself cum."

"Wow. Okay."

"So I'll leave you to that. And I'm going to call you next week."

"Fuck off and die."

"That's not what you want."

"You don't get to tell me what I want. Not anymore."

"I never did! Don't be annoying. Don't play a victim."

"Freud had it backwards," she says, looking at her cigarette. "Death is an unwished-for necessity. And there's no Heaven, you know. So, *blood to your dick*, fuck me, or give me my *auto-da-fé*."

He sits on the bed and puts his head in his hands.

Schubert plays in Nora's head.

String Quartet No. 15 in G.

That damning note.

A pretty girl, the dead maiden.

A silenced mistress.

She gets it.

"We were lovers, once upon a dream. Secret lovers. Go, it'll be like none of this ever happened."

"That's not what I want."

"Of course not, but this isn't your choice."

"You're acting weird. Weirder than usual."

"You're a memory now, Jacob Noyes. No longer a fantasy, just a memory; a fond one too, but still," She says to the window, looking out, as though she were looking ahead, to the future, to a future without him, without her golden sin.

To a future bereft of the very concept of sin.

He walks past her to leave. There's still some feathers in his hair. She doesn't tell him.

"Goodbye then," he says, opening the door.

"Goodbye then," she mirrors.

"Nora…" he stares into her eyes. "Chopsticks…"

"*Oh my God.*"

She shuts the door and locks him out. Looking through the peephole, she watches him stare at her door, raise his knuckles to knock, then lower them, thinking better of it, he rounds his shoulders, but before descending the stairs, he says, "Don't fucking kill yourself tonight. You're acting all weird and shit. And I don't need you haunting me for the rest of my life."

If only that were metaphysically possible, she thinks.

And for the first time she understands what it truly means to be alone.

. . .

Alone, with a black leather rose, an ibuprofen,
and a burnt palm.

. . .

In bed, lying flat on her back, in the corpse position, palms facing the ceiling, the sky, feet splayed open, right foot resting on Rufus, who is also on his back, legs spread apart, obscenely, in total upside-down kitty bliss. When the train rumbles by he doesn't even open his eyes, but continues dreaming, soft growling meows, followed by mouth smacking. He's dreaming of eating his prey, as Nora beside him does her best to concentrate on nothing, least of all food. Tchaikovsky's *Sleeping Beauty* blasting at full volume, to drown out the train, to drown out (draw out?) her blustering migraine, to draw out vulnerability and humiliation, she inhales her cigarette and ashes in an abalone shell, strategically placed arm's length away, so she can move as little as possible. She's waiting for her Vicodin to kick in, grateful she only had four drinks, but still, enough to wake the sleeping dragon who lives behind her left eye. Thinking about tomorrow, her stomach turns over. This is when she would've prayed to God, but she doesn't. And she doesn't miss it.

. . .

Everything smells like burnt feathers.

As if she were having a stroke.

She gets out of bed, makes herself some juice with apples, spinach, some daikon radish, a little bit of ginger, and a small wedge of lemon. She notices that Jiji's door is still open, that she never came home. She takes half a Vicodin with her juice then decides to forgo her morning cigarette. She also decides not to wear her Claddagh ring ever again.

The death of all gods, she thinks.

And with that she walks over to her jewelry box and takes the extremely expired Ibuprofen as well.

Feeling both heavy and light, she pulls the television out of its box next to the couch. She sets everything up to watch *Kill Bill*. Then she goes to her room and grabs her purple comforter and a sewing kit. She lays them both on the floor in front of the television and goes sifting through their craft box. She's looking for a particular piece of fabric, a red square covered in minuscule white hearts. The same fabric her mother once made a dress from for her. She has to unpack half of the box before she finds it. It's the perfect size. Then she grabs the blanket, which sends another brigade of feathers flying. She blows on the comforter, pulling the cotton away from the stuffing inside, cleaning it up as much as she can, she now sees that the hole is in the shape of a heart. A heart with brown, burnt, crisp, jagged, gritty edges. She threads the needle, presses play, then begins to sew.

. . .

The End

Catherine Borders is the founder and executive editor of Omnia Vanitas Review. She lives in "Chicago" with her husband, daughter, and two very necessary cats. *A Suburb of Monogamy* is her first novel. She regrets nothing.

...

Omnia Vanitas Review is a small literary erotica press. A delicate mixture of Féminine Écriture, New Narrative, and Clit Lit. We enjoy specific descriptions of sex written in white ink. Deflowering language. Multiple orgasms with multiple climaxes. The playful touching of intertextuality. Deliberately elusive linguistic weavings. Words penetrating the void. Words that slow dance with Aphasia and flirt with Amnesia. Words wet with formlessness. Words pregnant with child. With twins, with quintuplets. Words as bound flesh. In other words, pretentious porn.

We believe that there is nothing more risqué
than the desire to write.

Look at us, submit to us at OmniaVanitasReview.com

And check out our tumblr at:

omniavanitasreview.tumblr.com

Acknowledgements:

A book is a testament to all the other texts its artist has consumed. This book in particular, and with deepest gratitude, bows before and especially gives thanks to: Roland Barthes, Hélène Cixous, Shelley Jackson, Simone de Beauvoir, Jean-Paul Sartre, Dodie Bellamy, Christopher Hitchens, Marguerite Duras, Kate Zambreno, Georges Bataille, Dorothy Parker, Lyn Hejinian, Anaïs Nin, Theresa Hak Kyung Cha, Lidia Yuknavitch, Djuna Barnes, Frida Kahlo, Madonna, Patsy Cline, Wendy MacLeod, Franz Schubert, Philip Glass, and Disney©.

I will forever be in debt to my parents. I am a daughter sponge. But a very grateful one.

I'd like to thank Nick, Corey, and especially Roenna for making things interesting.

Rufus, my furry rock, I know you're nearing your eighth life, make the last two really long.

Goocha, my wild heartsong, everything is always all for you.

Also, my terrifyingly brilliant husband, who helped wrestle this demon spawn out of me. I'll love you forever.

And lastly: Lily Robert-Foley, the stunning poetess, my comrade in arms, my Jiji, you midwifed this book from stem to stern. Thank you.